A Long
the
River Run

Glenn Stuart
Beatty

First Published 2022
by Soap and Candle Press
18 Upfold Street
MAYFIELD NSW 2304
Australia

Typesetting and cover design by Rack & Rune Publishing
rackandrune.com

ISBN 978-0-6454585-0-3

To find out more about the author visit
glennstuartbeatty.com.au

Glenn Stuart Beatty grew up in the Lower Hunter Coalfields of New South Wales. He was educated at the University of Newcastle, University of Central Queensland and Macquarie University. He has worked in labouring jobs in heavy industry, in the music and theatre industries as a sound and lighting technician and has had held senior positions in the public service in areas of housing, community services and disability services. His first volume of poetry, The Saxophone Injuries appeared in 1991 and since then his work has appeared in a number of anthologies. He has been a member of Newcastle's Poetry at the Pub since 1988 and spent many years as President of this group as well as chairperson of the Hunter Writers' Centre. As a playwright, Glenn has had works commissioned by Newcastle's Mission Theatre and Freewheels Theatre in Education. A Loved A Long the River Run is the first of Glenn's novels to be published.

You can find out more about Glenn at:
glennstuartbeatty.com.au

Angela Sees the Fire,
Raining in the Sky

A loved a long the river run – if there was any water left, it would run through it, but the river dried, was not a river if it had no water, no longer a soul if it had no spirit, and Angela McGregor had enough of drought and all that came with it. Okies, she thought, that film based on Steinbeck, Henry Fonda and Rose of Sharon, the daughter suckling grown men, her milk the only comfort for the dying, rib bones on them like the boy men from Changi, pictures kept by her grandfather, he who hated japs and nips and slaphead slopes and krauts and eyties too, an Sassenachs the most. And maybe loved her mother 'though he never said and little Angela, 'though he never said, and Rex his kelpie, 'though he never said, and his old digger mates at the RSL, though he never said. He said, 'I am the law' and Angela says now 'I am the law' and wonders what that is, the law. We need a diviner, she thought, but look at the trouble Michael brought, and Andy Mac, she thought, and that perhaps he was Christ, Michael that was, not Andy Mac, or was that the Thane of Cawdor weltering in blood in the Trobriands or an old man up north, the Kimberleys perhaps? Too many gods and the river does not run, and the smoke is building in the north.

The fire flows like water, the man who lived in the block up the road told her once, 'it pours across the ground, thirsty like water, long red tongue tasting at the bush until the bush explodes and the tree tops, the tree tops explode ahead of the fire and it is like something from God, something falling from the sky, the embers ahead of the snakewater flames.' Angela thought that he thought that she thought that he was mad, a crazy coot with a big white beard and the King Gee shorts and old rubber thongs despite the brown snakes, and the chesty bond cliché blue singlet and the leather Barmah hat with the kangaroo hide band that's turned black from his sweat and the oil that came from the band of white hair that hung from the back of his head as if to mock the shiny baldness of his pate. The locals called him Killer.

Five years she had been there, hidden in the bush in the foothills of the Barrington Tops. Five years, she often thought, is half a decade, half a decade for her sins, 'pray for us sinners and now and at the hour of our death' she remembers, Grandma and the big church near the river and the priest, whisky breathed smile and a pat on the head, but she thought she got it lucky because she was a girl and it was the altar boys that must burn deep in the dreams of the old priest in whatever gaol cell he sits in, weeping she hopes, and not just for himself.

Judgement, the fire is coming like water to judge, that's what old Killer says. Killer the amateur self-taught butcher who was so named because the small holders, the city folk who hid in the valleys would raise a cow or a sheep or a pig and when it was time to despatch the beast, they would bring it to Killer who would knock the bleating beast in the head with a sledgehammer before cutting its throat. He took to the newly dead animal with a sharp knife and the owners let him keep the offal, the innards that he liked, Angela thought, much like Leopold and his kidneys. Killer said that he would face the river of fire and stand his ground, but that a woman like Angela had no business standing up to fire and besides, what business did God have in judging Angela.

The precious books, the books by Mick, the first editions were packed in a carton that had once held twelve bottles of a decent Hunter Shiraz she bought in the days before she had to count her money. Mick's books, she had come to call him Mick because that was his nickname, the name he was known by to family and friends, but Angela never knew him and he wouldn't invite her in when she made her trip after she saved her money, scrimped for years on her part-time tutor's salary and was awarded a small research grant. Mick opened the door at Harwich and told her that he was busy, and she loved him even more for that and loved it the moment he divined her face, with his own face a mask of puzzlement, and she thought him some curmudgeonly Greta Garbo, without knowing that he liked the company of men in the pub, the fishermen.

Killer carried the books to the car and wondered why it was that the flame haired girl would want to save, of all things, books, old books that smelled of dust and forgotten rooms in houses full of people.

The afternoon sun was falling towards the ridgeline to the west in a struggle against the smoke that turned the sky to grey and white and black and red. 'It won't be long' said Killer, heading down the path to the gravel road that climbed another three hundred yards uphill to Killer's rough sawn timbered house and Angela laughed at the way he always talked in yards and miles that stretched across the uncleared hills.

There were no birds at all today. The only sound was a rushing, roaring noise from some distance to the north west, out beyond the second ridge, the higher ridge of spicy smelling eucalypt and ferns that fronded in the valleys in between. Angela liked the valleys in the winter when the dew hung heavily and the frost would not thaw in the hours before noon and when, in August sometimes, snow would fall in thin white sheets upon the grass. It wasn't even summer and yet the land was burning and she knew that she had to leave, drive down the narrow road that followed the river until it met another river and then looped lazily to the sea and the city by the sea that she had left some years before in order to heal and she wondered as she listened to that roaring, watched as the sky turned red, whether she had found enough time to heal, if she had healed enough to face the town by the river's mouth.

Once upon a time. She laughed at that and thought that Mick would never start with once upon a time even when he was being as ironic as the horseman. Mick would have started with an image, perhaps simple and startling or perhaps an observation.

By time she reached the age of fifty-six, Angela McGregor had grown thick around the ankles and the red of her hair was mingled with grey. She lived alone since the brown snake, the summer before, had taken her tabby cat Osana, who, in old cat age, had lost his ability to wile and scheme. She cried for him sometimes at night. On other nights she cried for different things, worthy of tears but not more worthy than her companion cat Osana, with the yellow eyes that followed her around the little mud-brick house on the overgrown five acres of scented bushland backing down to the river that no longer ran. Springwater has burbled surfacewood some miles up the road so that here, at Angela's back door it was always just a river in name and little more than a creek or perhaps, in Suffolk, Clare might have called it a brook, but it no longer burbled bubbled and the drinking water tank had turned brackish and had to be filled by a gruff ruddy skinned man who had a large yellow plastic tank on the back of a Bedford truck and always said he charged a fair price to cart the water from the dam five valleys towards the sea where the river that hadn't dried up yet.

Killer killed the brown snake for her the day after the snake had killed Osana. He had taken the snake's head off with a long-handled scythe, as cool as anything. Angela asked Killer 'how do you know that it was the same snake that killed Osana?' 'Does it matter?', Killer asked, 'it's a bastard snake close to your house, better off dead for everyone concerned and if you see any others, give me a hoi'. And Angela was glad to see the snake dead and felt bad because she had hoped that the snake had suffered, had felt fear even if just for the second the rusty but deadly scythe arced through the air in Killer's steady hands, guided by Killer's steady brown eyes to remove the snakes head from its body just as it rose it off the ground to strike out at Killer's bandy bared legs.

Angela had never wished more for a death the way that she wished for that snake to die and when the sharp blade severed the head with the flickering tongue and bared dripping fangs, Angela was convinced that at the moment the head was removed, the snake had locked its eyes onto hers and she hoped that in her eyes that snake would know that she wanted it dead.

Bluestocking, that's what someone said to her years ago, 'I always knew that you'd end up a bluestocking'. That was when she had a job, at the university before austerity – tenure had once been the dream but then, the muckle financial crisis. Bluestocking, she never owned a pair of blue stockings. Had a black pair once when she thought that some young man or another might find them erotic, but they never commented. Young men seemed to be such a long time ago, long before she came to these mountains where now the brook had ceased to run, the dried up gully that had once been verdant, life giving and affirming, a dusty useless thing, a string of disconnected muddy puddles that might remember what a brook might have been, what it might have been to flow brookish. 'Bookish', Angela remembered that's what her mother called her when she was a teenager and it wasn't meant as a compliment. Babies, her mother talked of babies, weddings, engagements, petty affairs, betrayals, divorce and death as they sang out from the Herald classifieds each day with their little life stories in microcosm, the fathers' funerals with the mention of children by name but not of a wife, or the old women with three or four surnames proclaiming earlier widowhood or divorce and Angela's mother worried that unless Angela found a marrying type of man that she'd grow old before she had time to worry the classified compositor with any announcement other than for her funeral, and that there were no men to be found between the pages of a book who could later be found between the sheets of the marital bed in a consummation of happy suburbia.

Up here, the mud brick house had not seen a man between the sheets since Angela bought it from the couple who thought they'd like the bush until they realised it came without the theatre, music, pubs and cafés, and before illness clouded over their dreams.

In the first few years the herb garden prospered – the bitter herbs she liked to chop and spread on hand made pizza dough and hand cut pasta or in the sauces she made with the bits of animal innards Killer would share with her when had done a kill for the young folk down the road. She grew tarragon for the chicken that she'd sometimes get from Killer when an old hen had gone off the lay. Killer didn't like chicken all that much, which is why he didn't cook his own chooks, but Angela would give him half when she had roasted the old hen in garlic, butter and herbs and he seemed to like the way she did it. That was in the easy years when the brook ran, and the tank was full before the end days when the garden died, and Killer's chooks stopped laying eggs for good.

Killer said to leave when it started raining fire from the sky and Angela thought that those words sounded like a line from a song she vaguely remembered from when she was a child and there'd be 2KO in the kitchen and some American man singing and then she remembered the night she spent some years ago in Longmont reading Kerouac and she didn't know until she read the page that night in Longmont that Kerouac too had come to Longmont and she read the page while she was there and felt the Goosebumps, and Longmont was in Colorado and she remembered then the song was from John Denver and she remembered looking out at the Rockies in late Fall and they had their caps of snow and that was five years ago and there is no snow here although it would be a blessing rather than the sky the colour she imagined the open doorway would be in a crematorium furnace when they push in the casket and she remembered funerals, far too many, friends and family gone in puffs of smoke and the smokes are puffing wildly over the next ridge plus one like a thousand angry grandfathers, jap broken in their clubs all sitting around puffing Borkum Riff from bent Peterson briars clenched between their yellow teeth, or with white dentures coming loose as their old heads shrink.

The roar slowly growing, Angela remembered playing down near the railway line when she was a little girl and her friend, the strange boy called Dean who went each day in a little white bus to the special school in another suburb and who never played with the other kids in the street because they called him a spazzo and threw stones at him if he came to play with them on the vacant block on the corner where Mrs King's house burned down in a fire one night when Angela was very tiny but could still remember the people in the street shouting and sirens and the noise and the smells and she remembered Dean daring her to stand on the railway track where it curved around the hill on its run into the city and to stand there until the last possible moment and she remembered the white panic stricken face of the man driving the flyer when he brought the locomotive hurtling around the corner and before he could blast the siren or hit the brakes she jumped and rolled down the steep embankment where Dean laughed so hard that he wet his grey school trousers that he seemed to wear everywhere.

She thought she remembered the night that Mrs King's house burned down even although her mother told her, years later, that she was too young and could never remember these things, but she described lying in her little wooden bed that was a step up from a cot and meant that she might have been three or so, and she was bedazzled by the beams of red and blue lights as they danced around the walls of her room passing over the pictures of fairies and puppy dogs and she remembered what had woken her, before she saw the lights, was hearing the man next door, Mr Collins, yelling loudly and her mother and father talking urgently in the hall and her father on the telephone and that must have been why Mr Collins was yelling because they had the only telephone in the street and her mother later told her the neighbours always wanted to use the telephone and she said only in extreme emergencies but that didn't stop the neighbours giving their families the McGregor's number and her mother said that for years it was her job to trudge up and down the street bearing news of deaths and births and accidents and sickness and crimes and celebrations so that Mrs McGregor became known in the street as 'The News'.

Angela had a mobile phone at the mud brick cottage but to use it she had to drive further up the hill to get reception, not that it mattered all that much because nobody ever called her and she had no desire to speak to anyone and if she had something to say she preferred to put it into a text message so she didn't have to indulge in meaningless chit chat, and in a text she could get straight to the point using as few words as necessary. She thought she should have texted her friend, Ingrid, to say that she was running from the fire and ask if she could stay in Ingrid's glistening glass fronted flat that reflected the green grey water of the harbour and where, at night, the tug boats with their mournful fog horns seemed to cry for something lost but not forgotten out there, across the water. It was too late to send a text now, for to drive up the hill, to climb the ridgeline would be to face the rushing, breathing fire as it ate ravenously through the bush.

A man had come to her door some minutes before, dressed in yellow and red with a big red helmet and she recognised him as Kevin Cutler who ran the general store in the little village five kilometres down the road and Kevin was the captain of the fire brigade or whatever they called the volunteers who fought the fires in the bush. Kevin Cutler told Angela that she had to leave, that the fire was coming from multiple sides and if it reached the road below her, she could not get out. He was a gruff man,

Kevin Cutler, and spoke with the authority of someone who had lived in the valley all of his life and whose ancestors were buried in the yard of the tiny stone Anglican church, their graves with headstones covered in lichen sitting inside a blackened wrought iron fence under the shade of an oak tree planted to make the little church look more like England, or so Angela thought. Kevin Cutler organised an annual Settlers' Day with a fete and a parade and a Cutler family reunion to celebrate the way the Cutlers pioneered the valley and settled the land. It was a day of drinking beer and rum and singing songs and having fistfights by the bonfire with the loud men shouting in their loud voices and the children screaming out on voices fuelled with fizzy drinks and lollies and the women watchful, careful, measuring their words so not to inflame the conquering blood of the sons of settlers. The black people stayed away. Killer said there'd been a massacre once, not far away and up upon the ridge where the big cliff dropped into the other river, the one that ran to the north. Killer said that some nights he could hear the black children crying. Killer said that he was part blackfella himself on his mother's side. Killer said he hated Kevin Cutler.

Kevin Cutler waved his arms and said words like 'out of control' and 'runaway' and 'crowning' by which he meant that all the years of the Cutler's authority over the valley and the ridges and the people and the plants and the animals couldn't stop the blaze from reaching them. Angela thought that Kevin Cutler looked scared and broken and the young boys and middle-aged men on his truck reminded Angela of her grandfather, the Law's, photographs, that he had sent back to her grandmother just before Singapore fell, of men clambering on trucks in Malaya heading off to some place called Parit Sulong. The boys in Malaya smiled nervously at the camera like little boys waiting for the dentist and so did the men and boys on Kevin Cutler's truck.

'I suppose your idiot neighbour is going to stay and try and fight the fire?' Kevin Cutler said to Angela by which he meant Killer. Angela said that she assumed that he would because Killer had once said to her that the only way that he would be leaving the valley would be in a box and even then he would prefer it if, when he went, that some kind person would borrow Bobby Parson's backhoe, dig a six foot deep hole, roll him in and cover him up and not to bother with any headstones or grave markers but just leave him in peace.

'Fucking stupid old bastard' Kevin Cutler said, still referring to Killer and walked back to his truck where his boys all looked like scared puppies, eager to please their master but still expecting to get a firm toe in the guts. 'If he gets in the shit, we won't be risking our lives to get him out of it. If you see him, tell him that' Kevin Cutler said and jumped into the truck and took off up the road towards the ridge that marked the end of the valley and meaning that even though he would drive past Killer's house, he had no intention to stop and tell Killer to leave the same way that he had Angela. Kevin Cutler knew what Killer's answer would be anyway, so there was probably no point.

It was then, that what sun there was, completely disappeared beneath the hot clouds of white and grey smoke that was flecked with red and the roaring in the sky grew even louder and Angela MacGregor shivered and realised that in all of her years, in all of her travels, in times when she felt uncomfortable and even a little afraid, she had never really known fear the way that it pounded into her stomach and making her think that she might vomit and her skin was tingling like she was being pricked all over with hundreds of tiny needles as if she was undergoing acupuncture, but ten times, a hundred times worse than when she had allowed herself to be pricked with the little needles to help her give up smoking and it didn't work anyway and the only way she gave up smoking was through sheer willpower.

The ground was smoking now. Little puffs of smoke arose

where embers settled on the tufts of dry grass and there was a little fragrant fire smouldering in what was left of the herb garden and she could pick the different essential oils that surrendered themselves and their volatility to the coming fire. The wind had changed in front of the fire and was howling the way her grandmother had described the dritch skraich of the boodies in the glens at night. On the breeze a little leaf fluttered down and landed in Angela's hair and she saw that it was leaf from a gum tree, a eucalypt, perhaps a Stringybark and the strangest thing was that the leaf was in one piece, but without much colour and almost transparent in places and felt brittle under her fingers and Angela realised that the leaf had been baked at an intense heat for a very short time without burning, it was radiant heat and she remembered seeing the pictures of people in Hiroshima who had been killed and what they left was their shadow on a wall, a silhouette of suffering. Angela turned and walked to her car.

The Subaru Forester was the one luxury she allowed herself. Once, when she was a student, she caught the train to a country town in the New England with a boy that she was sort of seeing and, looking out the window somewhere near Walcha or Uralla she had mentioned to her friend that for people who were allegedly doing it tough, she was surprised that so many of the properties they passed had relatively late model cars parked in their yards and her friend had said to her that when you live so far out of town a reliable car can be the difference between life and death and that's why a lot of the people in the houses they passed might not spend a lot on material goods, but they had cars that could get them to hospital long before an ambulance could reach them. When Angela bought the mud brick cottage, she traded in her old Ford Fiesta for the Subaru and when she turned the key, she was glad that the engine turned over straight away. Killer told her once about a fire, years ago, that came through a neighbouring valley so fast that when the people tried to flee, they found that their cars wouldn't start because the intensity of the heat of the fire was vaporising the petrol in their carburettors before it could be pumped into the cylinders and that's why it was better to have fuel injection. Angela thought that Killer might have been making that up because you could never tell when he was spinning a yarn.

Angela drove fast down the hill towards the village and liked the way that the car, driven by all four wheels, felt sure of foot on the gravel road and she imagined that it was leading her to safety. She was never one of those people, like one or two of her friends, who anthropomorphised their cars and gave them human names but now, as she fled the fire, she was sure was coming after her, she felt that the car was a living breathing thing like a horse that was intent on delivering her to safety.

About two kilometres from her house she rounded a bend and saw that Tony and Alyssa, a couple that had invited her to their house for a meal a couple of times, were standing in their front yard next to a huge water drum on the back of a trailer and Tony looked like he was connecting a hose to a diesel pump. Angela stopped the car and wound down her window and asked if they were planning to stay and fight the fire. Tony and Alyssa were both in overalls that, when Angela was a girl, were called boiler suits, and all the men who worked at the dockyard and the steelworks and on the railway wore them. Tony and Alyssa were also wearing heavy black suede work boots with thick woollen socks into which was tucked the bottoms of the legs of their boiler suits and they had big felt hats pulled firmly down on their heads and bandannas around their necks that they could pull up around their noses and mouths and they both wore big clear plastic safety glasses.

'We'll give it a decent crack' Tony said and smiled.

'Where are you going?' Alyssa asked Angela and Angela told her that she was heading to the city and would be staying with her friend Ingrid who had a flat in one of the new developments along the harbour.

'I bet your friend calls it an apartment and not a flat?' Tony said and he and Alyssa laughed, and Angela found herself laughing with them and agreeing that Ingrid probably did call it an apartment or perhaps a unit but definitely not a flat.

A flat, what was a flat? A cold water two room part of the upper floor of what once must have been a grand house with a shared bathroom on the landing somewhere in London. Angela avoided Earls Court and Shepherds Bush but didn't stray too far from Kangaroo Valley when she stayed for a time with Georgia in South Kensington, and Georgia even got her a job pulling pints at the Queen's Head down near the King's Road. That was when Angela had decided to spend a year in search of Mick or, at least, a year when she hoped she could meet and talk with Mick because he wasn't missing or anything and was really pretty easy to find in his little fishing village in Essex. What was a flat? Something cold and expensive and a long way from home, not like Ingrid's place with its glass and views and appliances and swipe card entry and little dark grey cylindrical pods in every room that played music for you or told you the time or what the weather was going to be like that day or answered inane questions with equally inane responses. There was no peeling paint or rising damp in Ingrid's place, but Angela wondered whether, in time, the salt air would corrode all the appliances. Still, she thought, there would be time to replace them gradually when, for Angela, come tomorrow, all that she possessed might be the things that she had managed to squeeze into boxes and bags in the back of her car, some clothes, some books and photos and a few treasured knick knacks from her travels and adventures. Everything else by then may well be ash and soot. Ash, she thought, Ash Wednesday and the unit on Eliot she had taught her third year class on Modernism in English Poetry and how, some of them, would openly yawn in class and how she told one young girl full of giggles, in one of her other classes, who wanted to be a high school teacher, to fuck off and that she was a waste of space and had no business studying English because she was too dull to get the finer points of literature and how the Head of Department had suggested that Angela might like to take a sabbatical which was easy for him to say with his tenure and his annual salary and his long service leave and study leave and superannuation scheme and his dreadful talented wife who was some research scientist of something that the university thought was useful for its prestige and the fact that it bought in money, as if poetry, as if Mick and his strangers who may or may not be Christlike were of no importance but told us more about ourselves than any genome sequencing ever would.

Angela admired Tony and Alyssa for their courage, or maybe it was for their cheerful foolhardiness. She wasn't sure which. She called out to them to not stay if it got too dangerous and they waved and went on with their preparations, as the colour in the sky started to change even more. It was well into the afternoon and the sun was getting lower in the sky and the smoke kept billowing and as Angela looked in her rear vision mirror, she could see high on the ridge, up where the grim faced Kevin Cutler and his coltish nervous young charges had headed, that the crowns of the big gum trees were starting to explode ahead of the fire front and there were more and more embers being carried by the north wind and they were dropping on the road in front of her.

'The north wind is tossing the leaves,
The red dust is over the town,
The swallows are under the eaves,
And the grass in the paddock is brown'

Angela sung to herself as she sped down the last bits of windy road before it straightened out and the bush gave way to paddocks and the paddocks gave way to the little village of Allynsdale. A shop (that was also the post office and bank), a pub, the Anglican church and a service station sat on the four corners of the intersection where the road to Angela's place met the main road that headed down the valley towards Maitland, where she would get onto the highway and find her way to Ingrid's. Just past the pub there was a collection of vehicles, mainly crew cab utes, sitting outside the shed that housed the bush fire brigade. Outside the pub there was a station wagon with the logo for the national television broadcaster and a technician was setting up what looked like a little antenna like the ones the people in town had for their pay television stations and a young blonde woman in jeans and a chequered shirt was standing holding a microphone and looking up at the sky to the north and there was a crowd of people on the pub verandah, holding beers and looking at the reporter and wondering, Angela thought, what the fuss was all about and Angela knew that soon, the fuss would come roaring out of the hills and across the dry grass paddocks that were brown and she remembered that the song she was singing to herself was some Australian Christmas Carol that she had learned in Primary School and she wondered if she actually remembered it correctly of if, over the years, the words had gotten all mixed up in her head that was already so full of words of poems and songs and quotes from books and movies and plays and important political speeches and the words of her own Mum and Dad that may or may not have been words of wisdom or just repeated truisms to be imparted on their children in the hope that those children would maintain their own view of the world.

Her Grandma got angry with her Dad when he took Angela out of the Primary School with the nuns and their rulers across the back of the legs, or the back of the hands, and put her in the state school where she said the teachers weren't allowed to beat their pupils. Angela, aged eight, sat in her bedroom and listened to the raised voices of her Grandma and her father and her Grandma saying that her father agreed that the children would be raised in the church and would go to the church school and that was a condition of him being allowed to marry Angela's mother and she remembered hearing her father saying that he didn't need the permission of hypocrite priests and her Grandma saying that Angela's father was no better than the communists and her father saying that there was nothing wrong with the communists. Angela doubted that there were any communists in Allynsdale. There were some Greenies in the hills in mud brick houses like her own, and she suspected that the people in the little village thought that she was a Greenie, but they never asked. After five years, the gossips in Kevin Cutler's shop would still stop talking when she walked in to buy some supplies, so she went to Maitland once a week, making the two hour round trip to stock up on all she needed and to sit in a café on the levee bank and enjoy a coffee and a pastry and use the free wi-fi to make contact with what was left of her world. She would go into the little café section next to Cutler's shop every couple of days to check her E Mails on her laptop hot spotted to her mobile but never really talked to anybody and she never went to the pub since the night some bloke who must have been ten years younger than she was, dressed in hi vis work clothes and a greasy baseball hat that sported a picture of a horse's head and the word 'Broncos' that Angela vaguely knew was a football team, she thought from Brisbane, had propositioned her in front of his mates, that might or might not have been for a dare or a bet, and all she wanted was a beer because it had been hot and she had been working in her garden all day and only had wine and gin at home but it was a beer that she really wanted, the bitterness and the coldness and the bubbles and the slightly gassy feeling you get when you drank it and she told him to 'fuck off' and he looked hurt and angry and the more so when his mates all laughed and when she finished her beer and walked to her car the man in the hi viz shirt called out that he knew where she lived and she gave him the bird but when she got home she kept her doors and windows locked at night but refused Killer's offer to lend her his old shotgun, the one with the slightly bent barrel that he said wouldn't matter providing she got nice and close before she pulled the trigger, and he chuckled like the old coot he was and told her that from her description the bloke in the baseball cap was Kevin Cutler's nephew and that he was all mouth and had no brains but seemed happy enough without them.

Angela pulled into the servo to fill the car with petrol. She looked back up the road, up the hill towards her house and could see that the flames had crested the big ridge and would soon come flowing down the valley in a flood of heat, flame and radiant energy changing matter, laws of thermodynamics she tried to remember from chemistry, or was it physics, she doesn't remember and just did science for the HSC to keep her father happy because he wanted her to go to university and study something real like medicine, something he said that he could be proud of when all Angela wanted to do was read books and study English and her favourite, in Year 12, was Mick and his story of the rusty ships mast sitting in the ocean at Geraldton that might have been, for the little boy, something else and Mick had taken some lines from John Donne and her teacher, Mrs Jackson, a kind but whimsical hippy, had told her that John Donne was a metaphysical poet and when Angela taught John Dunne to her first year uni students, she wondered how many of them thought that metaphysics had something to do with spiritual naturalism and even witchcraft and not because of the use by the poets of conceit.

When Angela walked into the little service station shop to pay for her petrol, she thought that Anila looked scared and while Anila was scanning Angela's bottle of water and packet of jelly snakes, she kept looking out the window to the flames on the ridge. Anila's husband, Gerald, was out fighting the fires but not in Kevin Cutler's brigade. Gerald was in the brigade in one of the neighbouring towns and he and Kevin Cutler hardly spoke, and Alyssa said that it was because Kevin said unkind things about Anila when she came to Australia from India with Gerald when he returned to run the servo after his father died. Kevin had said that Anila could live in the town for the rest of her life, but she would never be part of the community. Angela always made a point of being nice to her and would thank Anila by joining her hands at the finger tips and bowing her head whenever she bought petrol or her jelly snakes.

When she walked back out to her car, Angela heard the sound of sirens in the distance but getting closer now and coming up the Maitland Road, and soon she saw a line of fire fighting vehicles appear from a number of the neighbouring towns and villages. They had been fighting these fires for a couple of days in the hard scrabble gullies and ridges but for some reason, some person, somewhere, sitting in an office perhaps with maps and white boards and radios and worried colleagues and thermos flasks of tea and unattended sandwiches going hard and curling up at the edges, had made the decision that whatever else was burning, Allynsdale was now the priority and, Angela thought, in the tropes of the cowboy films her father liked to watch on television on Saturday afternoons, the cavalry had arrived and she was pleased to see that one of the leading trucks was from the brigade where Gerald volunteered and he was at the wheel of the Toyota Landcruiser and gave Angela a wave and tooted his horn for Anila as he swept past the servo and the shop and the pub and the church and pulled up just past old Molly Thompson's house where it looked to Angela, who did not know much about the art of firefighting, that this was the spot where they had decided to defend the town and then Angela felt sick because, by not going further up the road, the fire fighters had already abandoned all hope for her place, or Killer's, or Tony and Alyssa's and perhaps Kevin Cutler and his band of boys had already entered the mouth of Dante's furnace.

As she watched, Anila came out of the shop and stood next to Angela, her hands twisting the bottom of the oversized polo shirt that she always wore with the fuel company's logo embroidered on the pocket.

'You'll be alright', Angela said to Anila, putting a hand on her shoulder, which she hoped might be comforting and which she also hoped was not culturally inappropriate to Anila, but was pretty sure it was ok to touch as long as you didn't touch someone on the head or touch them with your foot, 'Gerald's here now and he's got his mates and they'll protect the town.'

Anila just nodded in response as they watched the men and women unroll the hoses from the trucks and direct water on the gutters and eves of Molly Thompson's house and then one of the trucks roared off up the road another hundred yards or so. The embers were now causing spot fires on the edge of town and there were new puffs of smoke up the ridgeway, up towards Killer and Angela's houses and she was torn with the urge to get moving, to get to the safety of the city or to watch what she knew was coming bearing down on them and knew whatever she decided to do, she had to do it quickly.

Connecting
the Stagnant Ponds

A disconnected series of stagnant ponds. She remembered reading those words or hearing those words and maybe it was on the wireless or the television set, as she anachronistically liked to call her electronic media apparatus. A disconnected series of stagnant ponds she thought she remembered was a description for what had once been a grand old river out in the west of the state. One of those rivers where the paddle steamers used to come to collect the wool clip and now there were no paddle steamers and no wool clip and no river even, just the stagnant ponds that could not support the most basic river life.

A swamp was how a friend once described the city they had both grown up in and Angela had laughed at her friend because Angela thought she heard once that a swamp was an endlessly interesting and complex eco-system, and this is not what her friend meant in describing their city and maybe the friend should have called it a bog or a morass or some other word that meant those things that her friend had wanted the words to mean. A disconnected series of stagnant ponds might have been more apt if either of them had managed to hear that phrase all those years ago, when they were young and when they used to laugh and love and all the other foolish things.

Angela had driven some ten or fifteen miles south of Allynsdale and the valley was much wider than it was at the little village, and the river, still scarcely a stream and not like a grand river, the Thames or the Seine or the Rhine or the Rhone, was on her left hand side and had been there, just over her shoulder, since she crossed the little rickety wooden bridge that was just outside of town and always made her scared with the way it seemed to rattle and sway when she drove over it and she wondered how on earth it managed to allow the fire trucks with their heavy water tanks to get across. She knew that the fire was probably getting worse because a couple of times she saw helicopters lowering buckets into dams to get water to drop on the flames and there wasn't a lot of water in those farm dams anyway and she hoped that the firefighting helicopters wouldn't leave the farmers short of water for their stock. Starving stock, thirsty stock, she remembered once, a big dry, going to Queensland in her father's car and out in the West there were lines and lines of dead sheep up against the barbed wire fences for miles and miles and miles. Every now and again, as she drove, she could see irrigation systems set up to draw water from the river to fill up the big concrete water containers that the cattle drank out of but now there was so little water in the river that the drawing off from the river had been banned and the paddocks had grass that was stunted, brown and dead, with lots of patches of earth in between.

Further south the land would change again to the wide alluvial mud plains that, when she was a little girl and would go on family drives in her father's Kingswood, would be lush and green with big tall fronds of corn that rippled in the wind and once, her father stopped the car and walked over to one of those tall stalks and broke off a cob of corn and let Angela bight into the bright yellow juicy kernels and she remembered that as she drove and she smiled and she thought for some strange reason of Kansas and how, the year she went to Aztec to see where Mick had lived, that she had decided to do a road trip through the mid-west and drove through the miles and miles of corn plantations of Kansas that could feed the world, she thought, but the Grandfathers of Kansas, who Ginsberg said had holy cocks, had decided that the corn was best for ethanol and preferred to feed the cars of the wide grey interstate than feed the babies of the world. Moloch!

What year was that, she tried to remember, her journey in summer to New Mexico, the first night in Longmont to meet with a friend who didn't show at the funky pub where she drank dark beer and ate Jambalaya even though she was in Colorado and surely they would have had some local speciality, and the drive next day to Santa Fe and how her father, he of the Saturday afternoon cowboy films, would have loved the landscape from the I25 of mesas in the blue sky distance, thorn trees and cacti and the expectation that somewhere in the distance the ghosts of cowboys and Native American warriors were still spilling blood or leaving parched bones, whitened in the sun like the skulls of buffalo and cattle in the paintings of Georgia O'Keefe that Angela drank in, absorbed through her pores, the hot afternoon when she stopped into the museum in Santa Fe for the cool of the air conditioning and then later to wander around the old town square and then to a hotel to spend the night before the pilgrimage up into the southern part of the Rockies for Aztec and for Mick, and remembering that D.H. Lawrence lived in New Mexico, in Taos a long time ago, and the Professor, her tutor, her colleague and old man lover, loved David Herbert because he was from working class England and was complicated and died too young.

It was 2013, she remembered, her yearlong research trip to England and America, returning home and back to the halls of the university and how dreary it all seemed and how, when she was gone, the Professor had retired, grown too old to bother now with undergraduates and their flirtatious ways or the earnest young men who wanted to challenge him because he was old and grey and liked to share a flagon with his tute group of an afternoon after polishing off a bottle of white wine in the staff house. The Professor who had told Angela MacGregor, bluestocking tutor of the English Department, flame haired courtesan of poets, that she could not talk of such things as literature if she had not seen the world and that the words on the pages might be read in dusty rooms with a sad and pale sun streaming through a dirty window but they were written out in the streets of a foreign city, the ports and docks of Europe, the fabled streets of Manhattan, the great plains rolling west across another America where the sleepers of Jean Genet had fled. He simply told her open her eyes to something more than the steel city.

London was a dream and she knew the city backwards from all the books and plays and movies that she had read, could walk its streets, its parks and buildings with a map made up inside her head from culture. She though she understood a tiny bit about the singing of the country that her Aboriginal friend, Bob, had once described, but knew she never could tell him that because she would get a lecture that she knew she deserved about cultural appropriation and colonisation and all those nasty things. But here, in London, it all seemed different, known and unknown all at the same time and she had promised Grandma that she would make the trip up North to Scotland and maybe there, she would have some epiphany, where at long last she might know who, at last, she was, and if not in the Highlands of Scotland or the streets of London or New York, perhaps she would have her epiphany in the pueblos of New Mexico but she knew, that this twelve months would change her.

Angela had been given the name of the girl in South Kensington by a fellow they all called Ned, on account of his surname being Kelly, who had worked in London for a while and Ned had told Angela that she might have remembered Georgia from their days at uni although Georgia was a few years older than the rest of them and had finished uni when they were all still in second year but she might also remember that Georgia had once shared the house in Tighes Hill in the shadow of the steelworks with Andy Mac and a fellow called Patrick who had dropped out of uni and had some job in the mines. Ned reminded Angela that Georgia had wild multi-coloured hair and that Patrick's girlfriend had nicknamed her the Rainbow Warrior and that must have been in the mid 1980's because the Rainbow Warrior was the name of the Greenpeace boat that the French Secret Service blew up in Auckland Harbour when it was protesting French nuclear tests in the Pacific.

Georgia returned Angela's E Mail and said that she remembered Angela clearly from back in the old days and made some oblique reference to the fact that her flatmate, Andy, might have been more than a bit keen on Angela but all of that changed when Sophie came along, and everything changed for all of them. The mention of Sophie unsettled Angela a little bit because there were things that Angela chose not to remember and other things she preferred to forget completely. Poor little mad Sophie was the daughter of the Professor and seemed to live in his shadow, he being the great Promethean colossus who strode across the English Department exclaiming passages from Blake and with a fierce countenance to match his apocalyptic vision. Angela never knew if Sophie was aware that she, Angela, had for a time became the lover of the Professor sometime after he tried to seduce her with claret and poetry one night in his study while they were discussing what she might do for an honour's thesis and he was not impressed when she said she wanted to focus on Mick. She had thought of doing something on Joyce because he was her true love, the master of words, but she also loved Mick because he was the lover of something else, something untouchable, a mirage on the horizon across a salt plain, a song of a bird on the wind on a day that was so hot that it was brittle even though she always thought of brittle days as being days in winter, with a frost on the ground or what she imagined the crunch of snow underfoot would sound like, so, in the end, Mick won and she read and re-read and found that Mick wasn't the only enigmatic stranger but his books were filled with them, sometimes the redeemer and sometimes the destroyer, and time and time again and the more she read, that summer before her honour's year started, she began immersed in time and words to the point of not seeing anything around her and having her friends accuse of her of forgetting them.

Angela had never forgotten Andy, who wanted more than anything to be a poet because somewhere in his mind he had an image of what a poet was or what, perhaps a poet should have been, and maybe he had thought that through Sophie, he could have found his poet, and Sophie, poor little Sophie, who just wanted to be loved by somebody in a way she though that love should be.

Angela MacGregor had stepped through the door of the Qantas Boeing 747 into the airbridge that would take her to the arrivals hall, customs and immigration control at Heathrow Airport and she was clutching a brand new passport and it was the second day of the new year and she was forty-nine years, single and could, as of late last year, call herself Dr Macgregor, which she hoped would satisfy her father at last, although it was not a PhD in Australian Literature that he had in mind when he said he would like to see a doctor in the family, and apart from a few nervous hours in Singapore, this was the first time her feet had touched a foreign shore.

Fading back out of her dreams and memories, Angela was amazed, as she drove south from the fire, by the way that her mind wandered when she was in her car, dreams and imaginations multiplying with the movement of the car, the whoosh of the tyres on the road, that had turned from dirt to macadam at the edge of Allynsdale, right outside old Molly Thompson's house, amplified by the various sights that flashed in the windscreen like she was watching a movie of disjointed scenes and tableaus that somehow informed the story of her life in stolen images and childhood memories. There had been a CD playing in the car that she barely registered and she thought that perhaps that she should turn to the local ABC radio station where she might get some news about the progress of the fire and she thought that as now she would have good mobile reception that she should call her elderly parents and tell them that she was safe and she wished that they had owned mobile phones themselves so that she didn't have to actually go through the tedium of talking to her mother and could just send a text message with the basic information she wanted to convey, but no, she would have to have a conversation and her mother would want her to come and stay at the family home in the suburbs with them and her mother would tell Angela that her bed was made up in her old room and Angela knew that the old room would look exactly like it looked in 1981, when she left home, and that the Joy Division poster, the one featuring the cover design from Unknown Pleasures, would still be on the wall and would be even more faded now, and she knew that the books she read when she was a teenager, before she discovered literature, would be on the shelves and next to them would be the art book filled with her terrible poems and drawings and there would be the polaroid photographs stuck on the mirror showing her when she thought that she might like to be a punk just because it would cause the neighbours to raise their eyes and talk behind their lace curtains about the wayward daughter of Mr and Mrs MacGregor. She decided that she would stop in Maitland and grab a cup of coffee and maybe a sandwich and would then steel herself to telephone her parents and chuckled to herself about the way they were probably worried sick about her and how she was with the fire rolling down the hill but they wouldn't think to try and call her on her mobile phone because it would cost too much and the call might inconvenience her and she thought that she should stop sounding so tetchy whenever she spoke to her mother on the phone. She didn't get tetchy speaking to her father because, on the phone, he was just as gruff and taciturn as Angela, so they could communicate in as few words as possible and still convey their meaning in such a way that Angela thought that her father probably should have been a poet.

The little towns grew bigger, further down the valley, but quiet now on Saturday afternoon with the shops in the towns all closed, Saterdee, day for sports it seemed and as she entered Wallisville, on the outskirts of the town ten times bigger than Allynsdale which meant it must have held two hundred souls, she saw the men and boys in long white pants and collared white shirts with soft brim white and floppy hats, the outfielders standing straight and bored, hoping for some breeze and the slips fielders crouching in their cordon, ready hands and watchful eyes as the batsman nervously and rhythmically taps the bottom of his willow bat with a thick yellow handle on to the toe of his Dunlop Volleys while the bowler, tall and lean with big broad shoulders, thunders in like an express train, or perhaps a bushfire running down a ridge, and Angela is gone before the leather hits the willow but hears the crack, the thump, of a well struck ball even over the radio announcers soft voice of dire messages about the coming conflagration.

There's a different radio coming from the pub where she's forced to stop and wait for a big four-wheel drive, crew cab ute with dog cages on the back to reverse angle park into a narrow spot between two other utes and, for a second, winds her window down to smell the smells of Wallisville and smell the burning coming from the north. In Wallisville the radio in the pub is playing the sounds of horse races, excited voice of the caller getting louder, picking up speed, high pitched and nasally, sounding all the world like a middle-aged man approaching a rare and unexpected orgasm. The race ends while the driver is still trying to manipulate the crew cab ute into the narrow space and when the race has ended, some men in jeans and chequered shirts come out from the pub, glasses of beer in hand and unlit cigarettes in their mouths and a permanent look of disappointment on their faces and, as they light their smokes with their plastic Bics, they look and point to the clouds of smoke to the north.

Angela's Pa liked the races on Saturdays. Her father's father, not her grandfather, who was her mother's father and never liked anything much that Angela could recall. Her Pa liked the races on a Saturday, the tinny sound coming from the boxy portable wireless in a brown leather case that sat on the windowsill above the kitchen sink and her Pa would sit at the table and her Nana would make pots of tea and cook pikelets if Angela was there and cut sandwiches with boiled corned beef and tomato slices soaked in vinegar for Angela's Pa who would lick the tip of the stub of a Columbia pencil, Copperplate, red and black and white like the old German flag, and mark up the form guide he had taken from the middle of that day's Herald, ticking the bets he won and crossing off the bets he lost and at the end of the day's racing, if he had winnings to collect, he would get in his Hillman Hunter and drive to the Commercial Hotel backroom where Sal D'Amico, SP Bookie reigned.

Once her Pa won a lot of money and he shouted Nana and Angela and Angela's Dad to tea at the Chinese Restaurant in Belford near their homes and Angela was told she could order whatever she wanted and she looked at the menu and thought that she wanted everything because it all seemed so exotic and special and she never had Chinese before because her mother wouldn't have it in the house on account of her own father's feelings about the Japanese and Angela thought that the Chinese and Japanese were different and, anyway, Angela's mum said she had a headache and wouldn't come to the Chinese restaurant and her dad was happy because when they had gone to a Chinese restaurant, once before, Angela's mother would only order off the section of the menu that said 'Australian' and while her dad had tucked into his egg flour and chicken soup and his beef in black bean sauce and deluxe fried rice, her mother sat with a pursed face and a plate of fish and chips with a little salad on the side.

At last the man had parked his ute and hopping out, called

out some obscenities to the men on the pub verandah and they all laughed and Angela put the Subaru in gear and, easing out the clutch, continued on her journey down the river to where it joined the bigger river and ran, a river to the sea, but the road ran away from the river before it joined the other and crossed the valley floor and wended its way through farms with their rows and rows of chicken sheds and large brick houses with American style barns and children on loud little motorbikes and teenaged girls on ponies, to the place that had once been another little town like Wallisville but now was streets and streets of brand new houses on quarter acre blocks and was known to the local council as a suburb and every second house had a flagpole with an Australian flag fluttering in the strong north wind and at the edge of the suburb were two big barn like building next to one another, The River View Tavern and the Songs of Praise Revival Church and the church was empty but the carpark of the tavern was half full and a sign out the front said that there would be a band on that night after the raffles and the happy hour.

Angela rarely went to pubs these days, not like when she was a student and the university bar seemed to be her second home, downing drinks with her friends after class, listening to the bullshit that flowed between Andy and Brendan as they tried to outdo each other in how well read they were until Andy met Sophie and it all changed and Brendan started hanging out more and more with Lucy, who dropped him cold when he got himself busted and even though he managed to get off, his days of supplying weed to his friends was over as he wanted an unblemished record so, when he finished Arts, he could enrol in Law and have a glittering legal career. If she went to pubs infrequently she went to churches even less and had never actually stepped foot inside one of the big barn like happy clappy churches that seemed to be springing up in all the outer suburbs, where all the families lived, with their Macmansions and neat clothes and big cars and children who looked like they stepped out of some mid-western nineteen-fifties family sitcom, the type Angela would watch after school on the big black and white Pye with its polished wooden cabinet. She liked her churches old school with lots of incense and chanting and mystery, but not the priests with their roving hands. When she was in London, she went to church one Sunday, inspired by Nick Cave to climb the stone steps to Brompton Oratory where the mass was said in Latin inside the shadowed gothic vaults. Angela remembered feeling a bit disappointed that the stone steps were nowhere near as grand as she had imagined them from Nick's song and she had a vision of Nick, thin and black suit clad, climbing a high set of steps, majestic in his brooding darkness like some vengeful character from the Old Testament, burnt clean with the fire of redemption, but when she arrived at the Oratory, she found two or three low stone steps that didn't require any climbing other in the most symbolic sense of needing to ascend to the word of a God in which she had long stopped believing.

Angela thought that the bushfires might have brought out the happy clappers a day earlier, because, from the colour of the sky, the sun hidden, red and angry by the growing smoke that, she could see in her rear view mirror, was now taking up nearly half the sky, it might look, if you believed in such things, as the start of the end of days, the start of the rapture and that's what all the happy clappers were waiting for. She remembered the old Prime Minister, the nasty little one, the one who didn't appear to like women very much, describe the ISIS fighters as belonging to a death cult and this amused her greatly because she thought that the Christian Church was also a great death cult – the Catholics with their emphasis on the tortured death of the twisted and broken body of Christ and their saints and their heaven and hell and purgatory and the rewards that follow a good life, and then there were the happy clappers, who Angela thought were even more of a death cult, meeting in their churches, feverously praying for the end of the world, the end of days, the cataclysm that would come as surely as the sun would set and Angela thought that if she believed in such things, the red sky to the north might be all the evidence she would need of the imminent return of Christ to sort the sheep from the goats. She assumed that the happy clappers were probably all ensconced in their large air-conditioned houses doing whatever it was that they did behind closed doors and then she had a sudden desire, like she had when she was a little girl, to be rendered invisible so she could creep quietly into other people's houses to see how they lived, what they did and what they talked about. She would love to creep into one of those big houses on the edge of town to see what books they had on their shelves, if any other than the bible, or what food they had in their cupboards and she imagined that there was probably a lot of processed food and ready to eat meals but had no basis on which to think that this was the case.

She was glad that Maitland was close and hoped that her favourite café would still be open as it was getting late into the afternoon and she couldn't remember whether the café stayed open for dinner as she had only ever had lunch there and all this thought of food had made her realise that she hadn't eaten all day and needed a coffee to get her through the last half hour of driving to Ingrid's harbourside apartment and, if she didn't eat something soon, when she got to Ingrid's place she would probably eat her out of house and home and then Angela thought that she should stop on the way and get some provisions like wine and cheese and crackers and olives and cured meats.

In the last couple of miles to the bridge over the big river, Angela had passed a number of fire trucks heading north and from the names on their sides, she realised that they had come from lots of different places throughout the state and the call must have gone out for more volunteers. It seemed from the radio that there were a lot of fires burning in the mountains across the top of the ranges and all the way east to the coast where there were concerns for some of the little places where people went to retire or to stay over the summer for fishing and aquatic holidays. Angela had never had the desire for a holiday by the sea and she hated the way that her fair skin never tanned and just turned the same red colour as her hair, and when she was a teenager, she envied all the skinny girls lying in the sun at the Lambton pool in their little bikinis and skin that smelled like coconut oil while she had to wear a one piece that covered her body and she would slip on a light weight cotton long sleeve top and straw hat when she wasn't actually in the water having a swim. The cool girls from her school all said that she was a dag and sometimes the words stung and she wondered what the cool girls from school were all doing now and wouldn't have been surprised if they were all out in the suburbs with their tradesmen husbands and their adult kids still living at home because they had ADHD and couldn't get jobs or study and who spent all day playing games on the their X Boxes that involved stealing cars and shooting police officers and kidnapping prostitutes somewhere on the west coast of the USA.

San Francisco, she liked San Francisco and stayed for a couple of nights on her way back from searching for the spirit of Mick and D.H. Lawrence in Aztec and Taos on what had been the last leg of her big trip to London and New York and all the other places in England and Scotland. She bought so many books at City Lights that when she got to the airport, she had to pay an excess baggage charge and now those books were all on the shelves of the mud-brick cottage, waiting for the flames to reach them, if they hadn't already, and she suddenly felt a rise of bitter bile come to her throat from her stomach when she thought about her little house in the hills and what might be happening and Killer, who she saw in her mind's eye standing up to a wall of flame coming towards him and him screaming 'come and take me you fucking cunt bastard' because that's what Killer called everything he hated, a 'fucking cunt bastard' and if he said it in front of Angela, he would immediately blush and apologise for his language and she would tell him that words never offended her only actions and he would say 'I was raised better than to swear in front of a lady' and she would tell him that she was a woman and not a lady and that ladies had titles and lived in crumbling mansions they couldn't afford on large tracts of land in England and Killer would tell her that she was always a lady in his eyes and then he would blush some more and apologise some more and then find an excuse to get back home because he had to feed the dog or feed the chooks or water the tomatoes and as Angela drove over the long bridge into Maitland she almost found herself praying for Killer and his dog and his chooks and his tomatoes.

The café on the levee bank was still open and there were quite a few people who looked like they might have been lingering post lunch with coffee and cake but she still managed to find a table for one in the shade of a frangipani tree and thought of having some cake with her coffee, but decided on a sandwich instead and thought that if she needed an extra sugar hit she could have an affogato after the sandwich and café latte. She tried not to be annoyed at the children who were playing a chasing game around the various tables in the courtyards while their parents sat, feigning oblivion, trading gossip over the frappes and cappuccinos, but it took all of her effort and she tried to decide if she was less tolerant to children nowadays than she had been in the past or had she always been intolerant.

There was a point in her early to mid-thirties when it seemed like all of her friends were getting married and having children or, at least, partnering up and having children and over time she lost touch with the raisers of children because they preferred to do things with the other child raisers and Angela always felt left out of the conversations about whether little Hayley had started to walk yet or how advanced Sebastian's language skills were and how he could string together complete sentences which, to Angela's ears, still sounded like gibberish. Being an only child herself, she didn't have siblings with children, so she never got to play the role of aunty to anyone except in a couple of honorary situations but she just didn't click with the little ones and thought that perhaps she could rekindle some of the friendships she had with the child raisers once they became empty nesters and might be more interested in, what Angela considered to be, adult conversations.

As much as Angela preferred to text people rather than talk on the telephone, she decided, while she was waiting for her latte and chicken and lettuce sandwich to arrive, that it would be more polite to speak to Ingrid in person and tell her that she was on her way to stay, if that was alright, and she thought that it would be because had told her that she was welcome to stay anytime and even given Angela her own swipe card for the garage and the lift and Ingrid's apartment door. She hoped that Ingrid wouldn't be at work and didn't think she would be because a couple of years ago Ingrid moved into a management role at the hospital and didn't have to do to many shifts unless they were really short-handed in the emergency section where she had been a Registered Nurse for years and years and then, as she thought this, Angela realised that if the fires got too bad and if there were a lot of casualties, that it might be all hands on deck at the hospital.

'Hello stranger' Ingrid said when she answered the phone on only the second ring, 'what's happening? I've been worried sick; the fire is really bad, and I've been stuck in front of the telly. When you rang, I thought it might have been work calling me in and then I saw your name and thought, well at least you're safe enough to call'.

Angela waited until Ingrid drew breath, it was always like that talking to her. 'I had to leave, you know evacuate. I was hoping to crash at yours?' Angela said and instantly thought how silly it sounded, a middle-aged woman asking if she could crash with her friend as if they were all still uni students in their twenties.

'Any time, you know that' Ingrid said, 'where are you now?'

'Maitland, I just stopped at the café on the levee to grab a bite to eat and a coffee so I should be with you in under an hour. Is there anything you need me to pick up on the way?'

Ingrid told her that was nothing she needed, and she was going to put some tonic water in the fridge and that there would be a g and t in Angela's hand the moment she entered the door.

She couldn't see the river from the café on the levee as the banks of the river were too high and the river was so low and she always found it hard to believe that the river could rise so high that it could flood the town and had done so a number of times over the years but everyone thought that it was less likely to flood now the levee was in place but Angela wasn't so sure. Her dad had seen it in 1955 when it was one of the worst in recorded history, by which she knew, when people said that, they meant white people's history. Angela's dad had been doing his national service in the CMF, the Civilian Military Force of part-time soldiers and has her dad dismissively called them, cut lunch commandos and weekend warriors. She often thought she got some her self-deprecating humour from her dad.

Lance Corporal Macgregor, as he was then, was twenty two years old and was in charge of a DUKW based at the big depot on the harbour just below Fort Scratchley and he thought he was very important to be a Non-Commissioned Officer at such a young age where he had to give orders to the rest of the men in his DUKW, the driver and the signaller, who were both a few years older than him and had served in Korea. The DUKW was a type of truck that could travel in the water like a boat and was mainly used to move soldiers and material from ships to beachheads or to cross rivers and lakes and, in times like 1955, they were used for flood rescues. Angela's father had two main jobs during the flood. One of the jobs was to direct the DUKW up to the awnings and second floor windows of shops along High Street and take on passengers to be transported to safer, higher ground at Rutherford or East Maitland and he was very proud of that. The second job was one that he only spoke about during the last few years, and that was to retrieve bodies that had been spotted by the helicopters floating in the water, and he hated the way he had to lean over the side of the vehicle and use a hook, like a big gaff hook used in fishing, and pull the bodies to the side of the DUKW where he and the signaller would have to haul them over the side and then check them for signs of life but he said that you could always tell straight away that they were dead and it wasn't the fact that they weren't breathing and had no pulse but he said that you could tell that the life force or the spirit or whatever it was had already left them and they were no longer a person with feeling and dreams and desires and loves and hates but just a body, just a collection of organic matter that was, if they had been in the water for more than a day or two, already returning to the earth in its constituent parts. One night when he was going on and on about this to Angela as they sipped on a whisky during one of her rare overnight visits, where she stayed in her teenage punk bedroom, she wondered whether he had PTSD and then wondered to herself whether you could suffer from the effects of PTSD for sixty years, and assumed that if you kept all bottled up in there that you could, but when she broached the fact that maybe he should talk to someone about these feeling, he told her that he was just a silly old man and that it was just the whisky talking.

If it was the whisky talking, perhaps it would have had an accent like Angela's grandma, her mother's mother who never lost the accent of Fife even though she was only a little girl when she came to Australia and had never been back to Scotland, even for a visit. She liked a drink herself, Angela's grandma, and would sit down each afternoon with a cold glass of Cream Sherry or two, 'to taste the gab' she'd say to Angela, meaning to whet her appetite and as she got older, Angela would think that her grandma's appetite might have been improved with a more interesting diet that seemed to consist almost entirely of mince fried with onions and oatmeal (that she called collops), boiled potatoes and turnips and, on Friday, what with grandma being a good Catholic, it would be poached smoked cod, boiled potatoes and turnips. Sometimes grandma would cook a special meal for Angela's grandfather that would consist of tripe that was cooked until it was tender in milk and onions and would be served, like everything else, with the boiled potatoes and turnips. Angela liked good food but had never really bothered with learning how to cook anything more elaborate than a roast and her own diet was usually simple with some grilled or fried chicken or, if she cooked a piece of roast beef or a leg of lamb, she could live on the leftovers for days, sometimes cutting up the roast meet and putting it in a dish with some onion gravy, carrots, left over baked potatoes and peas and topping it with mashed potato and then baking it until the top was a golden brown and if she had plenty, she would put some on a dish and take it up the hill for Killer who said that Shepherd's Pie was his favourite and she reminded him if it was made with beef, it was Cottage Pie and he would laugh and say 'it's all fucking Shepherd's Pie to me love' and then quickly apologise for swearing. Killer always came back the next day to return the dish that had been carefully cleaned to an immaculate level including the removal of some of the burned on black bits on the bottom that Angela never bothered to clean. She had thought, sometimes, of inviting Killer in for a meal, particularly if she was cooking something he had given her, like the chooks gone off the lay, but she thought that it might make him feel uncomfortable and she suspected that he might not have the best table manners and while that didn't bother Angela, she thought it might embarrass Killer. They had known each other for years and would speak nearly every day and certainly there wouldn't be a time when two or three days passed without them having a brief conversation about something or other or borrowing something or lending each other a hand. Killer would help Angela with chores around the yard that were too big for one person and Angela would mend Killer's clothes when they needed a patch, or a tear sewn up. Given their closeness in some ways, Angela thought it was funny that they had never actually stepped foot in each other's house but had conducted all their conversations in the yard or sitting on the verandas of the houses.

As she sat with her chicken sandwich in the levee bank café, Angela wondered if Killer liked tripe. In the same way that Angela's grandma cooked tripe as a treat for her Angela's grandfather, her mother cooked tripe for her father and used much the same recipe and it became a favourite of Angela's as well, much to the horror of a lot of her young friends at school and later at university and it was a food memory that Angela missed because it was never on the menu in any of the cafes or restaurants that she would visit when she was in town on business and was rarely seen in the supermarket although she did manage to buy it once from the little butcher in Wallisville who had lots of interesting things in his display case including goods he smoked himself, like ham and even venison that he would buy from the hunters in the pub and turn into salamis and pastramis and other treats, and Angela had smiled and said to him that he was a real charcutier and the butcher eyed her suspiciously and said that no, he was just a butcher. She bought the tripe and took it home and let it simmer away with milk and onions and she was so looking forward to her dinner that night but when she ate the tripe, it was tasteless and had the consistency and texture of rubber that had been left in the sun. She thought that she would ask her mother for the recipe and that she would stop again at the butcher in Wallisville and, if it was any good, she would share it with Killer.

Her mind snapped away from her thoughts of tripe when

she realised that she might not have a house to go back to nor might Killer and if he stayed to fight the fire, anything might have happened to the old man because one thing she knew for sure, Kevin Cutler and his boys wouldn't do much to save old Killer and she pictured him, standing there by his little cottage as a wave, a tsunami, of red hot flame swept him and all he owned into its embrace and she hoped that he didn't suffer when this happened and that it would be mercifully quick and she wondered if, at that last moment, in the words of Mick, that Killer would think, like Herriot, that his soul was an old country.

The Ghosts in the River

Angela threaded her away down the streets that led her away from the river and the levee and the café towards the railway station where she would cross the line on the high level bridge, turn left at the roundabout and then be on the highway that would take her to Ingrid and the city and she would not see the river again until she reached Hexham and there it would be, much broader and a muddy kind of brown colour that was tidal, pulled by the moods of the moon, that harsh mistress, Angela sang to herself, and where, if the season was right, there would be a number of little boats, wooden prawn trawlers with chipped and faded paint work and bedecked with nets and ropes and bright orange buoys, making their way up and down the river catching the tiny but sweet Hunter River prawns that her dad liked so much on crusty white bread with lashings of butter and a little splash of brown malt vinegar. The river runs through the heart of the valley, drawing into it the other rivers and creeks and brooks and streams that run from the mountains to the north, west and south, the Barrington Tops and Liverpool Range and Wattagans. Apart from her year abroad, her year in London and New York and New Mexico, Angela had never lived anywhere else other than in this valley and, apart from the last five years living in the hills above Allynsdale, she had always lived in the once smoky city and its suburbs.

When she was teaching at the university, many of her colleagues were proud of the fact that they had qualifications from universities all over the country and the world and acted as if there was something quaint and provincial about someone like Angela who had completed her undergraduate degree, master's degree and doctorate all at the same small university. Angela, on the other hand, found that all those colleagues with their Oxbridge degrees were snobbish and clannish and she once earned a reprimand for saying in a staff meeting 'if your degrees from Oxford and Cambridge make you all so superior, why aren't you teaching in one of the great universities in the UK or an ivy league college in the USA or, is it that you see yourself in some missionary role to educate us poor simple colonials?' There was much huffing and puffing from her colleagues and lot of offence, both real and feigned, being taken, and they were probably even more offended when the Professor, who had himself earned his doctorate from Magdalen, laughed loudly and heartily and winked at Angela. She later learned that the Professor had spoken up for her when the head was considering not offering her a teaching position for the following year, and the Professor told the head that Angela's assessment was spot on and that the Oxbridge clique were exactly that, a clique of pompous jumped up snobs who, to a man, and they were all men, had come to Oxford or Cambridge via one of the lesser public schools and had decamped to the colonies where they could be big frogs in small ponds and that the Professor felt the university actually had an obligation to nurture and promote their own, to which the head replied, heavily with sarcasm, that the Professor seemed to be doing enough nurturing of students for the rest of the staff put together.

Angela thought it strange the way that her thoughts all seemed to come crashing into each other these days and she could be thinking about one thing, something she had seen or something she had heard, or a book she was reading or a film she was watching on television, or the noise of the birds and animals around her house and the thought that she was thinking would suddenly fly off to something completely unrelated like it was on a whim of its own and she could not control the randomness of her thoughts.

There had been nothing on the wireless for some time about the fire at Allynsdale and she couldn't decide if this was a good or bad thing. From what she could gather, the fire had swept across the ridges, pushed by the north westerly winds and then when the wind swung around more to the north and even to the north east, the fire had broken the containment lines that had been set and was sweeping down a couple of valleys and the valley to the east of Angela's valley had a couple of towns that were larger than Allynsdale, larger even than Wallisville and these were the towns of immediate concern and the many small holdings and hobby farms that made up most of the properties outside of those towns. The wireless told Angela that there had been evacuation centres set up in the high school at Cheltenham which was one of the larger towns at the foothills of the mountains and was at high risk.

Angela wondered what it would be like sitting in an evacuation centre fearing and expecting the worst. She thought that the fear was probably contagious and imagined that most people would be sitting around muted and stunned, but that it would only take one person becoming hysterical to cause that hysteria to spread faster than the fire from which they were fleeing. The children would be the worst, she thought, little partially formed beings responding more to stimuli than anything else, tasting and smelling the fear, but not knowing what the fear was about, other than the sense of either panic or despair on the faces of their parents and the other adults.

'Allynsdale', she heard the word 'Allynsdale' on the radio and it snapped her out of her thoughts about the children and she thought for a second that the word seemed strange and alien to her and yet, at the same time, something known and something comfortable. When she was a child she would sometimes repeat her own name to herself like a mantra and wonder if that is who she really was, a collection of vowels and consonants strung together neither randomly nor with any particular sense of order and was her Angela different to any other Angela spelt the same and that there were at least seven other Angela's in her school that she knew of and they all looked different, one was black skinned whose parents came from some place called Rhodesia and they were both nurses at the hospital, even the dad, which Angela thought was strange, a man being a nurse, another was Chinese but said that she came from Singapore and Angela asked her grandfather, The Law, if there were Chinese in Singapore and he said the place was full of them and that the Japs killed plenty during the war but when Angela asked the little girl from Singapore, she said that she didn't know anything about the war and that it was a long time ago and that her parents didn't like to talk about it and Angela said that her grandfather, who had been in Singapore on and off for over three years talked about nothing else and it made him angry and he would swear and then her grandma would rouse on him for saying naughty words in front of his granddaughter.

The man on the radio was saying that people were very worried about Allynsdale and that the fire had reached the edge of the little town and that there were a lot of spot fires from the burning embers and at least one house on the edge of the town was on fire and crews were fighting to save it and Angela had an image in her mind of Molly Thompson's doilies bursting, one after another, into flames on top of her sideboard and polished dining room table and wondered why she would think of Mrs Thompson's doilies above anything else and she couldn't even be sure that the house on fire belonged to Molly and anyway, it could have been one of a couple of houses that sat on the edge of the town and if it was falling embers doing the damage, they could have landed anywhere and started the fire and not necessarily on Molly Thompson's.

The man who owned the pub, Singo, was on the phone to the radio announcer and he said that the police and fire fighters had told the people in the town that they should all leave and they could wait at the showground at Wallisville where the Salvation Army and Red Cross and the Wallisville Neighbourhood Centre were organising meals and drinks and places to sleep in one of the pavilions if needed and that the RSPCA had sent volunteers to look after any pets and they had supplies of pet food with them. Singo said that a few people had left but that he was going to stay and fight the fire with his big hose and pump connected to the bore water that fortunately had not run dry. Singo said that they were worried because nobody had heard from Kevin Cutler and the Allynsdale firefighters who had gone to the top of the ridge early that morning and now, the police were saying, that the road was completely cut with fallen trees that were still burning and that Kevin Cutler's wife was staying until she knew that her husband was safe and that everyone hoped that they were just taking shelter in the truck while the fire front passed over them and that it was one of the newer trucks in the district and had a sprinkler system that they could deploy while they all huddled in the cabin under aluminium thermal blankets to diffuse the worst of the heat.

Angela didn't like Kevin Cutler all that much, but she felt sick at the thought of those men, huddled in the cabin of a truck while the fire approached, not knowing if they would live or die, and if those deaths would be quick and merciful from the smoke and toxic chemicals in the truck, or slow and painful from the flames. The radio didn't mention fatalities but perhaps it was too early to tell because nobody would be able to get up the road to check on Tony and Alyssa or Killer and there were a couple of other little houses down a side track between Angela's and Tony and Alyssa's. Angela said to Killer, as he was helping her pack her car, that she had heard a few cars on the road down the hill that morning and assumed it was the people leaving their holiday cottages and Killer said 'city people, piss off the first time they see a puff of smoke on the horizon' and yet, at the same time, he had been the one to encourage Angela to pack up her most valuable items and head to safety.

The highway followed the wide river and came to a stop at the traffic lights that were on the intersection of the main highway that led up the coast and there were flashing signs on the backs of trailers leading up to the ramp for the bridge that crossed the river that told drivers that the highway north was cut in a number of places due to bushfires and to check their apps and Angela tried to remember what people did before they checked their apps and thought that they would do exactly what she was doing and listening to the local radio broadcasts. While she waited at the red light she looked over to her right and was surprised to see an overgrown, weedy paddock with lots of concrete footings, foundations and pads and where the OAK milkbar had once been. She knew that it been closed down for years and years, but the building always stood there as a reminder of trips on a Sunday with her Mum and Dad. 'Going for a drive' her dad would call it and the drive usually took in one of the OAK milk bars with a short drive being to this one at Hexham or a long drive to Peats Ridge on the Central Coast and a medium drive to Freemans Waterholes where Angela always felt sorry for the sad kangaroos and wallabies locked up in a terrible excuse for a zoo at the back of the milkbar. Her favourite milkshake was chocolate and her dad liked spearmint the best which Angela thought was yucky, and her mother liked hers without any flavouring, just an extra dollop of ice-cream, or dairy delight, as it was called, and Angela thought that a milkshake without a flavouring was both boring and pointless.

The angry beep of the horn from the car behind her told Angela that the lights had changed and she hadn't noticed, so she raised her hand and waved at the driver behind her to say that she was sorry and when she looked in the rear-view mirror, the young man driving the large ute behind her flipped her the bird and then as she took off he made sure that he kept the ute just a few inches off the back of Angela's Subaru and this made her slow down, keeping him trapped behind her as the long line of cars in the left hand lane, the slow lane passed both of them. When she noticed a gap in the left-hand lane, Angela pulled over because, while she was enjoying toying with the bloke in the ute with the baseball cap and what looked like tattoos on his neck, she didn't want to be in the papers as a victim of some bogan westie's road rage and thought that this was the better choice. As the ute sped up and went roaring past her, she could see the woman in the passenger seat turn around and even over the radio playing in her own car heard the woman shriek in a good broad Aussie accent 'mad fucking bitch'. Angela smiled and said to the back of the rapidly departing ute 'you don't know half of it'.

Angela wondered if she had always thought of herself as mad or whether that it was a more recent phenomenon that came with the rest of changes she had been going through over the last couple of years. She thought, that by comparison to her own mother, she had a fairly benign menopause and that any madness she might have been feeling was not the result of recent hormonal changes, but had always been there, just bubbling under the surface, something that she didn't need to use a lot of energy to keep the lid on but had to be conscious of the need to anyway. She thought that she might ask Ingrid if she had noticed any changes in her behaviour, after all, she and Ingrid had known each other for more than thirty years and for a while, in their twenties, they had shared a house and come to know each other's ways and moods almost intimately.

As she drove passed the big cemetery at Sandgate, Angela realised that she was crying. Not great heartbreaking sobs, but hot tears were overflowing from her eyes and running down her cheeks. The road had diverted away from the river and she couldn't see the water but could see the course that the river took by the line of mangroves either side of the water and, anyway, she didn't need to see the river because it had been there all of her life and she knew its course around the base of the hill that had once been a migrant hostel before she was born, and she wondered what it was like for some of those people who had been in camps in Europe, to come to a new country, a new start and be in camps again but at least they weren't like the new camps, the human zoos for refugees, no, these old camps would have been hot in summer and cold in winter but they didn't have razor wire and the people were free to come and go to the shops and to the jobs they were encouraged to get and to visit their friends and relatives who had come out earlier and now lived in the old working class suburbs near the steelworks.

Past the hill where the migrant camp had once sat, the river ran in a straight line to the old steelworks now long since closed and Angela remembered that when she was a little girl there was this two story red brick building that stood stark and alone on top of a hill, in a middle of a big paddock with nothing around it and her dad had told her that this was an orphanage and that was where children who had no parents had to live and sometimes the children had no parents because the parents had gotten sick and died, or had been killed in automobile accidents and sometimes they didn't have parents because the parents didn't want their children and had handed them in the same way that when Misty her cat had kittens, her dad had taken them to the RSPCA where she hoped that they had been adopted, and her dad told her that she should remember the red brick place on the hill because it was probably not a very nice place to live and where the children probably got fed watery soup with celery in it, and Angela hated celery and her father knew, and that Angela wouldn't want to have to live there, but that's where she would have to go if she continued to misbehave.

Maybe that's what her tears where for, she thought, for the

migrants in their camp and the children in the orphanage and all the stories she heard when she was young and all the dead in the cemetery she had just driven past and her grandfather, the Law, who she didn't really miss and her Pa who she did, who were both laid in Sandgate, six feet deep but a long way apart with Grandfather in the Catholic Section and Pa in the Presbyterian Section and how, on Father's Day, her mum and dad would make the trek to the cemetery to place flowers on both the graves and how Angela knew that in the not too distant future she would probably be making the same trek to lay flowers on her parent's graves although she suspected that he mother would go on forever.

Wiping the tears from her eyes, Angela turned onto Industrial Drive and remembered how she used to get in trouble from her mother for correcting her when she would always call the road the Industrial Highway because it was new when Angela was a child and was four lanes wide and designed to speedily move trucks to and from the steelworks and the port and how, at night, it was brightly lit with large orange lights, unlike the weak streetlights in their suburb and how, therefore, a road so grand had, in Angela's mother's eyes and in the eyes of her friends who all used the same misnomer, to be a highway.

The closer she got to the city, the more she felt like home with the familiar suburbs from her student days in shared houses and the endless round of parties and backyard barbecues and she thought that maybe the tears were caused by nostalgia for her younger days when anything seemed possible and she didn't think she would end up in her fifties, fleeing from a bushfire with all that she treasured crammed in the back of a car.

As she drove along the road, past the site of the demolished steelworks and the huge coal loader with its lines of freight trains snaking in and out, bringing back the ground of the valley that had once been rich farmland and now was nothing more than a disconnected series of huge quarries like, she thought, the disconnected stagnant ponds of what had once been proud flowing rivers, she made the last minute decision to turn off the main road and drive into Tighes Hill so she could go past the house where Andy lived so many years ago.

She was struck by the trees. Huge Australian native trees lined the street and towered high, their spreading branches green with leaves and giving the street a dappled shady quality that must have cooled down the houses and then she remembered that they had all been planted by Andy's friend Patrick, the man who owned the house that Andy lived in and their other flatmate, Georgia who had kindly put Angela up for some months in her little flat in South Kensington when Angela was looking for Mick in England and looking for her soul in Scotland before going to New Mexico to look for her heart. She hadn't known Georgia all that well in those days other than as one of the many characters who inhabited the university bar and by time Angela was coming to the house to visit Andy, Georgia was already out working for the Education Department, travelling all over country NSW teaching teenagers about the dangers of drugs and alcohol and unprotected sex and all the other things that teenagers in the country thought of as being the only entertainment that they could easily get hold of.

The other thing that struck Angela was how quiet it was in the street compared to what it had been like thirty years before, which was probably the last time she had been in the street and, back then, the steelworks was in full production and the house being a few hundred yards from the main gate to the steelworks meant that you could hear every sound from the huge industrial monster that, to Angela, sometimes seemed like a living breathing thing, spitting out fire and smoke and dust and noise and light and all things that are transformative, changing, harbingers of all sorts of evil.

Angela tried to remember the last time that she had actually been in that house in the shadow of the steelworks. She thought that it might have been not long before she graduated with her honours degree and that it might have been a party, but it wouldn't have been to celebrate Andy's graduation because he had dropped out of uni for the second or third time and this time it had something to do with Sophie, the Professor's daughter. Angela remembered that Andy had tried to chat her up at the party and looked all hurt and sulky when she rebuffed his advances which is something she wouldn't have done before he had his thing with Sophie. Angela also remembered that she had an argument with Lucy about something or other but couldn't recall the details but then again, Lucy was always playing mindgames with people and trying to manipulate them so it could have almost been about anything. Everyone at some time or another had a falling out with Lucy, Angela remembered. She had a vague recollection of Lucy making some disparaging remarks about Angela being offered a job tutoring at the uni while she did her Masters and Lucy suggested that Angela was the sort of person who would never grow up and who would find safety behind the walls of the academy and, as she remembered this, she remembered it was Lucy, that night, who had been the person who had first called her a bluestocking as a form of insult and that Andy had joined in the teasing and she hated him for that and it was Andy who, a few years later, bumped into her at a big poetry prize announcement in the Regional Art Gallery, that Angela thought, he had expected to win, without having the smarts to know that the organisers always tell the winners beforehand that they have won so they'll turn up and have an acceptance speech ready, who had said that he always knew that she 'would end up as bluestocking'.

'And I always knew that you'd end up a dilettante' Angela had said to him as she turned her back and found a group of young post-grads from the English Department who seemed to enjoy drinking and partying and always invited her to their shindigs, and that always made her feel years younger and now she could no longer remember, or even imagine, what it might have been like to be thirty years younger, a girl, just a girl in her mid-twenties looking out at the world and all it had to offer, all its promises and all of its dreams that were yet to be dreamed.

Angela remembered the night that she had gone to Harry's Bar at the university one evening when she was still an undergraduate with some of the people who had been in her English tute group. There was Brendan, who thought himself a bit of a lady's man and who Angela had been on a couple of dates, but nothing came of it and mainly because Brendan had one big passion in his life, one big interest, one big project and that was Brendan. When Angela had started going out with Brendan, Lucy started to take an interest in him as well and that was the first time that Angela really had anything to do with Lucy and she suspected that Brendan and Lucy traded pot for sex and that Brendan had a mate with a good sized plantation up in the New England where Brendan's father was a magistrate and everyone in the town's establishment turned a blind eye to the doings of the favoured sons, the golden haired boys of the town and that's why Brendan was, in many ways, a spoiled and conceited prick. Angela and Brendan had also been joined briefly by Louis, another of their fellow students and Angela remembered how she had been disappointed that Louis was gay and had not the slightest interest in women in that sense and yet, he was absolutely charming, incredibly handsome with a wonderful cultivated voice and very much at ease in his own skin and who liked to sit in the bar downing gin and tonics and telling outrageous stories about which members of the academic staff had, what he called, 'closets with revolving doors'. And then there was Andy, sometimes the life of the party and sometimes the sullen and morose one with his big afro hair do and his old ripped jeans and combat boots, Andy who had dreams of being a poet and living a bohemian lifestyle and who, Angela suspected, had a crush on her, but was too nervous or uncertain around women to do anything about it and she thought that if he didn't make a move on her, she might have to take matters into her own hands and make the move herself and show some assertiveness.

As Angela remembered it, they were all sitting in the bar on some lounges that were arranged in a square around a large low table when this blonde-haired girl that Angela had seen around the campus came and sat with them and Angela could tell that Andy was instantly smitten. She wasn't particularly offended at the way in which Andy showed so much interest in Sophie and the way he paid her undivided attention, but she was miffed by the way he physically half-turned in his chair to face Sophie so that he turned his back towards Angela. She stayed talking to Louis and Brendan for a while and then left to catch the bus, which is something she would normally have done with Andy but she didn't even bother saying goodbye and when he didn't arrive at the bus stop in time for the last bus back into town, she had assumed that he had gone off with Sophie and that perhaps that she had a car of her own.

Angela was lost in time, sitting in the street in the shade of native trees that Patrick had planted all those years ago, remembering what it was like to be young and to think that all of those little heartaches actually mattered, actually meant something and wondering to herself if any of them at that time were ever really happy. Andy thought he was happy in those first few months that he was seeing Sophie to the point that Angela couldn't stand his company, the very few times she actually bumped into him, because all he could talk about was Sophie this and Sophie that, as if there was nothing else in the world that mattered and he never once asked her how she was doing, what was happening in her life of whether she had met anyone, which she hadn't but would have made something up rather than give Andy the satisfaction of thinking that he was the only one that was happy, or at least pretending to be. Angela didn't know what happened in the end but eventually Sophie and Andy split up and six months or so later

Andy left town. Sophie hung around and Angela didn't bump into her until a couple of years later when she decided to be sociable and go to the English Department Christmas Drinks in one of the pubs in town. Sophie walked into the pub arm in arm with one of Sophie's colleagues, a brilliant young man who was beavering away on his first novel and who had not long returned after doing his PhD at Princeton. Brad Shaw had started uni the same time as Angela but had managed to complete his honours degree in four years and get a first and then went off to the USA to grad school. Angela walked up to say hello to Brad when the Professor also rushed up and turned to Angela and asked her if she knew Sophie and that, Sophie was his daughter and, as he did so, the Professor put a proprietorial arm around Angela's shoulders and Angela turned a red brighter than her hair and thought that they would all be able to tell that for the last month or two she had been carrying on a torrid affair with the Professor who was old enough to be her father, even, perhaps older.

A couple of people had come out of their houses in Tighes Hill, probably wondering why this young woman with the car laden with bags and boxes was just sitting in the street with the engine idling and Angela thought that if she was one of the neighbours, she might suspect that she was up to no good, casing the place and she also realised that she had phoned Ingrid when she was leaving Maitland and that if she didn't turn up soon, Ingrid might start to worry. She thought about waving to the people watching her but decided in the end that it was probably a little cheeky and so she just pulled into the street and drove away from the house in the shadow of the steelworks and hoped that her presence hadn't unleashed any ghosts from the past who were still, in their endless loop of ghostime, unable to resolve the years of unfinished business.

It was one quick diversion to the big shopping centre in town that had a reasonable range of cheese in the supermarket and a well-stocked bottle shop to pick up provisions and then, in what seemed like no time at all since he had left her own house, Angela was fishing for the swipe card to open the door to the basement garage in Ingrid's building.

'Come in, come in' Ingrid said, hugging Angela at the front door of the unit.

'How safe is it down there?' Angela asked, meaning the garage, 'I've got just about everything that I treasure in my car and don't want it nicked.'

Angela suggested that they should at least bring the most valuable things up to the apartment and the rest can be stored in a heavy metal locker like a small garden shed that each of the residents had in the basement garage.

After they had lugged a couple of boxes and bags up into the spare room, Angela waved the unopened bottle of Pinot Grigio in Ingrid's direction and Ingrid said that she thought that Angela would never ask.

'I can only have a glass or two', Ingrid said, 'in case I get called in to work.'

'Has there been anything on the news about the fires?' Angela asked, pointing to the television hanging on the wall in the living room and Ingrid picked up the remote control and turned it on and flicked between the local commercial television program and the national news network. Angela sat down with her glass of wine and Ingrid sat next to her and laid her hand on the back of Angel's forearm.

'Was it bad up there?' Ingrid asked and Angela looked at her and nodded. The television news seemed to be mainly focussing on Cheltenham and Angela wasn't sure if this was because it was at more risk than Allynsdale or whether it was more newsworthy because it was a much bigger town. After showing scenes of people at the evacuation centre who were clearly in distress, the report then crossed to another journalist and Angela recognised straight away that he was outside the Allynsdale hotel.

'Emergency services can confirm that a number of houses were lost in the Allynsdale area, but containment lines and the use of water bombers appeared to have saved the bulk of the town including the small businesses on the main street' the reporter announced. 'Emergency services are gravely concerned about the local firefighting unit who have not been heard of for some hours after they headed to fight the fire in the ridges north of the village. Police said that is still too dangerous to attempt to enter the area by road and thick smoke is making it difficult for aircrew to see what is on the ground. Police are also concerned for a number of residents from the north of Allynsdale who are yet to be accounted for.'

'Did you tell anyone you were leaving?' Ingrid asked.

'Of course, I did, there was Killer and Tony and Alyssa and Kevin Cutler', Angela said and then quickly covered her mouth with her hand. 'Oh shit, Killer and Alyssa and Tony might not have got out, they were going to defend their properties and Kevin is the captain of the missing fire crew.' She turned to look at Ingrid with eyes that were wide with fear.

'O.K.', Ingrid said, reaching for her mobile phone, 'there's an information line for people to report that they have loved ones missing or to report that they're alright and I'm just going to call it and say that you're fine and that you're here with me and that way the police won't risk themselves going to look for you.'

Angela nodded agreement and took her wine glass and walked out onto the balcony that had views all the way up the harbour and out to sea, and the sinking sun was casting a bright red line tinged with gold across the top of the green water like a finger pointing its way to the sea and Angela had hoped to be able to smell the sea in all its saltiness that sometimes made her think of blood and sometimes of tears, but all she could smell was the acrid bitter taste of the smoke that was being pushed down the valley, following the course of the river, by the running wind. It would be night soon and the streets below the unit will be filled with cars and pedestrians heading to the restaurants and bars that lined the harbour where the old wharf sheds and warehouses used to be when Angela was a little girl and her dad would drive up the street that was so close to where the cargo ships were tied to the wharves that it almost seemed to Angela that if she leaned far enough out of the car's window, she would be able to touch the sides of the ships and put her finger on the Plimsoll Line that her father had told her was how they knew not to overload the ship and if the water line was above the Plimsoll Line then the ship could founder and sink and lives would be lost.

'What are you thinking about?', Ingrid asked, walking out on to the balcony to join Angela.

'Do you remember the Stockton ferry?' Angela asked.

'I sometimes catch it on a Sunday with a couple of girls from work and we go and have lunch and a few beers at the Washtub.'

'No, not the passenger ferry, the car ferry, the punt, well there were two of them I think, and they criss-crossed the harbour before the bridge opened.'

'Not really. When did the bridge open?' Ingrid asked.

'1970, I think or somewhere around then, I'm pretty sure that I was in Kindergarten at the time' Angela said, turning to smile at Ingrid.

'I was three that year, no wonder I don't remember.'

'We used to drive down the old road that was much closer to the water over there,' Angela said pointing to where some new buildings were going up right on the edge of the harbour, 'and for some strange reason I was remembering my dad pointing out the Plimsoll lines on the ships and I was wondering whether or night we might have our own Plimsoll lines, even if they're invisible.'

'I'm not sure I follow?' Ingrid asked.

'Is there some way that we can tell that we're getting close to being overloaded, being overwhelmed, before it's too late and we just founder, crushed under the waves and water, the oceans and seas of our lives and experiences, the tides of change, the winds of storms, the tempests of time?'

'Enough with the weather analogies' Ingrid laughed and Angela looked hurt for a second.

'Could you actually hit you breaking point and not actually realise that you were even close until it is too late, until you're over the edge and rapidly sinking?' Angela asked, looking back over at the harbour as the reddish golden line in the water seemed to get longer until it reached the point where it rapidly faded to nothing as the sun fell below the western mountains at the edge of the city and it was truly night.

'Maybe you should talk to someone' Ingrid suggested, and Angela turned back to face her.

'Isn't that what I'm doing?'

'You know what I mean, a professional, a counsellor.'

'A shrink?' Angela laughed just a touch too loud so, to Ingrid, it sounded forced and strained.

'At work, we have professional supervision once a month and is just a chance to sit and talk to someone about whatever's been on your mind or whatever has been causing you stress and anxiety and you'd be surprised how good it feels to get stuff off your chest, just to put it into words. I think you spend too much time sitting up there on your mountain and not talking to anyone and just stewing about a whole lot of unresolved stuff from the past.'

'I talk to plenty of people and I had enough talking to shrinks years ago remember?' Angela said and to Ingrid's ears, it sounded more like a petulant child speaking than a mature, intelligent and articulate woman.

Angela knew what Ingrid meant but she wasn't sure if she wanted to admit it, even to herself. It was true that sometimes she went days without speaking to anyone and even when she did speak to someone, it was usually Killer and, as nice as he was to her, they were hardly stimulating conversations and his topics were usually limited to the weather, what the neighbours were up to and then sometimes he would go into some diatribe about the 'clowns in Sydney and Canberra' and how 'none of them were worth feeding'.

Angela sometimes wondered about Killer's past and it seemed to her that he had been on top of the mountain in his little slab cottage forever. She knew that his family came from around Allynsdale and the surrounding hills and valleys, but she wondered if he had ever left, if he had some life somewhere else only to come back to the place where he had grown up. Angela had heard that's what people sometimes do although, for her, there was nothing she could think of that would be worse than returning to the suburb where she spent her first seventeen years, but, then again, when she made escape, it was only to travel a few kilometres closer into the city into the first of many shared student houses in the old run down suburbs with the sight and sound and smell of the steelworks. She never made the big escape, the running away overseas like a lot of the people she had met in uni did and it seemed, for a while, in her late twenties and early thirties, that just about everyone she had ever known was living in London or some other part of the U.K. doing all sorts of menial jobs in bars and restaurants notwithstanding their uni degrees. She would get the occasional postcard or aerogram letter from the likes of Louis and Ned Kelly describing all the sights and sounds of London and she even got a letter from Linda, the cranky Trotskyite who liked to taunt the Professor in class and call him a class traitor because he lived in a big house high on the hill overlooking the town. She heard rumours on the grapevine that Andy had been in London or New York and had scored some good gig with some media organisation or other, but she never received a letter from him or a postcard or an invitation to come and stay in London or Manhattan. In fact, the only person from the old circle at uni who didn't do the obligatory stint overseas or the move to Melbourne, and Angela often wondered why so many of the people she was at uni with went to Melbourne and not to Sydney and thought that it might have been a bigger statement to move that distance when Sydney was only two hours down the road, had been Lucy, and Lucy never even moved from the same suburb that she had lived in when they were students and as far as Angela knew, she might well live in the same house but she hadn't seen her for years and since she had moved up to the mountain, Angela didn't bump into anyone who knew Lucy.

Angela thought that when all of this was over, she would invite Killer inside for a cup of tea, because she thought that's what he'd prefer to drink and not the coffee she made on her Italian stove-top espresso machine, and she would ask him to tell her the story of his life and that it might make an interesting tale that she could write down and perhaps he had some mysterious past of great symbolic value, like one of Mick's characters from the outback. Angela gave a little gasp, which caused Ingrid to ask her if she was alright, when she realised what she was thinking and how, in all reality, Killer was possibly dead and even more likely was the fact that neither of their houses would have survived the fire.

'I'm alright' Angela said to Ingrid. 'I just keep kidding myself that everything is fine when I know, when I'm sure it isn't.'

'You can't know anything for certain. Do you want to come back inside and see if there's anything more on the news?' Ingrid said and took Angela by the arm and led her back in before she had time to answer.

They sat down in front of the television and the news was still all about Cheltenham and the live pictures looked even more like some vision from hell now that the sun had fallen. Cheltenham sat in a little valley on one of the rivers that fed the main river that ended up in the harbour under Ingrid's window. There were high mountains around three sides of Cheltenham and an ever-widening valley and farm lands to the south. It looked, from the television pictures, that there were large fires burning on the three sides of Cheltenham and the television reporter said that a lot of homes had been lost and in one little village, of five or six houses, up in the hills to the north, all of the houses had been lost but there were no casualties. The sky was angry, Angela thought, the redness glowing in the darkness and smoke illuminated by the rising moon to the east seemed to billow in rolling waves and she wondered if any of the valley would survive the night.

'Fools and madmen' Angela muttered to herself at one time when one of the firefighters appeared to be overwrought with emotion while describing to the television reporter how they were unable to save any of the properties in the little village to the north.

'What did you just say?' Ingrid asked and Angela though, from Ingrid's tone, that she was somehow being rebuked.

'This night will make us all fools and madmen. It's a quote, Shakespeare, King Lear when Lear is wandering around the heath during the tempest, with thunder and lightning and rain. It doesn't mean fool in the sense of foolishness, like folly or stupidity but in the sense of being made mad, being undone, so what seems real might be unreal and vice versa' Angela said without taking her eyes of the exhausted firefighter on the television.

'Thanks for my English 101 tutorial' Ingrid said, and Angela suspected she might be being a bit sarcastic.

'It's just like some vision of hell and enough to send anyone crazy and that television reporter is trying to get some sense out of that poor man who has just come out of the hills and probably thought that he would die up there.'

They watched for a bit more and ate some of the cheese and

olives that Angela had bought but she found that she didn't have much of an appetite but did think that she should slow down on the wine. Ingrid had drunk her ration of two small glasses because she was on call and Angela had polished off the bottle before starting on a second. Eventually, Ingrid said that she was going to bed and Angela said that she just wanted to keep watching for a little bit in case there was any news from Allynsdale.

Angela was just about to turn off the television when the announcer said that they were crossing to Allynsdale for some breaking news and Angela felt as if her heart had leapt up into her throat. The television crossed to the scene just outside the pub and the shop in the main street and it looked like there were a lot of arc lights on big stands further down the street at what seemed to be the smouldering remains of Mrs Thompson's house and Angela hoped that they had gotten her little dog to safety because old Molly Thompson would be devastated if anything had happened to her dog. The reporter outside the pub was interviewing a man who was completely covered in soot apart from the around his eyes where he must have been wearing goggles and he had his arm in what looked like a sling with bandages on one of his hands. Even with the soot and the heavy clothes, Angela could tell straight away that the man the reporter was talking to was Kevin Cutler and he had somehow survived to come back down the mountain and Angela didn't know whether she wanted to laugh or to cry.

Angela Dreams of Snakes

Angela didn't sleep much at all that night and was up in the kitchen, foraging around for something for breakfast, before the sun rose over the ocean, out beyond the entrance to the harbour, where the long beach arced its way to the long dead, dormant volcanos to the north.

When she had managed to fall into something that might have been sleep, she was bedevilled by all manner of dreams. At one time Angela felt a weight on her chest and in her half asleep, half-awake state, she reached her hand down to pat her little old cat, Osana, who liked to climb into her bed with her on the cold frosty nights in the mountain, but when she lowered her hand, Osana was not there and she remembered that he had been killed by the brown snake and that Killer had killed the brown snake and she cried for Osana and then she cried for Killer, who she was certain had been devoured by the fires on the mountain, and as she fell back into another fitful sleep she dreamed of the snake that Killer had decapitated with his old rusty scythe and in her dream Killer was wearing a hooded cowl and looked like the character of death in that Bergman film she had studied in first year, where the Grim Reaper played chess on the seashore with the Teutonic looking knight and they were very serious as the plague raged around them, an eerie portend of something unhinged and unworldly, a bit like the strangely dancing, twisting, living flames that, in her dream, were in the hills behind the figure of Killer as the Grim Reaper holding out the headless snake toward her, almost as an offering, and the snake's body still twitched and writhed and dripped blood and the bodiless head on the ground kept opening its mouth and baring its dripping fangs.

As she quietly made her coffee so as not to disturb Ingrid, who liked to sleep in on a Sunday, Angela tried to remember, from when she studied symbolism, all of the meanings that snakes can have in dreams and she tried to put them into some sort of order in her head.

There was the snake as a symbol of sexuality, or a phallic symbol, and Angela found it quite funny that the symbol of sexuality might also be linked in her dream to Killer who, out of all the men she knew, was one of the ones that she was least likely to sleep with, particularly if he was dressed as death, and she thought that maybe to sleep with him would be to encounter death because in her dream, he not only looked like the Grim Reaper in the Bergman film, but also the Grim Reaper that had been in all of the AIDS awareness commercials that had been in television when she was in her early twenties in the days when some of her friends assumed that it was just a matter of time before they all contracted AIDS despite the condoms and refusal to share needles and, anyway, Angela didn't use needles, shared or otherwise. She then remembered that the whole snake as a symbol of sexuality had, she thought, came from Freud and so she dismissed it out of hand because, whilst there were things she liked about Freud, she found it was his own sexual repression that informed Freud's writing.

The snake as a threat made more sense to her. A snake in the grass her father used to say when he meant that there was some man he worked with, or drank with at the club, who couldn't be trusted and Angela remembers really chiding her father for being racist, which he wasn't generally, or at least no more than most the white men of his generation, the time he referred to someone in the union who was white anting the latest campaign as being the 'nigger in the woodpile'.

The problem with threats was that they were everywhere, like a snake in the long grass waiting to strike bare ankles and calves and Angela always wore a pair of thick rubber gum boots when she worked in the garden or went to the woodpile at the back of the house to get fuel for her fire in winter.

The snake, she remembered could also mean a nasty person in your life or a friend who was about to betray you and Angela thought that this was unlikely and, besides, she hardly had any friends these days other than Ingrid. Killer was a friend, she supposed, but couldn't imagine how or why he would betray her unless, if he did get killed in the fire, it was a form of betrayal by leaving her to sift through the ashes of the life she had made without his help and his advice and his knowledge of all those things that old men who have lived on their own in the bush seemed to have gathered and stored for times when it was useful. Tony and Alyssa were nice people who she liked to spend some time with occasionally, but she hardly knew them or much about them apart from the fact that, like her, they saw coming to the mountains as some form of healing and Alyssa had once hinted that Tony had a high powered well paid job in the city until something inside of him broke and Angela thought that it must have been like some form of nervous breakdown that meant, even though they were both nice and friendly and would do anything to help their neighbours, there was a brittleness just under the surface of Tony and Alyssa that Angela thought could easily snap and she thought that their staying to defend their home might not have been the wisest option, but then thought that perhaps they thought the pain of losing everything was a pain they couldn't bear and so decided to take the risk. Ingrid, of course, was her best true friend and so she immediately dismissed the thought that anything to do with the snake of her dream could relate to her friendship with Ingrid.

The next piece of symbolism on Angela's mental list was that the snake represented something in her own subconscious that she was refusing to face up to, something buried deep that she did not want to think about, but also knew that it was something she would encounter at some time or another when she least wanted to face down whatever it was that was lurking there. She knew that she had buried deep within herself a sense of failure. The sense of failure was something that had been building in her for years and years and it was a sense, or a thought, that she had failed in everything other than becoming the recluse that many of her friends had warned her for many years that she would become. Her mother was disappointed that she had never got to become the grandmother that most of her contemporaries had been. It had only been in the last ten years or so that her mother had changed from dropping hints to Angela that the clock was ticking and if she didn't have children soon, it might never happen, and that Angela herself would find this sadder as she got older. When it became obvious that Angela had become too old to have children, her mother wore the disappointment of not being or ever getting to be a grandmother like the old Greek widows, in the suburb where Angela used to live, wore their black clothes as a mark of mourning for the rest of their lives. At least, as Angela had gotten older, her mother had stopped finding examples of women who managed to bear healthy babies well into their forties who she would hold up to Angela as examples of the sort of woman that Angela could be and not what she was. Bluestocking, Angela thought, bluestocking crazy woman in the hills without even her cat for company.

The other thing that Angela had found infuriating about her mother, and to a lesser degree, her father was their constant finding of eligible bachelors for Angela at their local Ex-Services Club. These men always had a couple of things in common. They were generally divorced and often had children that Angela thought might have provided her mother with some surrogate adopted grandchildren which, although not being as desirable of the ones made from her own DNA were close enough - any port in a storm, as they say. The other thing that Angela's mother would point out as being the selling point of all of these men was that they all had trades and some of them even had their own businesses and Angela's mother took great stock in having a trade because it meant that the man was educated. Her mother never particularly acknowledged the value of a university education, particularly in the arts and particularly for men. Sure, she understood why a man might want to be a doctor or a lawyer or something like that, if you came from the right family and went to the right school, but Angela's mother could never understand why a man would study something like Arts, why a man would want to devote his life to reading books and talking about them like a 'gaggle of gabbering old biddies gathered at the chook raffles', Angela's mother would say, and Angela would tell her that she liked her alliteration and her mother would scowl at her and say 'I know you think I'm stupid, that I don't know the meaning of the big words you and your lot of smarty pants like to fling about to hide things and to make fun of people.'

Angela's mother had never particularly liked any of the men that Angela had gone out with when she was in her twenties and had thought they were all a bit unusual with their long hair and their hand rolled cigarettes and the clothes they bought at op shops that made them look like 'Charlie Chaplin in them films your Grandma used to like, you know, the Little Tramp's what they called him, well that's [insert name of whoever Angela was currently seeing]' and it applied most frequently to Andy who, Angela had to admit, had been the scruffiest of the young men that she knew, but they had never officially been boyfriend and girlfriend and she sometimes wondered what might have happened if Sophie hadn't walked into the uni bar that night all soppy eyed and flirtatious.

As far as her father was concerned, Angela didn't think that he paid any attention to whoever she was seeing and probably thought that none of them would make the sort of son in law who would enjoy joining him at the Ex-Services club on a Friday night to watch the football on the big screen television and cheer for the team her father barracked for, because a good son-in-law always barracks for the same side as his father-in-law and anything less would be a betrayal. She suspected that her father thought that all her male friends were probably closeted gays and, in fact some of them were gay, and certainly well and truly out of the closet. 'Poofters' her father would have called her gay male friends, or 'queens' or 'shirt lifters' but never 'fags' because he said he couldn't understand the correlation between homosexuality and cigarettes.

Coming out of the closet, changing and transformation, the shedding of an old skin that was dull and lifeless, worn and torn for a new skin that was shiny, sparkly and unblemished was what snakes did and what Angela remembered as being another of the symbolic meanings of snakes in dreams.

Transformation, the changing of form, the becoming something new and in some Asian religions the transformative nature of the snake is also a healing force. Maybe, Angela thought, that her dream was really about changing, about renewal, about reinvention, about becoming someone different and she thought about that Cat Power song where Cat's voice almost cracks with emotion when she sings about becoming someone better and then she thought it was funny that she was thinking about Cat Power when it was the snake, the transformer, that killed her cat and bought her so much sadness.

Angela took her coffee and her toast out on to the balcony just as the sky in the east started to change colour from the deep black to a dark blue and the rays of sun started to appear and highlight the mist from the harbour that was being held over the water by the higher layer of bushfire smoke that seemed to seep into everything to such a degree that Angela almost forgot that she could smell it until a particular denser piece of smoke wafted by and caused her to cough and splutter and remember the fleeing from her home the day before, and then her stomach tightened as another wave of anxiety hit and flooded her stomach with bile that sat burning and uncomfortable with the mouthful of coffee and the bite of toast and vegemite she had at the bench in the kitchen before coming out to the balcony. Angela sat focussed and regulated her breathing until the desire to throw up had passed.

She wondered how her little house would have withstood the fire and whether the mudbrick walls would have survived the heat, or if they had crumbled and fallen. She had been told that mud bricks offered excellent resistance to fire but if the flames got up under the eaves, the timbers holding the galvanised iron roof would burn and the roof would have fallen in and perhaps the windows would have melted or been blown out by the force of the fire and then everything inside would have gone up, her furniture and furnishings and the clothes that she didn't pack and the books she had no room for in the back of the car other than the most precious of first editions and rare books that she had packed, ready, in boxes almost every summer that she had lived on the mountain, knowing that she'd have to flee someday. She had her laptop and her back up discs and drives with copies of all of her photographs and scanned newspaper clippings and was glad of the what she considered to be the extortionate amount of money she paid each month to keep all of these things, these records and memories in what they called 'the cloud', which, she assumed, consisted of large banks of computer hard drives somewhere in America or India or China or God knows where.

Thinking of her laptop, Angela remembered that she could listen to the local ABC radio station on it through her headphones. She had been wanting to turn on the radio since she got up but didn't want to wake Ingrid. Back at Allynsdale, up in the hills, she was still waiting for the promised broadband to be delivered and there was talk of installing small satellite dishes as it was too hilly for the wireless system, they had a bit further down the valley. Angela used to head down to town some days to sit in the little café at the side of Kevin Cutler's shop where she could tether her laptop to her mobile phone. She would get funny looks from Kevin's wife because Angela thought that she suspected her of trying to somehow hack into the Cutler's home and business wi-fi networks and she earned a sneer from Mrs Cutler when she told her that the café she went to in Maitland, like most others she knew in the city, offered free wi-fi to their patrons.

'This isn't the city and you're not a patron you're a customer' Mrs Cutler said, and Angela just smiled and sipped her cup of Lipton's tea made with a tea bag because the only coffee the so-called café served was International Roast out of a big tin that might have been months old.

Angela quickly booted up the laptop on Ingrid's balcony and was pleased that there was plenty of juice in the battery so that she could stay sitting out there and enjoy the sunrise. The local announcer was giving an update on the location of emergency evacuation centres and said that the fire commissioner would make an announcement that morning about the state of the fires and whether people would be allowed into some of the affected areas. There had been substantial building losses in the area to the north of Cheltenham and a number of people were unaccounted for. The announcer went on to say that there were also house losses and people unaccounted for in the Allynsdale area, particularly in the hills around the township but the people of the Allynsdale were celebrating what they considered to be the miraculous story of how their little bushfire truck and its crew had been spared after the fire had flashed over them and they were blocked by burning and fallen trees across the road and that the heat of the fire passing the truck had melted the antenna mount for their radio and burned through some of the connecting wires so the radio was useless. The fire crew could not be spotted by air because of the smoke and the wind that was like a mini tornado made it impossible to get a helicopter up to them. Kevin Cutler and his crew followed the fire front back down the valley extinguishing the fire in fallen trees and cutting them with chain saws or dragging them away with a chain on the back of the truck until they were able to get clear of the timbered land and come out on the river flat where they could make their way into town. There was no mention of Killer or Alyssa or Tony.

Angela had never believed in fate as in the concept of the future being pre-ordained, set in stone, unchangeable and unavoidable. In fact, she was quite the opposite and believed that everything in life was random and that where she was in life now, the person she had become, was a result of an untold number of minor events, encounters and random happenings. When she was a teenager, in her last year of high school, her best friend, Vicki Mankovski, was killed in a car accident when a driver, attempting to overtake a truck on the highway between Aberdeen and Scone, ran head-on into the car that Vicki's father was driving north to take Vicki to visit her uncle and aunty in Tamworth. Vicki was in the front seat and was killed instantly, as was her father, the police said, and the family in the other car suffered some terrible injuries. Angela often found herself thinking about Vicki and what sort of life she might have led had she not died on a foggy morning on the highway. Vicki was smarter than Angela and was well liked and attractive and was what was known as a good all-rounder in that she was academically gifted, played piano and violin to a high standard, could paint and draw and was a top hockey player in the local competition. Angela always contrasted herself to Vicki and thought that the only thing they had in common was their intelligence and, even then, Angela was only really good at English and not bad on Ancient History, where Vicki was good at the humanities and maths and science. Vicki, Angela thought, could have done whatever she wanted with her life and yet it was cut down at random one morning, heading for a couple of days break from studying for the HSC. Angela was troubled the most by the randomness of it, and all the what ifs, like would delaying their trip by even two or three minutes made a difference, or if the truck hadn't been on that particular piece of road at that particular moment or even if the truck was going a couple of kilometres an hour faster or if the driver of the other car had gotten an hours more sleep and was paying better attention or any number of things that reached a point of convergence at one point of time in one place and if it had happened how different the world might have been for everyone that Vicki would have touched throughout her life, including Angela.

There must be some comfort in religion, Angela thought, particularly those who were pre-disposed to believe that everything that happened in the world was pre-ordained and was part of some grand plan by God, that had some purpose that, perhaps, was only known to God. What purpose, Angela thought for a long time, was there in Vicki dying like that in the crumpled ruin of her father's bright red XY Falcon? Mrs Mankovski didn't cope at all after losing her husband and daughter and had to be hospitalised in the place that Angela's father called 'the loony bin' and the Vicki's big brother, Nico who had just finished his apprenticeship as a fitter and turner at the steelworks, had to act as mother and father for Vicki's little sister, Tracey, who was fifteen at the time that Vicki died. Tracey stopped going to school and was hanging around near the beaches and the pubs and clubs all over the place, wherever she could get in using Vicki's i.d. It wasn't long before Tracey was hanging out with a group who were in to all sorts of drugs and Angela would sometimes bump into Tracey when she was out seeing a band and every time she saw her, she thought that Tracey seemed to age and she was starting to look haggard and gaunt with lifeless eyes sunk into her head and Angela wasn't surprised when, one night a couple of years later, she was in a car with some friends heading back to their place when she saw, out of the window, Tracey shivering in the cold winter air wearing a tiny mini skirt that barely covered her butt and a tiny crop top boob tube that only accented her skinny ribs that to Angela made her look like the soldiers in her grandfather's pictures from Changi. Tracey had a cigarette in her mouth and was plying her trade, waiting for the next car to stop at the kerbside, with the grim determination and the sense of resigned despair that this was as good as it was going to get. Angela heard on the grapevine that Tracey had been found dead with a needle in her arm in the early hours one morning a few months later in the front yard of somebody's house, not far from where Angela had seen her doing her street work.

'A horse walked into a bar', Angela heard Ingrid say from the kitchen.

'And the barman said, why the long face?' Angela answered and they both laughed, and Angela realised that she hadn't laughed for a long time.

'I'm sorry,' Ingrid said, coming out on to the balcony, 'you've been through a lot, the last twenty-four hours,' and then pointing at Angela's laptop, asked 'any news?'

Angela shook her head. 'The roads are open up as far as Allynsdale. I think I'll head up there this morning and see how far up the hill I can get.'

'Are you sure?' Ingrid asked. 'I mean do you think you can cope if it's the worst-case scenario?'

'I can't cope not knowing' Angela said and smiled weakly and Ingrid put her arms around Angela and gave her a tight squeeze.

'I can come with you if you want some company?' Ingrid asked.

'What about work? Aren't you on call?'

'Not until six tonight. We have an on-call roster and I drew the nights this weekend. I get nights one weekend a month and I get days another weekend per month and then two weekends without being on call' Ingrid explained.

'What if you want to go away somewhere? Your options are fairly limited if you're on call half the weekends?'

'That's why I don't have a life,' Ingrid laughed, 'no man in my life, no pets and no serious hobbies. What's your excuse?'

Angela laughed and shook her head and, in her own mind, wondered what her excuse really was. The no pets was easy and she didn't want another cat since the snake, the transforming symbol or the evil reptile, had taken Osana. Angela thought about the way she had thought about the reptile, the brown snake, as being evil and what a stupid thought that was, not matter how much she hated the snake for what it did, it was just living its life as a snake, following its nature and it was no more evil than she was when she went to butcher's and purchased some lamb to make a curry. The excuse for not having a hobby was that she didn't need one and that she had plenty to keep her busy with her reading and writing and tending her garden, growing her herbs until the lack of water killed them, until the drought, the dry brittle earth, killed everything over time and what it couldn't kill by dryness, by the wind and the dust, it killed, in the end, by the most powerful of forced it could muster, the fire that swept everything away.

Mick would have said that it was a haunted land and that it reflected the violence that it had seen and had thrown back that violence on to the people a thousand fold, a million fold, for what they do to the land and what they do to each other and that there were sins in the land that needed to be expiated by blood. Killer wouldn't have been able to put it in the same words that Mick would have used, even in the books of his juvenilia, but Killer would have understood the sentiment and he carried with him the memories of the old people, the people who lived here first, the people it was rumoured to have been murdered just up the road from her house in the hills and maybe, she thought, the fire was fuelled by the restless spirits of the unmourned dead, writing their name in blood across the forested hills of their country and she thought of one of Mick's poems and how it was a woman who wrote her name in blood and how that name would abide, perhaps forever and what were the 'stations' of the poems title and she wondered why she hadn't really thought about that in any detail, and why she hadn't addressed it in her thesis, and when she first read the poem as a schoolgirl she thought that it just referred to stations in the context of farms, the cattle stations that Mick knew and wrote so much about, and then she thought of the redeeming stranger, the Christ figure that appears so much in Mick's work, and then she thought of the Stations of the Cross and how that might be the secret meaning of the poem's title. Stations of the Cross, Via Dolorosa, the fourteen set pieces from the passion of Jesus – Angela wanted to go through her box of books and dig out the book of Mick's poems, the first edition with it's strange purple, green and pink cover that was so very much a sixties artefact, because she couldn't remember how many sections there were in the Stations poem and she remembered that it was made up of a series of poems to be read aloud by three different voices and she was pretty sure that the total number of shorter poems that made up the whole didn't add up to fourteen and if it was meant as some form of Via Dolorosa, then it should be fourteen stations and maybe she was falling into her old academic traps of reading too much into things and looking for meanings that weren't there, riddles that were just simple words, solving mysteries that she herself created in order to solve.

'I've got no excuse', Angela said, 'and yes, I would love it if you could come with me today, I'd appreciate the company'.

'Good', Ingrid said, 'an outing in the country. Don't be surprised if, when we get to Allynsdale, they don't let us go any further.' She left the reason unsaid and that was if there were people who were unaccounted for, the police would be sifting through the burnt-out houses and sheds and cars looking for bodies.

'I won't be', Angela said, 'but hopefully, even if we can't get to the house, somebody will know what happened and hopefully my friends came out of it without too much drama, they're not silly, well, Tony and Alyssa aren't silly, can't assume anything about Killer because he's so stubborn but I'm pretty sure that Alyssa would have the sense to leave when they knew there was nothing more that could have been done.'

Ingrid nodded, but also knew from what she had heard around the hospital from firies and the police that the fires can come roaring down through the bush like a freight train and people think that it is someway off and will have time before they have to flee, but before they know it, it's too late and they're engulfed in flames and smoke and what was worse is that in a housefire, most fatalities are caused by smoke inhalation but in these rapid high temperature bushfires, the victims often burn alive.

Angela sipped her coffee and hoped that she wouldn't see any snakes.

The River Returns to
Its Source

Angela wanted to go for a drive along the beaches and harbour before they headed up the valley, following the rivers almost to their source, and Ingrid was happy to go along with that. The water sparkled in the mid-morning sun and the sky was blue, but out on the horizon there was a dirty brown smudge of smoke. The wind had shifted in the early hours of the morning to the south and had forced the fire back on itself to where there was not a lot left to burn, but on the fringes, it had found new fuel and the focus had shifted away to the other side of the ranges where new fires were bearing down on some of the little towns and villages.

Angela parked her car in the car park that looked down over Bar Beach and she and Ingrid got out and walked to the viewing platform from where they could see all the way down the coast to the Redhead bluff. The water was still a bit cool and there were no swimmers, only board riders in their sleek black wetsuits that made Angela think, that if she didn't know better, because of her gradually weakening eyesight, she might easily have mistaken the surfers for seals, much like the seals she had seen on the piers and wharves in San Francisco or up on the North West Coast of Scotland the year she went looking for Mick.

Angela's search for Mick had not only taken her to the United Kingdom, where he spent his last years in Harwick or to New Mexico where he wrote the book that first caused Angela to fall in love with his writing and his world, amongst the adobes and a blue sky that seemed to stretch forever. Angela had also travelled to Geraldton to walk the streets Mick walked as a child during the war, and she tried to imagine what that must have been like, the fear that any time there could be ships coming over the horizon carrying armies of Japanese and the way the propaganda at the time, and not always without justification, had people scared of the massacres that awaited them, the raping of the women, the slaughtering of babies and the rounding up of men to act as slaves. 'Monsters and savages' her grandfather, The Law, would rave on and on and had once told Angela, when she was in her early thirties, that she was forbidden to go to the new Japanese restaurant that had opened in town, but she went anyway with her friend who was married to a Japanese man studying at the university and the Japanese man bought another Japanese couple with them and Angela found that they were the nicest, gentlest and most courteous people that she had ever dined with and thought that she should tell her grandfather this and remind how things have changed and different generations see the world differently, but then she decided not to. She once thought that all of his hatreds and his desire to see something nasty happen to Japan and its people were the only things that kept him alive and how cheated he would have felt if he could have known that he was to die just before the big disaster at Fukushima.

The place that Angela hadn't visited was the Trobriand Islands where Mick spent some time as a young patrol officer. She very much liked the book he wrote based on his experiences there and Angela had even named her cat, Osana, after one of the characters in that book of blood and death and madness and superstition, that she thought owed more to Macbeth than anything, and not only because of one of the character's name but because of the witchcraft and the unfolding of fates and the motif of blood, the house bleeding out on the boy sleeping in the cool space below and thinking of that passage made Angela shiver so much that it was noticed by Ingrid.

'Bit of a nip in the wind' Ingrid commented and Angela nodded and thought of The Law again and the way that he always spat that word, 'nip' and he only ever used it as a derogatory term for the Japanese to the point that he constantly corrected the barman at the Ex-Services Club if he referred to a measure of alcohol as being a 'nip' by telling the barman that the correct term was a 'dram, a tot, a measure or even a snifter if you like, but never refer to something as enjoyable as whisky by referring to those little bastards.'

'Let's get this show on the road' Angela said to Ingrid and Ingrid laughed and shook her head as they walked back to the car. One of the things that Ingrid had always liked about Angela was the way that she was able to make a joke, or say something funny, even when her whole world seemed to be falling around her ears. Ingrid thought that if she had been in the same boat, heading off into the country where the fire had raged, to see if her house was still standing, that she would be crippled with anxiety and would probably be too busy throwing up and dry retching to make breezy comments and to drive a car but then again, Ingrid always thought of herself as the more highly strung of the two.

Another thing that fascinated Ingrid about Angela was the state of her car compared to her own little Mazda. Their cars, inside, were almost polar opposites and the interior of Angela's car was always spotless and there was nothing lying around, nothing in the cup holders or little storage pockets or binnacles and everything that Angela kept in her car seemed to be stored away in the glove box or the console. Ingrid's car, on the other hand, seemed to contain an ever growing collection of used take-away coffee cups, water bottles, parking meter stubs, odd bits of correspondence and papers and magazines and spare canvas shopping bags and empty deodorant bottles and paper bags from the sandwich shop and all the other detritus of a busy life that, when she had a passenger in the front seat, she would bundle up holus bolus and throw over on to the back seat until they spilled onto the floor.

'Your car's always so neat' Ingrid said to Angela as they pulled out of the carpark.

'As opposed to my psyche which is a completely shambolic mess?' Angela replied and, because she had had her eyes on the road, it was hard for Ingrid to read her face and know if she was joking or not.

'I meant compared to my car' Ingrid said, although, when she thought about, it wasn't completely off-track to consider that Angela's psyche was, at times pretty shambolic.

Ingrid thought that Angela had become a bit loopier after she had spent her year overseas and wondered if something had happened to her while she was away. There had been signs before she left on her trip, like getting in trouble with her boss for telling the young girl in her tutorial to 'fuck off' because she was too dull and there had been a lot of drinking and partying with younger people that all culminated with the big party that Angela threw to celebrate the dual events of turning fifty and heading off for her first trip to Europe and the United States.

Angela booked the upstairs room of a pub that sat on the harbour and had views over to the peninsula opposite and the big arc of the bridge that had replaced the punts that Angela remembered fondly from her childhood and you could see the tall Norfolk Pines that grew in the grounds of what Angela's father has called the mental hospital that was next door to what was once an old army base that had big guns, like the fort on the city side of the harbour, to protect the city and its industries from invaders and had once fired at the Japs when they shelled the city and Angela's grandmother would tell her how scared she was that night as the shells whistled over her Auntie's house in the East End where she was staying while Angela's grandfather was in Changi and when she told the story, Angela's grandfather would look thunderous and angry and thump the table with his fist and go on about the cowardice of some general called Bennett and how that's how the Nips operated, shelling defenceless women and children while they worked the men to death and how he had been to places like Hellfire Pass where his best mate, Doug, had died of cholera or beri beri or something like that and how the Nips beat Doug with clubs and rifle butts because he couldn't work very fast, what with his legs rotting away from the tropical ulcers and the bloody water that squirted out his backside under his lap lap and Angela would get frightened and later have nightmares because her grandfather never talked about the war, but when he did, usually after he had been drinking at the club of an afternoon, he would get on a roll, and it was a vision of hell scarier than anything the old priest could trot out when he described hell and purgatory and the judgement day.

At one stage, Angela with her head full of Joyce and Martello Towers had thought that she would have liked to live in the old fort that overlooked the beach, harbour entrance and breakwater at one end, and the city at the other end, and contained several old building and gun emplacements and plotting rooms and storerooms for shells and gunpowder and generator rooms and rooms where soldiers probably had meals and others where they probably rested when they weren't on guard and she wondered who she might write to and make and enquiry about the possibility, perhaps, of leasing one of the smaller buildings and maybe she could phrase it as a sort of research project for the university and that she could invite some of the more promising students to come and live with her in the fort and that they could spend their nights sitting around a fire place discussing Molly and Leopold and Stephen and plump Buck Mulligan and all the others, and that they could, when the spirit took them, wander around the streets of the old part of the city, the convict built bits running from the old barracks that was now a mental hospital with locked wards and all manner of craziness and chaos, where they could roister and drink and laugh and invent a poetry for her city, a legend of the city and all its interesting characters like Joyce had done for Dublin.

She would write long and complicated stories and invent new words and phrases from what she heard on the streets, the dockworkers and the steelworkers and the coal miners and sailors and the bogans from the western suburbs and the grommets from the beaches and the punks and rockers and the old bikers with their grey beards and Harley's and the single mums from the commission flats and the Greeks and Eyties and Yugos, who were crazy for football in a town where all the Anglos, the Skippys, followed their losing rugby league team, and the Vietnamese fishermen and prawners with their little boats in Throsby Creek that headed out to sea each night with little lights on their stubby masts, and the old ladies in moth eaten furs buying silverside by the slice in the deli section of the department store food hall, and the spivs in wide ties who sat in the bowling club wishing they were members of the big club on the hill that would never have them, and not just because of the money, and all those voices would form some new language, some cacophony of sound that could only come from that one place, at that one time and if she could get it down on paper, if she could find the rhythms, find the songs and the poetry, she thought, in a moment of exalted madness, that maybe she could actually find herself.

Keith the Poet always said that she had a song inside of her, but she just didn't know the words or the tune, or the rhythm but that she knew the colour of songs and that it was the colour that would lead her to all those other things. Keith the Poet had been one of the guests at Angela's fiftieth and a few of her other friends wondered why because Keith and Angela had never been all that close and Keith had a reputation for being a drunk with extremely poor personal hygiene that caused people to back away from him when he approached and he knew that this was the case and Angela got the sense that he wasn't so much embarrassed for himself with the reactions of those he encountered, but was aware of his effect and was sensitive enough to the feelings of others that if he was invited to something he would turn up to say thank you for the invitation and then would be gone in no time at all. Keith bought Angela a gift and it was a small book that he had picked up at a second hand bookshop that, much to her surprise, had been expertly wrapped in expensive gold wrapping paper with a little ribbon bow that Angela thought might have been done by one of the old lady volunteers from the Cathedral where Keith's parents used to worship before they died, who would drop in a weekly casserole to Keith in his commission flat across the road from the fort where Angela had wanted to live.

'Open it' Keith said when Angela went to place the gift on the table with the other gift and she realised that he wasn't planning to stay but wanted to see if she liked her gift before, he left.

The book was a slim volume of the Collected Poems of Alister Kershaw and Angela thought she knew the name of the poet but couldn't recall reading any of his work.

'Strange man', Keith said, 'spent most of his adult life living in France where he made friends with all sorts of people like Oswald Mosely, the fascist, but I think he liked Mosely for his intelligence and aristocratic bearing rather than his politics. Anyway, read him and see what you think, back in the day he was not liked by the Meanjin crowd or by the Reads or Nolan'.

Angela was impressed that Keith knew that she had a slight interest in John and Sunday Read and Sid Nolan, Albert Tucker and the rest of the Heidi crowd that was probably only eclipsed by her loves for Mick and James and old Thomas Stearns. The book was in one of the boxes that Angela had put in the back of the car when she fled the fires on the mountain.

Ingrid and Angela must have been on the same wavelength because as they drove past the old fort and the unit complex where Keith lived, Angela asked Ingrid 'Do you remember my fiftieth?'

'That's amazing', Ingrid said, 'I was just thinking about that evening upstairs above the pub, late summer and you were about to bugger off to Europe and leave me alone.'

'You weren't alone.' Angela laughed, 'you were head over heels in love with whatshisname, the bloke with the jet ski and Ralph Lauren polo shirts in every pastel shade you could think of.'

'Colin, the anaesthetist.' Ingrid said, 'and yes, you did leave me alone, or at least that's what it felt like.'

'I always said that the hospital employed Colin to save money. He'd just start talking to patients and they'd fall asleep without the bother and cost of drugs.' Angela said laughing at her own joke and then, more quietly, 'I had to get away, you know that, I had to try and find myself, to find who I really was and yes, it's a bloody cliché and would have been more applicable to some twenty something and not a fifty year old woman but I was scared that I was just going to die here, just fade away to dust, to ash even.'

'So, did you?' Ingrid asked.

'Fade away to ash? I think I might have come close yesterday.' Angela said, looking straight ahead as the road followed the harbour, almost back to Ingrid's place but they wouldn't stop but keep following the river west and north to where there was plenty of ash on the ground.

'Find yourself?' Ingrid asked quietly.

'I think,' Angela said, 'and I know that this sounds silly, but I sometimes think the closer I get to knowing who I really am, the further away that person seems to be, like I'm constantly trying to catch up, catch up to myself, if that makes sense?' Ingrid nodded but Angela wasn't convinced that it made any sense at all to Ingrid, so she changed the subject. 'So, what was it you were thinking about when you were thinking about my fiftieth.'

'How much fun everyone seemed to have that night and how I didn't realise that you were adored so much by so many people.'

'Don't let any of that lot fool you,' Angela said turning to look at Ingrid. 'They were only there because I paid for all the food and booze.'

'Rubbish!' Ingrid said and left it that.

Angela tried to remember who actually did come to her fiftieth and thought she'd have to open up the file on her laptop and look at the pictures to see if she could remember. She found it strange that she had difficulty in remembering given that it only been six years earlier. Her parents had been there of course, and her dad made a speech calculated to cause as much embarrassment to Angela whilst trying to appear to her friends that he was Mr Witty and Charming and her mum just looked embarrassed and, to hide the embarrassment, made a point of fussing over the plates and bowls of finger food that the waiters were bringing out on a regular basis. The Old Professor made a speech full of references to Blake which Angela's colleagues found hugely amusing and which her school friends and family found obtuse and incomprehensible.

Angela found it easier to remember who wasn't at the party. Andy of course and she had really hoped that he would come when she found an E Mail address for him after she did an internet search and sent him an invitation to the university where he worked in London. She had thought that she might be able to persuade him to share a meal with her if he was in London while she was there because, although he taught at the university, she had gathered that he travelled a lot doing guest lectures and consulting. There was too much water under the bridge for any regrets and she hoped that they could just be friends and she could tell him how proud she was about the way that his life had gone and how exciting it seemed to be buzzing around all over the place doing all the things he did.

She had thought of inviting Lucy, not because they had been particularly close in the day, but she was still part of the group that hung out at the uni and ran the activities in the student union with Angela and Andy and Liam Kelly, who everybody called Ned and who Angela thought had a crush on her for a while but he never asked her out. Lucy worked behind the bar of a club in the same suburb where she lived and had started working there while she was at uni and, despite her first-class honours degree in Philosophy, was still behind the bar twenty-five years later. Something had happened to Lucy over the years and Angela thought that it had to do with the drugs that she took and the deadshits that she hung around with, including one particularly creepy guy called Leon D'Amico who had been Lucy's dealer and sometimes lover. In the end she decided not to invite Lucy because she didn't think that she'd show up anyway and if she did, Angela would spend the whole night tippy toeing around like there was a hand grenade somewhere in the room with a dodgy pin that was just about to fall out.

Angela was overjoyed when Louis had decided to fly up from Hobart with his new partner Boris and they were the most dashing pair at the party with their dinner suits and perfect grooming and Louis told her that he had been planning to show Boris his old home town for ages and when the invitation arrived, it was just the excuse that he needed. Louis had found his dream job at the big modern art museum just outside of Hobart and Boris ran a little bookshop near the Salamanca markets and Louis told Angela that they had plenty of room in their warehouse conversion behind the bookshop and that she could come and stay for as long as she wanted and Angela said that she might take him up on that when she got back from her travels.

After her dad and the Professor had made their speeches there was an expectation that Angela would make a speech herself and she had been worrying about what she would say for days. The simplest thing would have just been to thank everyone for attending and to also thank them for their gifts, which she asked them not to bring, but was grateful anyway and she would acknowledge those people who couldn't make it but had sent their best wishes. That would have been the easy way out, but Angela never looked for the easy way out and she thought that she should say something profound about such a significant birthday and what she had learned from her seventeen thousand and eight hundred days on the earth (plus another ten or eleven to take into account leap years). She also wanted to impart some significance on her life to show that despite the fact she hadn't, like nearly all of her old school friends and much to her mother's disappointment, bred any children, that, as teacher at the university, she had enriched the lives of far more young people than her peers had done (except one or two who were school teachers and could rightfully say that they had some influence over many young lives although, when she looked at her friends who had become teachers, Angela wondered whether their influence had been positive or had it been just to create some suburban clones of themselves). She wanted to make the sort of speech that would make her parents think that she was awfully clever and sophisticated and cultured but realised that if she made too many cultural and literary references her parents, and a lot of her friends, would neither get the references or realise how clever and witty they were.

She thought of Andy and the whole business with Sophie and how Andy thought that by going out with Sophie, who had grown up in a house full of poets and artists and musicians, that somehow all that culture that she had been born into would somehow miraculously rub off him and rid him of what he thought was the stain of the coal mines, where his father had worked and the stains of the steel mills where he, himself, first worked when he left school, before he decided that he wanted to become a man of letters with his poorly written and overwrought angsty poems. Andy had been fun before he met Sophie, and for a long time afterwards Angela had not liked Sophie for the effect that she had on Andy and how all the things that made him so charming, like his no bullshit approach to life, suddenly disappeared and the few times that Angela had met up with him, usually at the uni bar, after he had started to see Sophie, would be frustrating affairs where Andy seemed to have no more opinions of his own and would start every second sentence with 'Sophie says' or 'Sophie thinks' as if any opinion he might have of his own was no longer valid unless it was in accord with Sophie's view of the world and Angela had formed the opinion that any opinion of the world that Sophie held was probably just as loopy as Sophie was herself.

Angela didn't think that she would miss Andy as much as she did when he first started seeing Sophie and then, when everything with Sophie fell apart, he left town and in those months between the end of the relationship with Sophie and his running away, as Angela called it, she was surprised at how Andy appeared the couple of times that they bumped into her. He was always scruffy looking with his big shock of black curly hair that was a wild knotted afro of a thing, but his hair started to look lank and greasy and he had horrible skin that was blotchy with white and red patches on his cheeks above his beard and he appeared to have lost weight and what was once a slouch of affectation was now, in Angela's eyes, a slouch of despair. She'd heard he had moved out of the house that he had shared with Patrick and Georgia and was living with some would be musicians who spent all their days drinking and smoking pot and telling people that they couldn't get jobs or study or do anything other than collect the dole because they were artists and Angela generally would not have had a problem with that apart from the fact that this household of musicians and their resident tortured poet, Andy, didn't ever appear to actually do anything creative like perform at gigs or try and get studio time to record their music. Angela sometimes thought that she should have done something to rescue Andy from himself, but she was never the rescuing type and, as it turned out, within a couple of years, he had pulled himself up by the bootstraps and was soaring through the world where it was Angela's world that, by time she turned fifty, seemed to be contracting every day.

In the end she gave a brief speech where she made a couple

of self-deprecating comments about the travails of the years but how good it was to have so many friends who she cared about and who cared about her and, even as she was saying the words, she was thinking to herself that she hardly ever had any contact with any of these people and she had been genuinely surprised that so many had bothered to turn up and honour her like this unless it was for the free food and drinks and she felt guilty about thinking that of her friends, so to dull the guilt, started to hit the champagne pretty hard.

'I don't think I ever saw you as legless as you were at your birthday party' Ingrid said as they motored up the big four lane road that ran along the creek that was glimpsed occasionally through the gaps between the towhouses that had been built where, for most of Angela's early life, there had been rows and rows of wooden woolstores where the big merino clips from the New England would be stored before being sold at auctions and sent off to the suit makers of Italy, or to China and India if the wool was of a lesser quality.

'I didn't get teary though, did I?' Angela asked.

'No tears, you were as funny as buggery, but I don't know if everyone appreciated your humour' Ingrid said.

'Well that's their problem' Angela said and smiled at Ingrid.

'That's what you told them on the night'

'I didn't?' Angela asked.

Angela and Ingrid kept reminiscing about Angela's fiftieth for quite a while and eventually they reached Maitland and crossed to the other side of the big river and Ingrid looked out the car window and was shocked.

'I don't think I've ever seen the river that low' she said, 'and brown and murky looking.'

'It's worse further up the valley', Angela said grimly.

The sky had changed colour as they were getting closer to

where the fires had been and where the fires were still burning and there was a yellow haze in the air that the sun was having difficulty shining through and they both commented that there weren't a lot of people out on the street and many of those who were going about their business were wearing the white face masks that were usually seen on young Asian tourists all over the world and always made Angela wonder whether they wore the masks to stop them from catching something or to stop them spreading something, but seeing so many face masks, she wondered if the young people she had seen wearing them in the past just came from smoggy cities like Beijing or Shanghai or Jakarta and were used to wearing them.

'Worse than Santiago on a bad day' Ingrid, who had travelled to all sorts of places and normally on her own, commented, and Angela remembered seeing a photograph that Ingrid has posted on her social media page of Santiago on a Sunday taken from high up on San Christabel and there was a thick brown layer of smog covering the city nestled under the towering snow covered peaks of the Andes.

Angela was pleased to have good air conditioning in the car and the filters, she thought, were cleaning the worst of the particles out of the air but even in the car, with the aircon blasting and the windows up, the closer they got towards Allynsdale, the heavier the smell of smoke became and there were still a lot of fire trucks darting about and Angela thought that some of them came from interstate because of their different badges and the names of little places she thought she had passed through on one of her trips to Bendigo to visit the art gallery and wineries and to eat in the hip cafes.

When they arrived at Wallisville, there was a roadblock at the edge of town and a couple of middle-aged policemen were leaning against a Highway Patrol car with a flashing light and a digital sign telling them to stop. One of the policemen asked her what her business was in the area and she told him that she lived on the other side of Allynsdale and she was hoping to check if her house was alright.

'Check in with the Police at Allynsdale. It's still pretty confusing up there and I doubt if they'll let you go any further than the town, but things might change later this afternoon' the policeman said and handed her back her licence.

Angela and Ingrid sat in silence as they drove, Angela navigating the narrow two laned bitumen road that ran along the side of the river towards Allynsdale. It seemed that they were the only people on the road. When Angela drove down the road the day before, there had been a lot of traffic with fire fighting vehicles heading north and people who had decided to evacuate heading south but now there was just a sense of emptiness and abandonment. None of the country they were passing through had been burned that badly, but there were the odd patches of blackened grass and, in some places, it was still smoking, and Angela thought that there must have been a number of spot fires that, perhaps, were caused by embers being pushed along by the wind and landing in the dry grass. She thought that some of the fire fighting vehicles she had seen driving back and forward along the road might have been patrolling for these sort of small spot fires that, unless they're dealt with quickly, can, given the dryness of the country and the heat in the wind, turn into an inferno. She hadn't turned the radio back on since talking to the policeman and the only sounds in the car that Angela could hear were the whirring of the tyres on the bitumen and Ingrid breathing and Angela remembered that Ingrid sometimes suffered from Asthma and thought that it might not have been wise to bring her up the valley towards the fireground where the smoke was still heavy in the air, where the river, up in the mountains, had its source.

Ashes Remain When the Fire has Passed

Allynsdale looked like a scene from some disaster movie or war film and there were more than a dozen fire trucks of various sizes and configurations parked in the main street at all sorts of angles and the weary crews, who obviously hadn't changed or showered and probably not slept from the night before, were sitting on the trucks or under the verandas of the pub and the general store and they all looked, in Angela's mind, absolutely knackered. Angela found a place to park the Subaru down passed the pub, just outside the tennis courts and the little folk museum in what had once been the district court house.

'What now?' Ingrid asked as they sat and looked up towards the mountains where the trees were bare and black. Across the creek, just past the ruins of Mrs Thompson's place there were a couple of big black glossy crows circling around, low in the sky and Angela thought that it would be a picnic for the crows that survived the fire, there would be barbecued carcases of all sorts of animals for the crows to choose from, whether it be cattle and goats on the farms, or pets, or wild animals in the hills who couldn't outrun the flames.

'I think there's an evacuation centre in the Scout Hall' Angela said and pointed back up the road where there seemed to be a lot of cars outside the weatherboard and iron hall and there were people milling about and some of them were wearing bright coloured vests to indicate that they were there to perform some sort of official function.

Ingrid and Angela got out of the car and walked up the street. A couple of the locals who recognised Angela gave her a nod or a little wave, but nobody said anything. As she walked up to the front of the Scout Hall, Angela noticed that Molly Thompson was sitting on a fold up chair with a couple of brattice bags by her side that had some clothes and framed photographs in them and sitting on Molly's lap was her little Silky Terrier and Angela was so pleased that she almost felt like weeping.

'Mrs Thompson, I'm sorry about your house but at least you're okay and so's your little mate' Angela said and knelt down in front of Molly and gave the dog's ear a pat.

'Scamp, that's his name', Mrs Thompson said, 'Gerald from the service station found him in the house and he had conked out so Gerald got him outside and gave him mouth to mouth and he came around straight away and the vet from the Department of Agriculture just had a look at him and said he's fine, and it was just the fumes in the smoke. Can you credit that, a man giving mouth to mouth to a little dog?'

'I think Gerald has a kind heart' Angela said and smiled back at Ingrid who was hovering around not sure what to do with herself.

'I'm sorry lass, but if I did know your name, I've forgotten it' Molly said and looked almost apologetic, 'but you live up the road, don't you, last property before Bernard's?'

'Bernard?' Angela asked and Molly gave a little laugh.

'You probably call him Killer like the locals and blow ins alike".

'It's funny isn't it?', Angela said, 'He was one of the first people I met when I moved here, and I speak to him almost every day, but I never knew what his proper name was. The first day I met him, he walked up to my front door and said that he was my neighbour and that I could call him Killer because everyone else does.'

It was like a rebirth, the day that Angela took possession of the keys to the little mud brick house and thanked the real estate agent in the main street of Maitland who had told her that she had managed to get a bargain and that he thought the vendors had agreed on a lower price than what the land and house was actually worth because they were sentimental and wanted the house to go to someone like Angela which left Angela to wonder what the real estate agent thought somebody like her was like. The couple who sold her the house had built it themselves in the late seventies and it had originally been their weekender until they decided to move into it permanently. David was a school teacher and Tricia was a public servant and so they both jumped at the chance to take transfers that meant that they could live in Allynsdale on a full-time basis. David managed to get a position at the Primary School in Wallisville and Tricia got a position in Maitland and told people that while it was some distance to travel, in Sydney she was used to spending an hour each way in her car but up in the valley there was an ever changing scenery as the days shortened and then lengthened and then shortened again and the colours changed with the season whereas, in Sydney, a good percentage of her hour behind the wheel was spent looking at the car in front and waiting for the traffic light to turn green and hoping that she would get through the intersection before it turned red again.

David had turned sixty-five and Tricia was not far off it and they decided that it was time to retire. Both could have left their public service jobs years before with pretty handsome retirement benefits but David told Angela, when she came to inspect the house, that he really liked teaching and loved the kids and the sense of community in the little school and he also worried that after forty years together in which they both worked full time and only spent lengthy times together when they made their odd overseas trip, that he and Tricia might have gotten on each other's nerves. They had only just retired when David was diagnosed with a fairly aggressive cancer and had to go to Newcastle fairly regularly for treatment and even sometimes to Sydney to see particular specialists. To Angela, when she met him, David looked like a very sick man and she didn't think he had much time. They had bought a small apartment in Newcastle with views of the ocean and Tricia settled into the role of full time carer that would only end when David got too ill to stay at home, although he kept telling her that he wanted to die at home in the mud brick cottage they had built, but Tricia was having none of it and told him that she wanted to have him around as long as she could and that meant getting good support and medical treatment.

Angela had been a bit surprised when, after she had the first inspection of the property and put in an offer with the real estate agent, she received a call from the agent saying that the vendors wanted to meet prospective purchasers because having what they called 'the right person' buying their hand built house was even more important to them than how much the person was prepared to pay. Angela agreed to drive up the following weekend and that's when she had her first and only time with the people who built the house that Angela very much wanted to be her home.

The biggest challenge for Angela was getting the money together to make the purchase. She had barely any savings to speak of and the job prospects were pretty poor and besides, unless she got tenure, and she was told that wasn't happening, it wouldn't be worth her while to drive all the way from Allynsdale to do a couple of hours of tutoring at the university. She had an inheritance from her grandparents and being the only grandchild meant that it was fairly substantial and she was finally able to convince her father to lend her enough money to make up the balance of the purchase price but at least when the deal was done and she had the keys in her hand, she was able to say that the house was hers and not the banks or anybody else's and she thought she could make some money doing odd jobs like cleaning and waitressing the way she had when she was at uni and hopefully there might be some local kids who need some English tutoring to help them get through the HSC.

'Is there any news?' Ingrid asked Molly.

'News love?' Molly wrinkled her brow in puzzlement.

'About Killer, er Bernard, Angela's been worried sick.'

Molly Thompson looked fretful and kept gazing up the road, beyond the ruins of her house which was not much more now than a tall brick chimney rising out of a pile of charred black timber and twisted and buckled sheets of corrugated iron that looked even rustier than when it had sat for years, unpainted, serving as Molly's roof. Her old gnarled hands, with fingers twisted and bent by arthritis were stroking Scamp's silky, freshly washed coat quite rapidly and Scamp was looking up at her, his tongue lolling and his breath panting with what Angela thought must be a doggy sort of love and she thought that with all hell breaking loose, some kind person had taken the time to give Scamp a bath.

'I think he must be gone love' Molly said to Ingrid and a solitary tear rolled down her face. 'Nobody could survive that' Molly shook her head.

'Kevin Cutler did' Angela said and surprised herself by the level of defiance in her voice that made Molly look at her a little startled and then she screwed up her eyes.

'The devil looks after his own' Molly said. 'There's talk that they didn't get caught in a flame over or whatever it is they call it but found a safe passage around to the back of the fire front and then just sat it out in safety.'

The devil, Angela thought, isn't that what The Law, not her Grandfather but the other Law, the narrator of one of Mick's books called Michael, the Christ figure water diviner when he came to the little town in the desert? No, she remembered, The Law called Michael Lucifer and for some reason, Angela always related Lucifer much more to hellfire than she did the Devil, or Satan, or Beelzebub, or the Anti-Christ, or the Dark Angel or whatever other name people used to describe the force that was the opposite of goodness. Maybe the association with Lucifer and hell fire had something to do with the way that her grandfather used to use the name Lucifers for the matches that he would strike to light his pipe and she remembers him patting his pockets and looking down the side of his armchair and on the coffee table and the side table where he kept his pouch of tobacco and his ashtray and the little silver tool her used to clean out the bowl of his pipe, scraping off the thick black tarry deposits, and when he couldn't find what he was looking for, he would call out to Angela's grandmother and say 'have you seen my lucifers'. Her grandmother would bring in a fresh box of matches from the kitchen and Angela's grandfather would point to the picture of the lady on the box of matches and say 'they should call them Angela's because they've got a picture of you on the box' and, sure enough, there was a woman with scarlet hair on the matchbox and Angela would giggle and laugh and say 'that's not me'.

'That's rot Molly and you know it' said a male voice from behind Ingrid and Angela and Angela turned and saw that the voice belonged to Rodney Cripplegate, who was a councillor on the local shire and drove the school bus that took the high school students down to Maitland each day for their studies.

'You're probably right', Molly said, 'but when I heard it, I wanted to believe it.'

Angela didn't know how many people disliked Kevin Cutler and she thought it might have just been her and Killer, but it was apparent that for the self-proclaimed Mayor of Allynsdale, there were a number of people who would be happy to see him lose his crown.

'Have you registered inside, Angela?' Rodney asked and Angela was taken aback at first that he even knew her name because she couldn't remember ever exchanging more than three of four words in the last five years and even then, it was probably just a polite 'excuse me' or the like when they were both in the general store.

'I was just about to' Angela said and smiled at Molly.

'Good,' Rodney said, 'Nobody knew where you were and they all assumed that you were dead, up there in the fire. We're waiting for the ok from the police and fire bosses to go and search for bodies.'

'Anila from the servo knew that I was leaving town. I spoke to her yesterday on my way out' Angela told Rodney.

'Yair, well you could have changed your mind and come back and besides, you know how that lot get things confused and mixed up,' he said with a sneering curl to his upper lip.

'What lot?', Ingrid, who had met Anila a couple of times when she was visiting, asked, 'service station proprietors?'

'And who are you anyway?' Rodney said, stepping forward so that Ingrid thought he was about to push his pumped-up chest into hers. 'This is a disaster zone and we don't need rubber neckers from the city coming to gawp.'

'Fuck off Cripplegate, she's with me and she's an emergency nurse so she might actually be able to do something useful other than poncing around pretending to have some authority.'

With that said, Angela stomped into the hall and went up to the table where a young woman, wearing an orange vest with the state government logo and writing saying Disaster Recovery was sitting at a fold up card table. As she entered the door, Angela heard Rodney spitting and spluttering behind her while Molly had the first decent laugh she had for days.

Angela told the young woman that she lived up the road, further up the hill in the forest and that she had left the day before and had stayed in the city overnight and didn't realise that she was considered to be missing. The young woman looked at a list that she had on a clipboard.

'You weren't listed as missing. Anila from the service station told us that you had gone to stay with a friend. We just didn't have any contact details to confirm that you were ok and to let you know when it was safe to come back.'

'So, my house was saved?' Angela asked and the young woman told her that she didn't know about any individual properties at that stage, but some houses had been lost up the road and they were preparing for the worst. 'And casualties?' Angela asked and the young woman said that she couldn't say anything and then made some gesture to some people across the other side of the room.

An elderly couple wearing white shirted and bloused and black trousered and skirted uniforms of the Salvation Army came over and the woman took hold of Angela's upper arm and quietly suggested that she come and sit down and have a cup of tea and a chat.

'So what part of the district are you from?' the man asked and then introduced himself a Captain Collins but said that Angela could call him Reg and his wife, who was also Captain Collins, could be called Daphne.

'Up the hill', Angela said, 'about half way up to the top'. She tried to discern if the expression of Reg and Daphne gave anything away, but they just nodded with concerned looks. 'I'm neighbours with Killer, sorry Bernard, and I don't know his last name, on one side and Alyssa and Tony Rossini on the other, if that means anything to you.'

'Alyssa is in hospital' Daphne said, 'with some nasty burns to her hands and some more superficial burns to her body and legs that the paramedic said were caused by radiant heat and not directly by fire and she has some smoke inhalation but the doctor who came up on the helicopter told us that he thought that she would pull through ok.'

'And Tony?' Angela asked, her eyes darting from Reg to Daphne and they both lowered their own eyes until Reg cleared his throat and spoke in a soft voice that was almost a whisper.

'He didn't get out. We expect the worst. Mrs Conti said that she and her husband had argued as the fire approached. She wanted to leave, and he wanted to stay. He told her to go if she wanted to and she said that there were a lot of spot fires, now what did she call it? That's right, an ember attack and that's how she burned her hands, opening the gates. She said that she drove out on to the road and thought that Tony would see sense and join her and she could see the flames in the distance and heard the fire like an express train coming down the hill, and travelling just as fast and before the main fire front had even reached her, the house just exploded and Tony had been on the veranda with his hose and she knew that it was too late and she said she drove as fast as she could with the fire behind her like a demon at her heals'.

By time Reg had finished speaking, Daphne was dabbing at her eyes with a white plain handkerchief and Angela felt that she should be crying herself but couldn't summon the tears just yet. She felt a hand on her shoulder and turned to see Ingrid looking down at her with a sympathetic half smile.

'I can call work' Ingrid said. 'They would have taken her to the John for assessment, it's got the only decent heli-pad but if the burns were too bad, they would have transferred her to Concord by now.' Angela nodded.

'And Bernard?' she asked Reg who just shook his head and told her that was no news.

She wondered why Kevin Cutler hadn't checked out Bernard's place and Alyssa and Tony's if it was true what he was saying, that they made their way back down the road to Allynsdale after the fire front had moved through and swung around to the east.

When Angela closed her eyes, all she could see was an image of Tony Rossini turning into a column of flame, undergoing a chemical conversion that would release pure energy in the form of light and she thought of the images she had seen in a book of the English martyrs, burning in Oxford and how, when she was in Oxford, she had stood at the Martyrs Memorial where Latimer, Ridley and Cranmer had been consumed by the flames for their beliefs and she wondered what beliefs Tony had, and what he might have thought at that exact moment when his body exploded and if he would have even known what was happening other than a brief flash of excruciating pain.

Angela imagined the scene when Alyssa was begging Tony to leave, to abandon their dream home in the bush to the flames, everything that they worked for years to establish, the chook pens where the free range hens produced the eggs that Alyssa hauled off to farmer's market every week along with her jams and preserves and pickles that she cooked up in the old kitchen, the workshop where Tony had his lathes and chisels and a whole lot of other tools that Angela didn't know the names of and that Tony used to make the beautiful bespoke furniture from old timber he foraged in the forest and sold online or through his friend's trendy and expensive boutique in Sydney. Angela knew why he would want to stay and try and save all of that, and she could imagine him saying that the house, the shed and the garden where his life but, in the end, his life was something much more precious or, perhaps he was right and when everything he loved went up in that ball of flame maybe it was both figuratively and literally true that it would be his life that would also be consumed by the fire.

Angela remembered seeing a picture on the internet of a billboard with some community health warning that said 'Hundreds of Australian Men Will Die This Year of Stubbornness' and some wag had hand painted, in big black letters underneath the message 'No We Won't' and when she first saw the picture, Angela laughed and thought about all of her male friends who refused to see a doctor unless they were really sick but now, she knew if she saw that picture again, it would be Tony she would see, a stubborn standing column of flame that quickly turned to ash where he stood.

Daphne asked Angela if she had somewhere to stay if she wasn't able to return home and told her that the people from the Housing Department were somewhere in the room and that they could organise a hotel or motel for her, but it might have to be in Maitland because the pub in town only had a couple of rooms that were let to regulars and the two pubs in Wallisville didn't have accommodation options and that quite a few people had stayed the previous night on camp stretchers that the various charities had set up on the floor of the scout hall and that they had managed to get everyone fed when the mobile kitchen had turned up but it had now gone to Cheltenham where there were a lot more people in need.

Angela told Daphne that she would be staying with Ingrid and Ingrid nodded to confirm this and that all Angela really wanted to know was if anything was salvageable from her little house.

Angela Becomes
the Darlinghurst Push

The mega crack-up began with Angela's thesis for her Master of Arts degree that was titled *The Odyssey of Stephan Dedalus to the Streets of Darlinghurst – The Influence of James Joyce on the Caldwell Street Push.*

Darlinghurst in the nineteen thirties, where well-thumbed stained and battered copies of Ulysses were furtively passed from hand to hand between the poets and novelists and playwrights who gathered in darkened rooms, soot stained by the open mouthed coal fire, gathered in the yellow glow of the paraffin lamp on the polished dark wooden table in the parlour of Mr Seamus Plunket's house in Caldwell street Darlinghurst, and dreamed that maybe one day in the streets between the brothel worlds and sly grog worlds and razor men, that there might be a sainted thinker, a Stephen Dedalus who, one bright day might take a stroll from Woolloomooloo, up to the Cross, ten stations, rosary and the holy king and down the hill and up the hill by the grim sandstone walls of Darlo, the floggers triangle and gallows, then saunter left up Oxford Street to Paddo, turn down the hill, long march to Rose Bay, Qantas Empire Flying boats to Blighty then to home, before a walk along the water run through FelixBlackburnDoubleRushcuttersElizabeth and back by six for a beer or two in the loo. Or so Angela dreamed it, wrote it down, dissected, argued, shaped and invented a literary school.

Seamus Plunket, writer of words, Antipodean Irishman who claimed to have been there in Dublin, sixteen, sweet sixteen, with Pierce and Connolly and the others, who had claimed to have been to Trinity and him, the son of a cobbler, working the counter at Marcus Clarke's and scribbling in his leather-bound notebook by late night's candlelight, telling stories of the backlane saints of Surry Hills.

Ten years before, when the unbanned Joyce had not been held in his hands, Seamus Plunket was a balladeer of a bush he'd never seen, a chronicler in verse of hardy stockmen burning in a dust dry drought, running from runaway bushfires, swimming swollen creeks in flood, sucking the venom from the legs of mates, snakebitten and dying miles from the wattle and daub hut in the run on the Cooper or up near Barcaldine.

Two years before the war and the unbanning for the first time of the book, Shim Plunket, shop assistant, poet and novelist of Caldwell Street Darlinghurst had a salon and Angela MacGregor hovered over it in her imagination dreaming of the hurried words, the scraps of paper with poems, plays and bits of novels, the cheap fortified wine in enamel mugs stained brown by tannin from the tea.

Angela MacGregor became absorbed and then obsessed in finding any scrap she could in dusty diaries in the Mitchell Library, references in other books, recollections of people now in their eighties who hadn't been taken by booze or fags or killed in the war or murdered or suicided or succumbed to the slums, before they were cleared or because they were cleared. Angela MacGregor entered into one world and left another one behind, thinking herself in the 'thirties, cutting her hair in the style, seeking out the vintage clothes in op shops, country towns and cities. Angela MacGregor became the embodiment, transformed in time and space, of the Caldwell Street Push.

The doctor said it was overwork, her mother called it a breakdown and her father fretted much and said very little while Angela MacGregor, with a head full of Lithium just smiled and slept. There were too many things rattling around in her mind, Joyce and Seamus Plunket and his cohort, the unpublished novels found in an archive at the Fisher Library, the poems in yellowing journals in binders in the Mitchell Library and there was the sad figure of Plunket's wife, who in his letters that had survived, the woman he had called Molly but whose real name was Siobhan and, who according to a newspaper report published in the Sydney Morning Herald had at last, one Spring day in 1939, been released from Callan Park and upon hearing Mr Menzies announce that that the country was at war with Germany, for no better reason than Neville Chamberlain had committed the United Kingdom at war, and probably remembering the way she had been treated by her own father who had come home from the Somme with all of his madness and suicidal rages, brought about from the blood and mud and the mates dismembered, had taken the tram to Watson's Bay and thrown herself off The Gap.

Angela became obsessed with Molly and at times despondent because there was so little that she could find, just the odd references in correspondence that had survived by Plunket and some of the other members of the Caldwell Street Push, the occasional mention in a newspaper article about some literary event and some words in a couple of gossip sheets that suggested that Plunket and Molly and the others indulged in all sorts of scandalous vices.

There was a book that Angela found and read that had been written by a Colin Quigley who she had gathered from Seamus Plunket's correspondence, had been a member of the Caldwell Street group and may have even been Seamus' closest friend for a while. Angela assumed that the novel might have been autobiographical and it was called *The Portrait of a Young Man on the Hungry Mile* and was mainly about the travails of an unemployed wharf labourer in Sydney during the depression and consisted of poorly written polemic tracts against the government and the big shipping companies and the stevedoring companies and the unions and seemed, somewhere in its dense and at times unreadable sections, an apology for the New Guard, the protofascists active in Sydney at the time. There was one great long section when the protagonist talks about how he slept with the wife of his best friend and how the best friend had given Colin, who in the book he called Francis, his wife, who he called Norah, as some sort of gift to show how great the bonds of the friendship were but didn't say how Norah/Molly/Siobhan felt about this and Angela tortured herself for weeks trying to discover the true story and if Quigley had slept with Siobhan and, in more lucid moments, wondered why she cared, why this was important.

Quigley kept a diary and this was in the archives at the National Library and so, one chilly day in July of 1990, Angela drove down to Canberra with a bag full of pencils and blank notebooks and her IBM ThinkPad and a bottle of whisky and a bottle of valerian root tablets and checked into a cheap hotel near the centre of the city, across the lake from the Library and Art Gallery under the watchful gaze of the parliament on the hill and the lustful silver bodgie.

The whisky and valerian helped sleep find Angela, tossing on an ocean, drowning in poly-cotton and chenille, air conditioning too hot, fearing what she would find in neat faded copperplate, cheap Indian ink, lampblack mixed with water and drawn into the body of a black resin pen, sucked up out of the little mixing bottle to settle for a while and then slowly bleed on to the pages of a notebook that Angela fretted she would not be able to decipher, in a language of a secret land, a land of men of lusts and dreams, and legends half invented of themselves that sounded, in their drunken telling, so heroic, and yes and yes, there would be some telling of Siobhan/Molly before she disappeared into the swirling torment of the eddies of Callan Park and then fell one more time, not to rise, in the swirling eddies of The Gap where, in its day, all the desperate of Sydney made a journey with Charon, a blue serge suited and peaked cap Sydney tram conductor.

Angela dreamed of The Gap and that moment standing on the edge of the cliff, watching the black waves wash over the rocks to recede and wash again and, in her dream, she found, a crystal moment of clarity as she clambered over the fence that barely stopped the hundreds of suicides, who had made the same awkward climb over the years, as if each one had preceded her own fall, shown her the way, guided and directed her, whispered in her ear so softly that the words were lost on the waves and the wind of the things that Molly/Siobhan must have felt that day in early September 1939, thirty years old and three years older than Angela who was twenty seven and in her dream her friends were raising glasses and toasting 'Jim and Janis and Jimi – she was a rock star, Angela, rocks on the black rocks of the shore.'

The emptiness of waking after such dreams washed over Angela and she lay in bed for what seemed like hours until the pale Canberra winter sun peeked through the gaps in the curtain and down below, on the street, she could hear the people going about their business, off to work, grey bureaucrats with briefcases and newspapers and take-away coffee cups. She had a plan to go to the library, do some research and then, after lunch, go the National Gallery to take in the Nolans and the Tuckers and the Hesters, if they were on display, especially the Hesters. She only had to drag one leg over the edge of the bed, followed by the other and then lift her bum from the mattress and take five steps to the shower and her day could begin, but taking that first step was becoming impossible as if her leg weighed one hundred kilos and she didn't have the strength to lift it and yet, in her dream the night before, she clambered over the fence at the Gap with the poise and grace and speed of Nadia Comaneci attacking the beam. She could lie in bed all day but sometime in the morning there would be a knock and housekeeping would enter the room to make her bed and put fresh towels on the cold metal rack, no warming racks for towels in two and a half star motels. Angela thought about housekeepers and wondered how many times they opened doors to find a body, homicide or suicide or natural causes, gory scenes of blood and viscera, scenes of people looking peaceful, calm asleep, signs of struggles or despair, scenes like the dead ex-politician still wearing a loaded condom, suicide notes and empty pill bottles on the nightstand next to the half-finished vodka. Angela didn't know who found Molly/Siobhan, broken on the rocks, washed clean by the ocean, and perhaps some passer-by had seen her jump, had called the police who would have sent a boat around the heads from the harbour and down the cliff lined shore.

If she could find the energy to get up and place the 'do not disturb' sign on the doorknob on the outside of her room, Angela reasoned that she should use that energy to take a shower, get dressed and try and face the day. She had been excited during her long drive down to Canberra, through the sheep country around Goulburn, glimpsing what looked like the sun reflecting off the snow on the mountain tops way down to the south and anticipating the thrill of the chase, the pure research of seeing primary sources and the speculation of what that might mean but, somehow and for reasons she could not explain, the excitement turned to anxiety and then the anxiety faded, leaving her feeling totally emptied of all emotions and tired and weak and listless.

She found the energy to shower and dress but the thoughts of breakfast made her stomach churn and as she walked through the hotel foyer, she had a wave of nausea from the smell coming out of the breakfast room where visiting business people on a budget could be seen piling up their plates with scrambled eggs (and it was the smell of the eggs that was making Angela sick), and bacon and mushrooms and baked beans and sausage, (and Angela thought that the smell of the greasy sausage might also be making her sick), and hash browns and fried tomatoes until the mound of food became so high that bits and pieces would fall from the top to be ground into a greasy paste on the floor in front of the bain-maries by the worn but polished Windsor Smiths and Florsheims of the suited business folk.

Outside it was an early Winter Canberra day with a dazzling

blue sky and some high cirrus clouds, horsetails Angela's dad called them, and the slight breeze off the lake still had the lingering chill of the morning frost that the sun had burned away by time Angela had found the strength to get out of bed. She left her car in the hotel car park and walked to the library across the bridge. Angela had e mailed the library the week before and put in her request to peruse the diary of Colin Quigley, so she hoped that when she arrived, she would just have to show someone her library card and then the diary would be delivered to one of the reading rooms where she would have all day to read it and take whatever notes she could and, if she wasn't finished, it would be held overnight for her to come back the following day. Angela hoped that she would only need one day, possibly two and had only booked her hotel room for the two nights.

A young breezy woman in a uniform that consisted of a blouse with the library's logo on the pocket, under a name tag that said Liesl, and grey skirt, short socks and joggers that allowed her to move around quietly and not disturb the readers, brought the box containing not only Quigley's diary but some other papers to Angela and told her that when she was done, to buzz Liesl on the intercom and she would come and collect the box. Liesl said 'happy hunting' to Angela, smiled and was gone in a second of quiet, fluid and graceful movement.

Angela thought that she would have to use gloves to handle the diary but Liesl didn't mention it and none were offered, so Angela just plucked the quarto sized thick leather tome out of the box and started turning the pages. She assumed that the lack of gloves was because the library didn't consider Colin Quigley to be someone whose work had to be protected from the damage that is caused by oils from fingers on the old brittle acid paper and that the risk was so minimal because nobody ever asked to see Quigley's diary. Angela had also received, in the mail, some information from the National Archives including his military record from the Second

World War. The first thing that struck Angela when she looked at the diary was that it was identical to the leather-bound diary of Seamus Plunket that was held in the Mitchell Library which, seemingly odd, could also easily be explained by the fact that they probably both shopped at the same stationer.

The diary started in 1937 when Colin Quigley was twenty-three and he had written a brief autobiographical sketch at the beginning of the diary that described how he grew up in the streets of Glebe, one of two children, he was the youngest and his mother was a war widow after his father had disappeared at Lone Pine on the Gallipoli Peninsula, his body never found, but there is a marker in Gallipoli above an empty grave waiting in case some bones with a dog tag turn up one day in a farmer's field. Young Colin enjoyed school and could read and write by time he was five and called himself 'a bit of a teacher's pet'. He wanted to go on and finish high school and perhaps even get a scholarship to Sydney University that wasn't far from the slum he lived in, down at the end of Glebe Point Road. His mother was a sick woman, and, in his own words, his brother was 'a simpleton', so it became Colin's job to become the breadwinner. He got a job as a stable hand for a bloke who had teams of big Clydesdales and drays who'd cart goods from the wharves at Darling Harbour to the warehouses in Kent Street. Colin loved the big gentle horses, but the competition had set in and soon the horses were all sent to the knackery to be replaced by motor lorries and Colin was too young to drive and too small and wiry to be the offsider for the lorry drivers. He got a job as a junior at a foundry down the other end of Glebe Point Road near Rozelle Bay and Angela found herself being moved by Colin's descriptions of 'doing the work of the devil, in the furnace of hell' and how he was being shaped from boyhood into manhood 'by the casting sands and molten iron and the furious sparks of a new form being shaped'. She wondered when he first started to write poetry and if he was doing it as a young man because this diary was, at this point made up of recollections and the contemporaneous entries from March 1935 commenced a few pages in. Colin stayed at the foundry until 1930 when it closed and Colin, who was only sixteen was out of work and he wrote that he did whatever he could to survive, stealing things from the back of shops, going with a gang of mates down to Dixon Street where they would terrorise the Chinese market gardeners and steal their wares and on one occasion, Colin managed to grab a duck and wrung its neck on the trot and his mother said that it was the best meal she had for years. His older brother had been suffering from consumption, as Colin called it, or tuberculosis as it is called today, Angela remembered, and died in 1931. They couldn't afford a funeral so the brother, who was not mentioned by name in the diary and just called 'my brother' or 'my big brother' was buried by the church in a paupers grave at Rookwood and it broke Colin's mother's heart that she couldn't visit her son and when she died of the same disease less than a year later, Colin risked gaol by breaking into houses in the better suburbs like Vaucluse and making off with silver to sell and repay the loanshark who had lent him the money to bury his mother.

Colin covered the next six years in less than a page and described an itinerant life that included picking fruit in the Riverina, road building in the Blue Mountains and a year at the steelworks in Newcastle until he scored a job in the warehouse at the big Marcus Clarke store on Broadway not far from where he grew up in Glebe and where he first met Plunket and presumably Siobhan. Plunket encouraged Colin to write and provided him with advice and soon Colin was turning out poems on a regular basis and there were some clippings of his poems in the back of the diary but Angela was unable to tell where they had been published and she had already accessed online a copy of his collected poems that were published posthumously by Plunket and so had already read the ones that were in the back of the diary.

In his first entry for 1937, Colin Quigley talks at length about writing an epic verse novel that would be about life on the docks during the depression and the people who Quigley called 'exalted in their struggles and sainted in their dignity' and it struck Angela that it was a bit like Kerouac but written twenty years earlier and how, had he survived, Quigley might have embraced the Beats. A few pages into the diary, where he had been describing the process of writing without thinking too much about the words and just scribbling late into the night, he talked about how the great work was going to be a novel of epic proportions and set over the course of one day on the docks and adjoining streets and it would start just before dawn and end just before midnight and it would follow just a couple of characters with one of them based on himself. Angela thought to herself that he was a bower bird who was intending to shamelessly copy the themes and styles of Joyce. She also thought to herself that he knew so little about writing to think that Joyce had just spewed words haphazardly onto the page when every word he wrote was so carefully considered and how Joyce's writing must, at times been painfully slow.

Quigley also referred to coming home and it was obvious that he was living in the Caldwell Street cottage with Seamus and Siobhan, but he too, like Seamus, kept referring to Siobhan as Molly and it was obvious by his choice of words that he was quite attracted to this Molly. There were numerous entries about the drinking parties they held with a group of poets and writers and how everyone there loved Molly and how immensely proud Seamus was to have a beautiful young wife fifteen years his junior and how Colin thought that she would have made a better wife for him, their ages being closer and how he teased Seamus about this and about how he would flirt with Molly but she never flirted back but looked at him with sad eyes if he patted her knee or held her too close in a dance to a gramophone record.

Angela kept reading, her fingers trembling as she turned the pages and she thought that she could hear her own blood pounding in her ear with each entry she read until she came to December the 25th 1937.

> *What greater gift can a man share with his friend than his most treasuredpossession as a way of making an irrefutable bond of friendship. Last night after supper and copious toasts to our good health and enduring friendship and felicitations for the season, my dear friend Seamus looked at me quite solemnly and taking my hand in his said 'you are a good friend, a brother and this Christmas I wished to give you a gift of great value and one that is beyond the contemplation of mere pounds and shillings in its worth. I am giving you Molly as a gift, not to keep but to share as true brothers.'*

Angela was immediately intrigued and repulsed at how loathsome a man Seamus could be and how Quigley thought that the loathsomeness was something noble and how, notwithstanding the ways of Molly Bloom, it was a betrayal of these men to think that their actions were noble and maybe even Joycean and that Molly Bloom's philandering were her choice, her unbridled passions and lust, but Plunket was just treating Siobhan as a chattel.

> *My boon companion, my friend, my brother, urged me to take Molly by the hand straight away and to take her to my bed which I did as I had been dreaming of this since I moved in with them. Molly was so gracious and spoke not a word as she stood and allowed me to lead her into my bedroom where we consummated our passion although, she was quiet and nervous and returned shortly after I was spent to Plunket, but he sent her back telling her that she was to stay the whole night with me because that was the gift he was giving.*

Angela closed the diary and felt that she could not read anymore, and she looked at her watch and realised that she had been reading for nearly six hours without a break and that she was hungry but felt sick to the stomach, needed a drink and needed to go to the toilet.

She had enough for one day and decided that she would come back the next to finish the diary. The overwhelming thing that Angela thought was disillusionment. She had started doing her research with a romantic view of the Caldwell Street Push as being trailblazers of Australian Modernism who had been rejected and scorned by the establishment because they were poor and working class and hadn't graced the gothic vaults of Sydney University nor were they proud Australian chauvinists favoured by the Bulletin or Smiths Weekly, but cultural outlyers, but, reading Quigley's diary, what in his novel had seemed bohemian and joyous, now seemed seedy and ugly and most of all there was the forlorn figure of Siobhan forced to sleep with her husband's friend, their lodger.

After leaving the National Library, Angela made her way to the National Gallery and spent a couple of hours looking at the paintings and becoming quite absorbed in some of the modernist art and when she walked through the gift shop on the way out, she treated herself to a large book of Sid Nolan's paintings and she thought about Sid and Sunday Reed and how complicated that relationship must have been but that they had both gone into it willingly and enthusiastically unlike poor Siobhan who had left no writings of her own behind or, if she did, they might have been destroyed by Seamus Plunket. In his novel, Colin left the reader with the impression that Siobhan, or Nora as she was called, was smarter than her husband Francis and that the Francis character resented this and tried to put her down. Angela wondered how Seamus felt about the book and the way his relationship had been described by Quigley even in the guise of fiction.

After a boring dinner in the hotel dining room that consisted of some concoction of dried chicken breast and tinned apricot, Angela went back to her room and looked at the pictures in her Nolan book for a while and then watched some dreary Australian television drama about an inner-city doctor's surgery. She watched the program until the end and noticed that while she was doing it, she had drunk nearly half a bottle of whisky and her head was spinning a little as she turned off the television and the bedside light.

When Angela woke up the next morning just after the sun had risen and streamed in through the windows where she had forgotten to close the curtains, she laid in bed and ran her tongue over her teeth that felt furry, and she had a taste in her mouth that Andy had once described as being 'like the bottom of a cockie's cage'. She had a slight headache and she felt clammy and her sweat had left an acrid smell on the sheets and pillowcase, but she was glad that she hadn't dreamed the night before and the slight unwell feeling wasn't too high a price to pay for not dreaming.

She decided that she would put in four hours at the Library and that should be enough time for her to skim through the diary, take some relevant notes and citations for her thesis and still manage to drive home before it was too late in the evening.

The diary went on with much the same stuff, stories of parties and gatherings in Caldwell Street, Quigley struggling with trying to write his novel of an evening and early in the morning, the goings on at Marcus Clarks and every now and again a reference to Molly that gave Angela the very strong impression that the ménage a trois was an ongoing arrangement but that it was an arrangement between Quigley and Plunket and that Siobhan didn't have much of a say in it and Quigley alluded to the fact that Siobhan was drinking a lot and even hinted that she was using cocaine which was something Angela didn't know people did back in those days and made a note to look it up.

In late May of 1939, Quigley had made a note in his diary that said that '*the cops took Molly to Callan Park last night, maybe some peace and quiet for a while*' and that was it, no mention of the reason or what had happened or why the police had been involved and Angela made a note in her notebook to consult the Sydney newspapers for that period. The diary then became sporadic with days going by without any entries and then the entrance for the 4th of September 1939 that simply said that war had been declared and that Colin was thinking of joining up because it would be decent pay. The next entrance was for the following day:

> *The wallopers called in last night, that big bastard Sergeant Truscott from Darlo station. He looked a bit awkward when I opened the door and he asked to see Shim and I wondered what he had gotten himself into. Shim came to the door but wouldn't let Truscott in so Truscott stood in the street and told Shim that Molly was dead, that she had thrown herself of The Gap and Shim said he wasn't surprised.*'

And that was it, Angela thought, the death of his lover glibly reported in a total of seventy-six words without a shred of emotion or sorrow. Molly didn't get another mention throughout the diary and Quigley didn't join the army straight away because he got an offer to publish his book that he had managed to finish, but it didn't sell all that well and he lost his job and Plunket threatened to evict him for not paying his rent but Quigley thought it was because Plunket had found another girl, even younger than Molly that he wanted to move into the house but that the same arrangements they had in sharing Molly weren't going to apply. Quigley's last entry was to say that Plunket was going to look after his papers while he was away in the army and how he was looking forward seeing the middle east and the pyramids and there the diary ended in the middle of 1941.

Angela knew the rest from her research. Colin didn't get to see the pyramids. What he got to see were the jungle and rubber plantations of Malaya where he was part of the same fighting retreat as her grandfather and, like him, Quigley ended up in Changi but didn't go to work on the railway. Quigley got what he thought was his dream prisoner job unloading ships in Singapore Harbour and managed, every now and again to smuggle food into the camp until he was caught and severely beaten. The second time he was caught he was tied to a post in the hot sun for three days until, according to a witness, he had spat and swore at a passing Japanese guard who stabbed him in the stomach with the long blade on the end of his rifle. Angela thought that she might ask her grandfather, who was still alive and not long turned eighty-five if he remembered Quigley or had heard of him.

As for Plunket, he seemed to disappear into obscurity after the war apart from a few odd poems in Angry Penguins, but he did edit and pay for the printing of a collection of Quigley's poetry. There were no more novels although he did leave some scraps of autobiography that covered his younger years where he claimed to have been in the 1916 Easter uprising and there were some other scraps about what it was like living in Sydney during the war and how the whole place became lively when the yanks arrived and how his new young girl left him to work in the Cross, dating, as he called it, the American servicemen and even, he noted with some distaste, Angela thought, the black ones. There was no mention of Siobhan/Molly in any of the scribbles Plunket left and he soldiered on, trying to trade in on his bohemian past until he was taken by a stroke in 1963.

When Angela got back home she was fatigued from all the research and the way her head was spinning with what she had found out about a group of people she originally admired and thought of as harmless larrikin would be intellectuals but all that changed and she realised that she was trying to view the whole Caldwell Street Push through Siobhan's eyes but couldn't because Siobhan never told her own story or, at least never left her own story, and all that Angela could find was snippets in newspaper clippings and Colin Quigley's diary where Angela tried to imagine being Siobhan and feeling what she felt.

Her supervisor told her to re-write her thesis and to just concentrate on the writing and to put it into the context of the time and to analyse how these writers, and others in the push, not just Plunket and Quigley, all tried to emulate James Joyce and got it so terribly wrong so that their work ended up being pale imitations without originality or literary merit and how it was symptomatic of the cultural cringe of the time but he did suggest that it would benefit some analysis of how women's voices were silent and that whether one agreed with what Molly Bloom had to say, Joyce had given her a voice whereas Quigley and Plunket took Siobhan's from her.

Angela worked around the clock finishing her M.A. thesis and survived on instant noodles and plunger coffee and the odd meal Ingrid would make for her and leave in the fridge to be microwaved. Angela finally submitted her bound copies of her thesis and then went out on a bender of massive proportions. She remembered getting out of the taxi at her front door and then the next thing she remembered was waking up in hospital with Ingrid and her parents standing at her bedside and Ingrid was in her green scrubs and looking very concerned.

Daniella Dabs, Siobhan, Mick and Other Ghosts

They swept over the Tarro railway bridge and caught sight of the muddy river in the moonlight at Hexham and knew they would be home soon or, at least Ingrid would be at home and Angela would have another night on the spare bed before repeating the drive to Allynsdale the next day.

'You've not said a word since we left Wallisville' Ingrid said, more as an observation than anything else.

'I was thinking of the mega crack-up' Angela said, using the name they both used for Angela's mental collapse nearly thirty years earlier.

'Well you never did things by halves' Ingrid said and patted Angela's leg.

'It's funny, but the next ten years after the mega crack up now seemed like they were a lost ten years until I started to work seriously on Mick and my doctorate, and then I had a good twenty years with some ups and downs and even losing my job wasn't so bad because I could buy the cottage, but now I'm scared that I might be lost again and this time there might not be a way back.'

'There's always a way back' Ingrid said. 'You've done it before, reinvented yourself and you'll do it again.'

'What if I've run out of Me's to reinvent?'

'Oh, I think there's plenty of Angela MacGregor's in that head of yours waiting to burst out and take on the world.'

'God! You make me sound like Sybil. I might be a bit loopy but I'm not completely insane.' Angela said to Ingrid as they kept following the river towards the sea.

'You know what we should do?' Ingrid asked, and went on

before Angela could reply, 'Go out tonight like we used to in the old days'

'What?' Angela asked, 'A couple of cougars hitting the town?'

'I didn't mean trying to hook up, I'm over that crap' Ingrid replied, and Angela turned to gaze at her for a while.

She had never told Ingrid the reason for the 'mega crack-up' because she wasn't always sure of the reasons herself, and it was easier to fall back on what her parents thought the reasons were and that was burning the candle at both ends, trying to complete her thesis, do part time teaching at uni and private tutoring for kids doing the HSC and partying too hard with her friends. The reason she suspected, and then discounted as being silly, was she believed that somehow Siobhan had entered her soul and that she was being tasked with the almost impossible job of rescuing Siobhan from the twisted vision of Molly that was held by Plunket and Quigley, that was all that existed in the world of Siobhan because there was hardly any record of who she had been, or where she came from, or if she had family. With a name like that she was obviously Irish or of Irish extraction but apart from that there was nothing. The newspaper reports of her incarceration and suicide didn't mention her by name but just referred to a twenty-six-year-old woman and Angela only assumed that it was Siobhan because of the dates in Quigley's diary and the fact that he kept the clippings. Births, Deaths and Marriages said they couldn't help with just a first name and an age and she never appeared on the electoral role for Caldwell Street. Mental Health told her the records for Callan Park for 1939 had been lost but Angela suspected that they might have been spinning her a line and she knew that in the days and weeks leading up to the 'mega crack-up' that she often sounded like she was on the verge of hysteria.

'Can I take a rain cheque?' Angela asked. 'I'm done in and I want to be up early in the morning and head back to Allynsdale in case they finally open the road.'

'How about pizza, wine and some Netflix?' Ingrid asked and Angela said it that it sounded like a recipe for a good night in.

By time they got to Ingrid's flat, the television news had finished and there was some program on about people building interesting houses in the United Kingdom and Ingrid said that it was one of her favourite shows, so they decided to watch it while they waited for the pizza to be delivered. The program was about a young couple who had bought a tiny block in South Kensington in London where they were keeping the shell of an old workshop but building some big ultra-modern multi-level house inside that looked on the plans like it might have been a Tardis in that it seemed bigger on the inside than the outside.

'I thought I recognised it' Angela said excitedly, 'that's my old street, the one I stayed in with Georgia in London back in 2012'

'I was surprised that you actually came back' Ingrid said, pouring the wine.

'I thought about it', Angela said, 'and you know, if I had the courage to take off overseas when I was a lot younger, the way that Ned and Andy and even Georgia did, I think I might have stayed there forever. It's just harder, the older you get.'

'If things turn out for the worst up in Allynsdale, there's nothing to stop you packing up stumps and going. The house was insured I hope?' Ingrid asked.

'Not for a lot of money but I could sell the land and after I paid back Dad, I'd have enough to live on comfortably for a couple of years at least, I don't actually spend much money these days other than fuel for the car and some decent wine and cheese.'

'Would you go back to London?' Ingrid asked.

'It would be the easiest in terms of getting a long-term visa thanks to my grandparents although I'm not sure if I'd want to live in London after all the years in the bush but perhaps a small village would be nice, somewhere up north, Scotland maybe, in the highlands. If you're near a train station, you're only ever an hour or two away from a decent sized city. The place I'd really like to live in, at least for a year or two, would be New Mexico.'

'Santa Fe?'

'No, maybe Aztec or maybe Taos' Angela said, remembering her visit there in search of Mick.

Her trip to undertake research on Mick, which she hoped to use to write a critical biography or a study of his work, had come about when the head of department suggested that she needed to take some time off and thought a sabbatical would be a good idea. Angela later came to think that the offer of the sabbatical along with a research grant was a smart strategy to ease her out of her job. She hadn't been granted tenure and, anyway, tenured positions on campus were pretty much becoming a thing of the past in the twenty-first century and Angela, like many of her colleagues were offered an annual contract each year.

Angela knew that by the start of the first semester in 2012, she was starting to get unreasonably tetchy with everyone and constantly felt tired and she put it down to not having had much of a holiday because she had been helping care for her sick grandmother who was refusing to go to hospital because she claimed that's where you went to die.

'Look at your gutcher, your grandaddie, never had a day in the ospital his whole life, even when he came home from the war, his ribs sticking out and all skinnymalinkie like, and then the doctor says he has to go for tests and he was gorn corbie the minute he set foot in the place, daid in three days.' Angela's grandmother said when Angela and her mum suggested that grandma might be more comfortable in hospital.

On Hogmanay, Angela sat up with her grandma and sipped whisky and watched the New Year's Eve fireworks from Sydney and her grandma pronounced that they were 'grand, but not as grand as Edinburgh'. Grandma died a week later, in her sleep, in bed, just short of her ninety-third birthday.

Angela organised the funeral and then took care of the estate, getting probate and putting the house on the market and by the end of February, she had been joking to family that she was looking forward to going back to work to get a rest.

She had begun to hate teaching and found that she'd be running a seminar and half the students would be sitting around the table with their phones in their hands ignoring her and any student that deigned to take an interest in the topic that was being discussed. A lot of the students didn't bother reading the assigned books and she could tell by their seminar papers and essays that a lot of them just looked up the plot summary on Wikipedia or hoped that there was a film or television version they could watch and had no interest in the language, style or structure. She suspected that some of her students had ended up studying for a BA by default, it's where their end of high school marks had led them, and they then planned to become school teachers for no better reason that the fact that they couldn't think of what else you might do with an Arts degree.

There was one student in Angela's third year seminar group on Australian Literature who, the previous year, she had taken a dislike towards. Daniella Dabbs was, in Angela's opinion just plain dumb and never had an original thought about any of the books they had studied in British Fiction Between the Two World Wars the previous year and once, when Angela asked her why she chose the elective, Daniella said that one of her friends did it the previous year and told her that a lot of the books had been made into movies and the timetable suited her because the class finished just before happy hour. Daniella managed to scrape together a pass for the subject by attending all the seminars and by submitting an essay that was worth a decent pass but not a credit and which Angela suspected, but could not prove, had not been written by Daniella.

In the first couple of weeks of the new semester, Angela found herself seething every time she looked around the room and laid eyes on Daniella, twirling her long blond hair between the fingers of one hand while looking down at her phone that Angela could not see, but knew was sitting in her lap or on her shapely thighs. Angela hated the way that Daniella would turn up to class in short shorts and little crop tops that showed off what Angela considered to be a very good figure in some people's eyes, predominantly boys who liked that sort of thing, flat stomach, pert boobs that were not too big and held up without a bra, long legs with thigh gap, long shiny blond hair, blue eyes and a little nose with a slight upward tilt that sat above full rosy lips. Angela hated the way that Daniela would laugh at anything she didn't understand, and to Angela that seemed to include a lot of things.

Sometimes, Angela would single Daniela out in the seminar to ask her opinion on whatever was being discussed and was always rewarded with Daniela not having a particular opinion on anything and if she did venture one, Angela would find ways to criticise whatever it was that Daniel said and when she did, Daniela would just look blankly back at Angela, shrug her shoulders and then pick up her phone as if it was all a joke that took too much effort.

Four weeks into the semester and it was Thursday afternoon and the warmth of the late March day was disappearing but that didn't mean Daniela wouldn't be wearing the briefest of clothes and would be carrying her little leather bag that never contained the books that were on the syllabus but her wallet, sunglasses, mobile phone and a little shorthand notebook that she would use to jot down something in class, but only if the lecturer said that it was important.

'Bimbo', Angela caught herself thinking as she walked into the room and saw Daniela sitting with her chair tipped back and her long smooth legs on the desk crossed at the ankles. Angela resented everything she saw that day and had developed, in her own mind, and entire life story for Daniela that might or might not be true. Princess Child in a big house near the beach, probably Merewether or maybe on the hill, a short walk down to Bar Beach where she would lie in a skimpy bikini while the surfer boys drooled over her on their way to the rolling breakers and they would make lewd comments to each other and Daniela would hear the comments and smile because she'd lead the boys on, their tongues hanging out and their dicks getting hard and then head off back to home, back to Mummy and Daddy where she was always Daddy's girl, but would be nasty to her mother and make little comments to put her down about her clothes or hairstyle or the food that she cooked and her mother wouldn't say anything, just wait until Daniela came out of the bathroom and then go in and pick up the swimmers and clothes and towel that Daniela would have left on the floor in a damp and sandy pile before going to her room where she would look at herself in the mirror, checking out her body from different angles and then flop on her bed with the ear buds from her phone in place where she would listen to someone like Ariane Grande for a while and maybe walk over to a bookshelf that held no books, just photographs of Daniela and her friends and the friends were all less attractive than Daniela, in that wholesome surfie chick way, because she didn't make friends with girls who were more attractive, but she didn't make friends with the girls she considered ugly either. Eventually her mother would call her to dinner and Daniela would go downstairs and announce that she didn't want to eat what was in front of her and announce that she wanted something different and her mother would get up from the table and let her own dinner grow cold while she prepared an alternative meal for Daniela and Daniel's father, tired from a long day as a senior accountant for a dodgy builder and property developer would just sit at the table and smile at his daughter who Angela had decided was some sweetly smiling, spoiled princess monster.

Sweetly smiling, spoiled princess monster was how Angela had described one of her own tormenters from her teenaged years and thought, for a second, while she looked at Daniela laughing at some YouTube clip on her mobile phone, that she wasn't hating Daniela so much, but channelling the hatred that she still held for Louise Milligan and her cohort of nasty tongued, narcissistic harpies who flaunted around Everton High School with their too short skirts and their too tight blouses and their too red lipstick despite the school rule prohibiting girls wearing makeup and their droning voices with an upward inflection at the end of each nasty sentence they would spit out when they were making judgements on the plainer girls like Angela and would always say things like 'I suppose the red hair isn't that bad but you'd hate the complexion that goes with it' or 'I'm glad I haven't got boobs like yours, they'll be sagging down to your waist before you're thirty' or 'look out, here comes thunder thighs' when Angela thought that her thighs weren't all that big, and while her boobs weren't pert and were rounder and fuller than Louise's and her friend's, they weren't all that big and things got really bad when, in Year 12, Angel had to start wearing reading glasses because of the headaches she was getting on a regular basis and how Louise and her friends would never need reading glasses because they never read and how Angela wished that she could have been a bitch too and made comments about Louise's teeth when she had to get braces and ended up with a tramline in her mouth and how her friends, even the ones who had perfect teeth all ended up with braces and how Louise announced loudly, just after her sixteenth birthday, that her doctor suggested that she go on the pill and made all the girls think it was because she was having sex with one or more of the boys in the Rugby team, Angela knew from one of Louise's friends who had been ejected from the gang that Louise went on the pill to help combat the raging acne that kept flaring up no matter how many litres of Clearasil she bought and Angela wished that she had the guts to call Louise 'pizza face' but didn't because she never liked confrontation.

'Daniela', Angela asked when she walked into the classroom and realised that she had almost called her Louise, 'please tell us what you think the symbolism of the ship's mast means in *Merry-Go-Round in the Sea*.'

Daniela looked blankly for a second. 'What ship's mast? Isn't it a merry-go-round? There's a merry-go-round on the picture on the cover.'

'You know,' Angela said calmly, 'why don't you just fuck off out of my class. You obviously don't want to be here and, in my opinion, you're as dumb as all shit and just a complete waste of space. You don't have to turn up each week when you're going to get someone else to write your assignments for you. Does Daddy pay them?' Daniela sat dumbfounded, staring at Angela amazed that anyone, let alone a university lecturer would speak to her like that.

Angela turned her back for a second to organise her books and notes on the desk in the front of the small classroom and when she turned around, Daniela was still staring at her.

'I'm serious,' Angela said, 'Fuck off out of here, I don't want to have to spend the next two hours looking at your stupid face or hearing your inane dumb comments when you do bother to make a contribution about whatever book you haven't read this week. Go and find something that will challenge you intellectually, like watching the Kardashians.'

The other dozen or so students were deathly quiet and sat looking back and forward between Angela and Daniela while Angela just stared Daniela down. Daniel's face crumpled and she burst into tears and then tried to run from the room but struggled in her platform sandals so that she stumbled in the leggy way of a new born thoroughbred and Angela watched her teeter from the classroom and shook her head and said 'you look fucking ridiculous' so loudly that it set Daniela off with another big sob in the hallway that the whole room heard.

The rest of the class were amazed when, as soon as Daniela had left, Angela took up her usual position, sitting on the front edge of the desk, dangling her legs and launched into a twenty-minute monologue about the role of the imagined merry-go-round and the illusion of the unobtainable without seeming to draw breath until she asked some questions of the class.

That night, when Angela walked into the student bar she got the sense that a number of the students were talking about her and pointing her out to each other and she thought that her little explosion would be all over the campus by the end of the week so she was not surprised when half way through the following day, she got an E Mail from the head of department inviting her to a meeting in his office that afternoon.

Angela thought that she would be sacked outright but the head was surprisingly pleasant. He told her that he had received a complaint from Daniela's father, who struck the head as being an oafish and aggressive buffoon who kept dropping the names of local politicians and business people into the conversation and was demanding that Angela should be sacked immediately. The head told Angela that she would not be doing any face to face teaching in Australian Literature for the rest of the semester and that perhaps she should use the time to get some articles published as this would help her when contract renewal time came around at the end of the year. He then suggested that she should think of taking a sabbatical and that he could help with getting a university research grant because, as a non-tenured staff member, she was not entitled to a paid sabbatical and would have to use her accrued long-service leave which would only last a couple of months. The head suggested that she take a year and when Angela said that her contract would be up half way through that year, the head smiled and said that she would be offered a new contract when she got back if she was still away, and if she came back she could cut her sabbatical short if she wished but it would mean repaying some of the research grant. Angela thought that this was her opportunity to write her book about Mick, who had become her new obsession to the point that she had almost forgotten about Siobhan and Plunket and others from Caldwell Street. She decided on the spot to agree to the Sabbatical to start at the beginning of the next semester and that she would first go to England and hopefully Mick would agree to meet her and she could ask him the questions she had been dying to ask for years but had been reluctant to put into writing, fearing that Mick would find them stupid and clumsy, but if they could be part of a conversation, Angela thought that it would be so much easier.

Angela had been living on her own in a little two bedroom cottage she rented near the bowling alley in Mayfield and the man who owned it had been suggesting to Angela for years that she should buy it and her father had even offered to help with the deposit until the money from her grandma's estate came through, where Angela would receive half her grandma's assets and so wouldn't need to borrow much, as her grandma's house was worth much more than her rented cottage. In the end, Angela decided that she would take some cash to help with her travel costs and to extend the scholarship money and that she would ask her landlord if she could sub-let the house with a view to buying it when she came back from abroad. The landlord huffed and puffed a bit and finally said that she could sublet it, but she was responsible for making sure the rent was paid on time and for any damages.

There had been a small farewell afternoon tea for Angela on the last day of the semester and a number of the staff turned up and some of the part-timers came in specially and even the old Professor, who was now Emeritus Professor and pretty well retired, but allowed to keep an office, turned up and dominated the room with his loud recitations from Blake and he gave Angela a big hug and told her that he had made a list for her of all the things she should do and see in England and she thanked him and whispered that she had no regrets, meaning the affair they had for a while in the 'nineties. The head of department had sent his apologies and said something about the Vice Chancellor calling a last-minute meeting which caused great amusement amongst the staff when the Vice Chancellor herself stuck her head in for five minutes to wish Angela the best. Before he left, the Professor told Angela that the head had planned to sack her on the spot after the business with Daniela, but the Professor told the head that he would make a fuss the likes of which the head had ever seen and it would certainly mean the head being blackballed from the Settler's Club, the gentleman's club on the hill that the head had been hoping to join and which the Professor sat on the board which was a strange thing to do for a left wing Geordie poet.

Ingrid had wanted to throw Angela a proper farewell party, but Angela said no because it would just make it more obvious to her that most of her friends, her real friends, other than Ingrid had buggered off overseas years ago and that she just wanted to slip away unnoticed. Instead, Ingrid said that she would drive Angela to the airport and because Angela was on an early flight to Singapore and then on to London, they would go down the night before and have a night on the town, but not too big a night because Ingrid didn't want Angela doing her first big overseas trip with a hangover.

When the architecture show finished, Ingrid and Angela watched an English murder mystery program that they both enjoyed.

'It took me forever to get into this show,' Angela said as the credits rolled over the top of the spooky music and graphics that she thought were supposed to look like blood dripping off the letters. 'I took it seriously and thought that it was, I don't know, a bit twee and then I realised that it was, in fact, really funny with lots of black humour.'

'That really surprises me', Ingrid said, 'because of everyone I know, you're the one who can find the humour in the darkest things and the darkness in the funny things.'

'It's the gloomy Celt in me', Angela said with half a smile. 'I'm mostly Scottish but I also have Irish in me from Dad's mother's side, the O'Hara's. You know what they say about the Irish, that all their wars are merry, and all their songs are sad.'

Thinking of the Irish, Angela shuddered a little but not so much that Ingrid would notice, and she thought that the shudder was caused by some remnant of the ghost of Siobhan who was still inside of her and was still chasing some unfinished business in Angela's heart, mind and soul.

Siobhan had been absent in the years that Angela was writing her thesis on Mick, *The Christ of Barren Landscapes – The Redeeming Unknowable Stranger in the Fiction of Randolph Stow*. Angela's head became full of men because the books she was reading were full of men, and men who were full of troubles and ghosts and demons of their own, who inhabited mainly barren lands to such a degree that even when Mick wrote about the tropical islands to the north or the green rolling lands of Suffolk, there was always the sense of barrenness that could only be expressed, she argued, by a man who had looked out over vast landscapes and distant horizons and who, in his time and perhaps for most of his life, was lonely and isolated. There were women in the books and most of them were good women, particularly in the later works and these women were the nurturers the supporters the mothers and grandmothers who were much loved by their sometime wayward me.

Siobhan's short life was so much different. There were no distant horizons in Surry Hills or Darlinghurst except, perhaps, the last far horizon of the edge of the Tasman Sea that Siobhan must have gazed at from the gap and, for the first time in ages, Angela wondered whether or not Siobhan stood on the edge for some time gathering her strength before taking the leap into darkness or whether she was fast, sure footed and certain.

Mick knew of suicides and breakdowns and the 'mega crack-up'. His books were full of them, the crack ups, suicides attempted and successful, and the recovery, and Angela had sought some solace in Mick's English story, his Suffolk fables when she was emerging into the light from her own dark days. She had read most of Mick's books, starting with the merry-go-round book when she was still in high school and also, when she started tutoring and later lecturing, the one about the old man on the Western Australian coast. She sought out Mick's earlier books, the books he wrote when he was still a very young man, before he found his voice as a writer, but still enthralled, captured by the vastness of the land and the smallness of the people in it and the ghosts that they all seemed to carry.

'What was Scotland really like?' Ingrid asked, 'it always looks pretty in pictures and I always thought that I'd love to go there some day.'

'The highlands are beautiful but in this strange, bleak way and sometimes eerily quiet and the weather can be treacherous and changeable and a lot of people who aren't prepared get caught out going on relatively short hikes. Glencoe is spectacular, the bare granite hills looking over the glen, the yellow gorse and the purple heather and the wind that howls that sends a shiver up your spine like it's the women keening for the men who were killed there all those years ago, massacred by the army for not swearing allegiance to King William after the Glorious Revolution, I think. I'm not always that good on history but when I was there, standing in the glen, hearing the crying wind, I had an overwhelming sense of sadness and started to cry and my tour guide cried too, and she said that the place often had that effect on people.'

'Sounds depressing' Ingrid said, 'not what I was expecting'.

'That's just me. You'd love Glasgow and all the groovy bars in the West End full of uni students and musicians and artists and comedians and heaps of good bands and plenty of drinking and dancing.'

As much as Angela did the tourist things in the U.K., it wasn't meant to be a holiday, it was meant to be work. She had packed paperback copies of Mick's books apart from the first two which she only had in hardcover, and first editions at that, and she made sure they were in her carry-on luggage because they were rare and would be hard to replace, but she wanted to have them with her as talisman and touchstones that were connected to the beginning of Mick's life with the pen. She spent the first couple of days travelling on the tube to all the sites and was awed by Westminster Abbey and the Tower and St Pauls, loved the Tate Modern and National Portrait Gallery but decided the cost and waiting times for the Eye were too much and that it was too much a touristy sort of thing to do. What Angela did do was set herself the task of reading all of Mick's books over a two-week period and to do this, she would get the tube to Russell Square and walk down Great Russell Street to the British Museum where she would set herself up for the day under the dome of the large reading room and think that just by being there, she was somehow absorbing all of the history and culture, the books and songs and plays that London had to offer and that, finally, she had become not just an academic, not just a university lecturer, but a scholar.

What is Saved, What is Lost

Monday morning dawned cool and overcast and there were even some light drops of rain falling and Angela hoped that the rain wasn't just confined to the coastline and had found its way inland, to where the fires were still burning. Ingrid had already left for work before Angela had gotten out of bed, pleased that for the first night in a long time the dreams hadn't come crowding in to her mind, whispering in the way of dreams, swirling, kaleidoscopic, ghosts of the past flowing endlessly as she tossed on her bed.

For the second time in two days she took the road that followed the river that gave the valley its name. All the fire warnings had been downgraded and while the bush was still burning in the hard to reach ridges and valleys to the north, there was no longer any risk for any of the areas around Allynsdale and surrounds and Angela was pretty sure that she'd be able to drive up the road to see if anything was left of her house. She was certain, deep inside, that it would be in ruins and wondered how she would face that moment when she saw her house for the first time. Everything would be ruins she thought, everything she had tried to build lost to the ash that she could smell in the air, taste on her tongue, the bitter ash, and it was not yet Wednesday, and she wouldn't know again what it was to hope that there might be something peaceful, something calm in the future, but liked the little joke that she had made with the bitterness and the ash.

She remembered that the rosary was there at the end of the poem that was about ashes and Wednesday and hope and time being time, and she thought that she would like to read that poem again and remembered that the poem was now probably ashes because she didn't think it was one of the precious books that found their way into the carton that went into the back of her car only two days before, and she had a vision as she drove of the book seeming to open itself as the heat blast hit the house before the flames arrived, and opening on the pages of that poem in particular, and the pages curling and contracting and slowly starting to smoke until there was a bright spot of flame in the centre that soon consumed the page and the other pages and then the other books and then all those useless words that she had spent her life reading and discussing and thinking about, until all the words ended up as ashes on the floor amongst the other ashes of her life, a life where it seemed to her that all she had managed to do was to get the better of words.

She started to see the world as words, jumbled and disconnected, not forming clauses or sentences, not making any sense of anything, like a useless collection of artefacts that has ceased to have any purpose and perhaps no longer any value, and Angela thought that perhaps this is what all the ashes meant at the end of the day, that her world would be reduced to ashes and, as her world was words, they too would disintegrate into powder in the heat of the fire that had driven her from the mountain, her peace and solace. When she thought this, she was gripped with a fear that she was heading for something bigger and much worse than the mega crack up and there was a tightening in her chest and her breath was becoming more rapid and shallower and she just managed to pull the car off the side of the road before her vision started to blur and she thought 'this is it, it's not the mega crack up but the big one', the heart attack that she thought was coming fast, bearing down like the firestorm off the side of the mountain.

Angela stumbled out of the car and leant on the bonnet hoping that some passer-by would see the distress that she was in and call for an ambulance and, if this happened, maybe this wasn't really the end after all. She felt like somebody or something was watching her and when she turned her head slightly she saw, in the paddock on the other side of the fence, a grey kangaroo standing quietly, quite tall on its back legs and tail with its short front paws dangling in front, some grass in its mouth which it had stopped chewing, and its big brown eyes, quietly and calmly watching her. Angela was surprised that it hadn't hopped away when she pulled over because the kangaroos in that area were quite skittish and were used to being shot at or chased to the point that Angela actually couldn't remember when she had last seen a kangaroo in that part of the valley.

Angela had been told that the drought and lack of food and water was driving a lot of kangaroos out of the forests and into the farmlands and even into the towns so that the old cliché that foreigners think kangaroos come bounding down the main streets of towns was now turning from a silly joke into a sad reality. This kangaroo had probably been driven out of the hills by the fire and Angela remembered hearing stories from of the old timers like Killer of how you knew the fire front was approaching because of the wildlife desperately trying to get out of the way and how kangaroos and wallabies would come flying down the mountain in a panic and would crash through barbed wire fences and slip rails and keep hopping away as fast as they could and sometimes their fur would be singed and smoking from the flames.

Angela looked closely at the kangaroo in front of her to see if it had been injured at all and even though she was no expert on such matters, she thought that the kangaroo looked surprisingly healthy and uninjured given the drought and the fire, and its coat was shiny and not covered with ashes and she thought that it looked like it was pretty well nourished. She wondered what the kangaroo was making of her as it stared back with the occasional blink of its eye and showing no intention of moving away and it had stopped chewing the grass in its mouth so that a few straw-coloured strands just stood there between the kangaroo's lips.

Angela noticed that her breathing had slowed back down until it was almost normal and that she no longer felt the pain in her chest, and she was no longer sweating. The longer she stood there, her eyes locked into the kangaroo's eyes, Angela started to almost feel a kind of calmness washing over her like a delicate warm wave and she was no longer frightened of what she might find up the hill and it no longer mattered and, yes, she thought, she would be very sad at losing everything to the fire, but that the feeling of sadness would, in time, pass and what she lost was only the material things that could be replaced in time, and there was something that she couldn't put her finger on, but it was like a voice saying to her that there was something greater than words and something greater than the ash of those words and she would know what it was when she found it.

Angela straightened her back and stood up a little taller and almost at the same time, the kangaroo sat back, most of its weight on the base of its tail so that it too was a little taller and all the time it never took its eyes of Angela. Angela let out a big sigh and it was almost as if she could feel the breath pass across the space between her and the kangaroo and the kangaroo twitched its nose like it was smelling Angela's breath and then it seemed to nod its head slightly, turn around and gently bound away down the paddock towards the creek and the little water there was and a stand of trees where the fire hadn't reached. Angela stood watching the kangaroo hopping away and then turned and got behind the wheel of her car amazed at how, in such a short space of time, she had gone from a full blown panic attack that she thought was the precursor to something even bigger than the mega crack-up, to feeling so unbelievably calm and ready to face whatever it was that she was to face when she followed the creek up the mountain, almost to its source, and see what was left of her home.

The service station was open as Angela rolled into Allynsdale and she was glad because it reminded her that she needed fuel and if she didn't fill the car up, she wouldn't make it back to Ingrid's and apart from the service station at Wallisville, there wasn't another one that would be open later in the day until she got back to the highway at Maitland.

'How's it going? Is your husband alright?' Angela said to Anila when she went in to the shop to pay for her petrol.

'Yes, he is. Thank you. He is out with the truck doing some back burning and clearing some of the roads from trees that fell over in the fire.'

'Do you know if the road up to my place is open?' Angela asked thinking that Anila would know which roads were open and which were closed and would be one of the people that would be asked by locals returning from wherever they had spent the last couple of nights, hiding from the fires.

'You should check first with the police if you are planning to go up there. I think it is still a bit dangerous with trees falling. There is a constable down at the Scout Hall and I think she will tell you what you need to know.'

There wasn't a lot of activity in the town as Angela drove the short distance back to the Scout Hall and it looked like a lot of the services that had been there the day before had packed up and moved on. There were still no confirmed reports of the number of houses that had been destroyed and there were still a number of people missing and the police had not released the names of the dead and the missing and the spokesperson on the radio said that it was pending notification to victims' families. Killer would be one of those people, dead or missing, Angela thought, and she hoped that there would be someone, somewhere, to grieve for him if he was dead and to worry for him if he was missing. Nobody knew anything the day before, but since she left the previous night, Angela hoped that at least somebody would have gone looking for Killer. All these little towns, she thought, liked to pride themselves on their sense of community but they are all riven with fractures and feuds and petty jealousies that bubble under the surface until something or somebody comes along and shines a mirror into their faces and then it all comes out and you realise that it isn't a community at all just a desperate bunch of individuals and Allynsdale was just the same as dozens of other little towns across the valley and was populated by the sort of people who had been there for generations, dirt poor strugglers, scared of the world outside their little town or there were the blow-ins, the people like her, who had come to the little town to hide from something and that something that they were hiding from was usually themselves and it took something major, a catastrophe for the people hiding from themselves to come out into the light and they didn't always make it.

She felt the eyes of some of the locals on her as she parked outside the Scout Hall and walked up the pathway. There was a group hanging outside of Kevin Cutler's shop, leaning on the bonnets of their crew cab utes and a few of them, the young blokes in their twenties were drinking from cartons of flavoured milk and Angela thought that there was something interesting in how these boy/men liked flavoured milk and it was not uncommon to see a young farmhand or tradie duck into the shop first thing in the morning for his milk and Angela imagined that they probably didn't drink tea or coffee but hung onto to the tastes of their childhood although, she countered that argument in her own mind by remembering that quite a few of them would buy a packet of cigarettes with their milk and most of them liked to knock down schooners on a Friday night and the older locals knew it was time to leave the pub when the schooners stopped and the Bundies and Coke started.

Senior Constable Brenda Ramzan was sitting behind a little makeshift desk that held her cap, a clipboard, a police radio, mobile phone and a thermos. She was bored with this assignment and most of the locals had now been accounted for, and those who weren't were going to be a job for the cadaver dogs in the next day or so. Brenda wondered if the burning and the ash and smoke made it harder for the dogs to sniff out a corpse and made a mental note to ask the specialist cadaver dog handlers when they turned up, because she didn't think that the normal dog handlers attached to her command would know.

'Hello' Angela said from the doorway to get the police officer's attention.

Brenda Ramzan snapped out of her daydream where she was remembering the sight of bodies being cremated on the banks of the Ganges the time her father had taken her to India when she was fifteen to meet some of her extended family. It was her first trip to India and was a real eye opener to the middle-class girl from Maitland who was the daughter of a respected GP and high school teacher. Her mother's family had been reasonably well-off graziers, growing wool in the New England, who hadn't entirely approved of their daughter marrying an Indian, but the disapproval was somewhat mitigated by the Dr Ramzan's profession and when Brenda came along, she was the apple of her grandparents' eye. Brenda knew that there were poor people, of course, and there were a lot of poor in some of the suburbs of Maitland and the outlying rural towns, but she had never experienced such overwhelming poverty as she did in India. Much to her parents' disappointment, Brenda dropped out of school in Year Eleven suffering depression that she believes was brought on by the huge attack on the senses from being in India. Dr and Mrs Ramzan had hoped their daughter would take up a profession, medicine and law were high on their list but, instead, after working in a number of clerical jobs and being a pool attendant, at twenty, Brenda Ramzan went to the Police Academy and was posted back to Maitland where she had been for twenty-five years, had no children and had married an older sergeant who split with her a couple of years previously and run off with a probationer nearly thirty years his junior.

'Yair? You need something?' Brenda asked Angela, hoping that it was just directions or something simple.

'My house', Angela started, trying to find words that hadn't turned to ash. 'My house is up the mountain on the Allyns Peak road' Angela said, pointing vaguely in the direction of the road that ran out of town to the north.

'And?' Brenda asked and Angela didn't think that this police officer could be more disinterested if she tried.

'It's a free country, or so they say', Brenda said reaching for her pen and clipboard. 'What's your name?'

Angela told Brenda her name and Brenda frowned for a moment and then consulted a printed list that was on her desk. 'Says here that you're missing?'

'I was here yesterday and reported to someone that I was alright and staying with a friend in the city and my friend had also phoned someone the night before.'

'Did you speak to one of the volunteers?' Brenda asked and when Angela nodded, Brenda sighed and scribbled something on her list. 'Bloody useless they are, bloody volunteers.'

'They seemed nice and caring,' Angela said, feeling the need to defend Reg and Daphne Collins who had been so kind to her the night before.

'Good for a biscuit and a cup of tea, crap with the paperwork. Right, that's you sorted' Brenda said, putting down the biro and clipboard. 'Your house was up the road you say?'

'Mud brick place, about half way up.'

'I haven't been up their myself, but what I do know is that not a lot was left standing between Mrs Thompson's house on the edge of town and the National Park so, if you're going up there, be prepared, that's all I can say. I'd go with you, but I've got orders to stay here and man the desk.'

'Do you know anything about my neighbour? Bernard, I forget his last name?'

'Killer?' Brenda asked and Angela nodded and hoped that the way the police officer responded with his nickname meant that he might have turned up unharmed.

'Missing, presumed dead. Sending the dogs up there later today.'

Angela was dumbfounded by the total lack of empathy that the police officer displayed. It might be the case that the police officer had been working long hours and was tired or that it was even a cumulation of all the terrible things that she must have seen over her career, all the horrible things people can manage to do to each other, all the miserable and sad ways there were to die, until the person witnessing it all comes to suffer from what Angela once heard described as 'compassion fatigue'.

'Anything else?' Brenda asked as a way of dismissing Angela and Angela just shook her head and walked back out to her car.

She sat in the driver's seat for several minutes drinking from the bottle of cold water she had purchased off Anila when she got her fuel and, as she sat there thinking, Angela thought that she was struggling to find the strength to turn the ignition key and start the car because there was nothing left now but to head up the mountain and see what, if anything, the fire had left untouched. Angela thought about the way change happens and what you think of being a momentous event is just the point of realisation and the thing that actually changed your life probably happened sometime earlier and you just didn't know for whatever reason, whether that be circumstances, or wilful blindness. As she sat there, in the car, Angela thought that this was one such moment. She had that feeling, that heavy oily feeling deep in the pit of her stomach, that the next half hour would probably change her life and yet her life was changed the moment the fire came racing down the mountain and it was just that she didn't know what those changes were.

What surprised her as she drove up the mountain road and

into the forest was that even though the burning was pretty severe and a lot of trees, both fallen and standing, were still smoking, she could see, here and there, patches of green where the flames hadn't touched the undergrowth and there were also areas where the tops of the tall trees, the crowns were burned but the shrubs and ferns beneath had somehow survived and Angela, not knowing much about the nature of bushfires, thought that this might have something to do with the absolute speed at which the fire front was running and some things behind the front, plants and areas of land that were dry and brittle burned and other areas, shaded damper areas, withstood the initial burst of flame. She remembered hearing Kevin Cutler talking about things like fuel load at one of the town meetings in the dining room at the pub at the start of the fire season and the importance of reducing the fuel load around your home so that if a fire front came through, it would not be able to take hold and without fuel, the fire would die out as the larger front of fire also sucked all the available oxygen from around it.

Once, Angela had complained to Ingrid that she didn't seem to be able to keep friends or maintain relationships and Ingrid had said that it was because when Angela was manic, she sucked all the oxygen out of anyone who came into her orbit.

'Then how come you've stuck around?' Angela asked Ingrid.

'I used to do scuba diving when I was a teenager, remember?' Ingrid replied.

'And your point?'

'You always make sure you've got good reserves of oxygen, so you don't run out or have to surface too quickly and get the bends, and when you do surface, you do it in stages and rest between each stage which is why you have to calculate your oxygen. When you're being a bit crazy, I just back away a little bit and gently, and that's how I can preserve my oxygen. The other thing is not to panic when something goes wrong, if you panic you breathe faster and use up your oxygen more quickly.'

'So, it's all calculated?', Angela said, 'And there I was thinking it was just you doing the Norwegian Ice Maiden act.'

'No,' Ingrid said, 'it's just being your friend.

Angela turned the key in the ignition, took a deep breath and pulled out on to the road and started to head up the mountain. She didn't look at the burned out remains of Molly Thompson's house as she passed it on the edge of the town. The ruins were still smoking, and Angela wondered what a person like Mrs Thompson does when she has lost everything and has nowhere to go and then Angela realised that she didn't know much about Mrs Thompson at all and perhaps she did have somewhere she could live, perhaps with adult children in another town or some other relatives who would take he in. This led Angela to ponder where she might have to stay if her own house was destroyed. She knew that she could stay with Ingrid for a while but then again, she didn't want to impose on her friend and while they had a lot of fun as housemates right up into their thirties, Angela knew that they were both very set in their ways after living alone for so many years.

Her parents would be happy if she moved back in with them and her mother could probably do with some help with Angela's father who had been reduced by time to trebles, pipes and whistles, but still had his own teeth, or at least a couple of his teeth, and he had his own eyes that were helped with a pair of thick lensed glasses that Angela thought might not be all that helpful because they always seemed to be smeared and greasy so that it was hard to see his milky eyes behind the wall of grubby glass. Never the dutiful daughter, Angela had moments of guilt, but to move back home, at her age, to live under the roof of her parents, to sleep in her narrow bed under the teenage posters, would be to give up, and it would be her, not her father, hovering on the edge of dementia and knowing that it was coming, who would be the one reduced to a child again at the ending of her own strange and eventful history.

Angela expected that her tears would flow when she turned the bend in the round and came to the remains of Tony and Alyssa's house in its bush clearing. She pulled up and gazed at the house but the tears she expected did not come. There was some blue and white police tape across the drive way where the stone gateposts stood but the iron gate was lying twisted and buckled on the ground. There was nothing much left of the house, just the brick stumps and piles of charred wood sticking out from under what remained of the corrugated iron roof that had collapsed into the wreckage of the house. The big shed was also completely burned but nearby there was a smaller building, another shed where Alyssa kept her pottery wheel and kiln and it looked to Angela to be pretty well intact apart from some scorch marks and one window that appeared to have been broken and she marvelled at the way a fire can destroy so much and yet leave other things virtually untouched. She thought that she should have bought some flowers and left them where she remembered the veranda to have been which is the last place that Alyssa saw Tony standing. There were some fresh tyre marks in the dirt and ashes leading across the burned grass between the gate and where the house had once stood and Angela thought that this must have been made by the vehicles that would have come now to retrieve Tony's body in the last few hours before the road was re-opened because she reckoned that they wouldn't have let people drive up the road if Tony's body was still visible to any passer-by and there were no check points leading out of town so it was possible that anybody could have driven up this way.

As she stood thinking about Tony and his last moments on this earth, Angela was surprised to hear bird calls and realised that it was crows she could hear and that there were a number of them flying around and she thought that they would be having a field day, the crows, as they mainly ate carrion and that there would be plenty of dead livestock and wildlife and the murder of crows would be having a barbecued smorgasbord and then she had a vision of a glossy black crow with a sharp beak and shiny eyes further up the road somewhere picking through the burned rough leather skin of Killer to get through to the easier digestible innards and she thought that Killer probably wouldn't have begrudged the crows a feed from a body that was no longer of any use to him. She thought of the sky burials in Nepal and Tibet that she had read about once, where the flesh is stripped from the dead bodies and the bones pulverised and then it is all left on top of a tower like structure for the vultures to eat and this was done because there was not enough wood or other fuel for cremations and the rocky hard ground cannot be dug deep enough for a grave. Angela liked the idea of the sky burial and thought that apart from the fact that some people would find leaving bodies out in the open like that, even when they've been dismembered, somewhat distasteful, she thought that there was something appealing about having your body consumed by other creatures so that, bits of you become bits of them.

Her thoughts about the sky burial and the calling of the crows was interrupted by a more mechanical noise from further down the road and when she turned to see where it was coming from, she saw a fire truck coming up the road but it wasn't Kevin Cutler's crew and when it pulled up, she saw that Gerald, Anil's husband was in the front passenger seat and when he recognised Angela, he hopped out.

'Heading up to your place?' Gerald asked.

Angela nodded. 'See what's left, I suppose'

'Dunno,' Gerald said, 'First time we've been up here, just making sure there's no spot fires still burning.'

'Kevin Cutler didn't say anything about my place?' Angela asked.

'We just heard that most of the houses up this road were gone, which ones, I don't know. If you like, you can wait here, and we can go and take a look and see it it's safe to go on to your property and then come back and let you know?'

'Thanks Gerald, but you've got work to do and I'd rather just take a look myself and, anyway, it's a bit creepy right here, right now.'

Gerald looked over at the remains of Tony and Alyssa's house. 'Poor bloody Tony Conti eh? He had no chance.'

He did, Angela thought. He had the chance to get away with Alyssa but chose not to, he sealed his own fate.

'Do you want to follow us?' Gerald asked and Angela nodded and then went back to her own car and when they saw that she was ready, Gerald's crew started to drive slowly up the road for a kilometre or so and, for Angela, the drive seemed to take an eternity. There were a couple of tracks of the road that disappeared into the bush and at the end of each of the tracks there had been houses in small clearings but Angela didn't know the names of any of the owners as they were all weekenders and there were different people in them all the time who Angela suspected rented the houses on Air B&B and, according to a few people in Allynsdale, the renters never seemed to spend any money in the town and must have brought all of their provisions with them. She imagined that these houses probably weren't the highest priority for the fire fighters but from what she had heard, Kevin Cutler's crew basically took shelter up the top somewhere and then made a racing retreat down the mountain behind the fire front without stopping to put out any fires other than those in burning trees blocking their path down the road.

The brake lights on the truck in front came on and it slowed to a halt and Angela looked down at her hands on the wheel for a moment and noticed that they were shaking, and the perspiration was sticking to the back of her shirt so she felt like she might have been glued to the car seat.

Angela slowly looked to her left at the same time as she heard the doors open on the fire truck in front of her. She slowly got out of the car and walked to the side of the road and then felt her legs turn to jelly and she started to sway for a second and, as she sunk down, she felt Gerald's hands slip into her armpits to stop her collapsing on the ground. Her little mud brick house appeared to be unharmed apart from some soot and ash and scorch marks on the wooden shutters she had closed over the windows before she left.

'I'll be fucked' she heard one of the young firies say.

Of Ashes and Men

Angela turned to Gerald for some explanation of what she was seeing in front of her and he just shook his head and whistled.

'It happens, sometimes, well rarely. I've never seen it myself.'

They started to walk closer to the house to inspect the damage that the fire had left behind as it made its way down the valley. Angela's little garden shed that had been made out of aluminium was slightly distorted and it looked like one side of it had blown out. One of Gerald's crew members pulled at the door to the garden shed and said that it was still warm.

'Did you keep fuel in there?' Gerald asked and Angela nodded and said she had a tin of fuel for the whipper snipper and mower and kept a small tin of spare fuel for her car. 'That would have caused that. The fuel would have vaporised in the tin from the heat and blown the lid off and then an ember's set the whole thing off. Would have went off like a bomb.'

'But what about the house?' Angela asked.

'Whoever built it must have known what they were doing.' Gerald said walking around the little cottage. 'The mud bricks won't burn of course. What normally happens is that the fire gets in under the eaves and into the timber in the roof or blows out the glass in the windows, but your shutters would have helped prevent that. Some fire passed over the house but not the main front I reckon. You can see the scorch marks on the timber on the shutters, but they held out and look under the eaves. There're no gaps, mud daub over any potential gaps or exposed timber.'

Gerald asked one of the crew members to grab a ladder off the back of the truck and when he was handed it, Gerald grabbed the ladder and climbed up and looked in the guttering near where the down pipe led into the stainless-steel rainwater tank that had been down to the last 100 litres. Angela had been getting a man to fill the tank each month or so for a hefty price with water from his tanker. Gerald pulled out of the gutter what looked to Angela to be balled up plastic shopping bags.

'That helped', he said, 'Blocking your downpipe and filling the guttering with water so the dry leaves in it didn't catch on fire.'

'I didn't do that' Angela said.

'You must have a guardian angel looking over your shoulder. It would have taken a bit of work to get up there and to fill the gutters.'

'I could see the fire starting to crest the top of the mountain when I left', Angela said, 'it couldn't have been more than half an hour before it reached here. Well, who knows, what do I know about bush fires, but I didn't pass anyone between here and town, only Tony and Alyssa and they were busy preparing their own place.'

'Maybe someone came down the mountain behind you and stopped to check your preparations.' Gerald said. 'You want to check inside?'

Angela went back to the car and fished her house keys out of her bag while the firies stood around, a little impatient. They had seen all they needed to see and one of them was writing some notes on a sheet of paper on a clipboard.

'Kevin Cutler and his crew went past, and he was the one who told me to leave' Angela said, 'but nobody got out the truck and they took off up the road towards the fire.'

'Killer?' Gerald asked.

'Must have been' Angela said. 'I spoke to him just here, just before I left, and he helped me load some things in my car. He said he was going back to defend his place.'

'Wouldn't have stood a hope in hell' Gerald said, taking off his helmet and wiping the sweat from his forehead as the heat of the day started to build up. 'You know what his place was like. Those old dry weatherboards and the rusty tin roof and all the big gum trees with the branches hanging over the side of his house. It's the oil in the eucalypts, they go off from the heat before the flames reach them. Big branches would have exploded and dropped on his roof and fell through the rusty iron and roof timbers, burning everything. When the fire hit It would have been over in seconds and we wouldn't have been able to save it if we had fifty fire trucks on the spot.'

'Why didn't he leave?'

'He must have come back here and filled the gutters. Look over there, your pot plants, look like they've been moved.' Gerald said and pointed to where some large tubs of shrubs that had sat on her veranda under the windows had been dragged out into the yard and were now blackened with the once green plants now burnt and dead.

'He never made it into town' Angela said. 'He told me that he was staying. Said he'd only ever leave the place if he was in a box.'

Gerald took the keys from Angela's hand and told her to wait for a second until he made sure it was safe but was pretty sure by the state of the exterior that it would be. She waited until Gerald came back out a minute or so later, satisfied that the house was safe to enter.

'Bit of smoke damage and it smells a bit and there's a bit of ash and soot that probably came in under the doors but otherwise, you've dodged a bullet' Gerald said, handing Angela the keys. 'We'll leave you to it. Go and check out Killer's place but I don't think there'll be much left.'

'Let me know' Angela said and left the sentence hanging, knowing that Gerald knew what she meant.

'Cops had a look at first light and didn't see anything but then they don't always know what they're looking for and if he was in the house, well, they're bringing some dogs up later, specialist sniffer dogs.'

With that, Gerald and his crew got in the truck and Angela heard it slowly make its way up the road and, in the silence, heard it stop again out the front of the entrance to Killer's block. Angela stood, not knowing what to do and felt uneasy at how empty she actually felt. She wondered how many people would grieve or mourn Killer and hoped that there would be some in the town, like her, who would miss the cranky old bugger.

She thought that she was starting to suffer from the onset of survivor guilt even though nothing had been confirmed and for all she knew, Killer might have had a change of heart about staying until the end, come down the road in his old ute, did the couple of jobs at her place to make it safer and then hightail it out of there. He hated Kevin Cutler, and the way Kevin Cutler thought that Allynsdale was his town would have meant that it was unlikely that Killer would have stayed in the town and could have ended up anywhere, but she also thought that once the emergency was over, he would have been like her and came back to inspect the damage and, if that was the case, somebody would have seen him and if they did, word would be out because there were no secrets in Allynsdale.

Most of her possessions seemed to be intact, not that she cared much about them except the books and the records, and the books seemed ok except for a gritty feel and a bit of ash and soot and she was surprised that the records hadn't warped in the heat of the passing fire and supposed it had something to do with the mud bricks being good insulation and the way the records were packed tightly in a couple of sturdy crates. The food in the refrigerator had gone off when the fire burned down the power lines cutting her electricity and without light, she didn't want to stay the night and, besides, the kerosene she kept for her emergency hurricane lantern went up with all the other flammable material that was in her lawn locker. She'd have to go back to Ingrid's place for the night and knew that wouldn't be a problem and, anyway, she didn't think that it would be too healthy to sleep in the house with all the smoke and ash that was still around and she even admitted to herself that it could be a bit scary on her own, and this came as a shock because she had lived alone in the bush for years without a moment of fear, but somehow, having Killer just up the road a bit made her feel safe for some strange reason because, if anyone did attack her at night, there's no way that Killer would know what was happening and be able to do anything.

On her drive back up to Allynsdale that morning, Angela had started to think about what Ingrid had said about packing up stumps completely and perhaps heading off overseas for a bit. She had started to think through the logistics and knew that she could easily get residency in the United Kingdom, but if she wanted a work permit, that would be a bit harder but not impossible and she also entertained the idea of moving to New Mexico but knew that staying long term in the United States without a work permit and a job was nigh on impossible, but, somehow, she was pulled by the romanticism of New Mexico and it wasn't just Mick having lived there in Aztec or David Herbert in Taos but she had also become quite fond of the works of Georgia O'Keefe and could see herself in a nice little pueblo on the outskirts of Santa Fe and now, there would be no insurance, so she'd have to sell the house and given all that it seemed someone, probably Killer, had done to save it for her, she was reluctant to upset his ghost if that's what had become of him, a wild spirit of the mountains inhabiting the trees and rocks and animals, looking out for her into the future.

Angela felt compelled to go and see Killer's house for herself as if, by being there, she might get some sense, some intuition of if he had made it off the mountain alive or if he was still there and Angela believed that if Killer had not made it off the mountain that she would able to sense this in her bones. She walked up the roadway that she had travelled many times over the last five years, and she used to enjoy the walk through the bush, listening to the small birds and the animals that would scurry in the undergrowth as she passed and she once stopped to admire a glossy red bellied black snake as it slithered across the road and this was before Osana and her coming to hate all snakes and wish every single one of them dead and she suspected that not many of them would have survived the fire but then again, if her house did, it wouldn't be much of a stretch to think that some of the evil serpents could have slithered deep under a cooling rock until the fire front past.

Angela couldn't remember when her thoughts, when the words that were in her head, had started to take on a distinctly biblical tone but she did realise that she was using words like serpent instead of snake more often, at least when she was talking to herself which she did more frequently, and she hoped that these old words weren't starting to creep sneakily into her conversations in such a way that people would think that she was just the crazy old woman on the mountains, the bluestocking, and she also hated the way that word, bluestocking, kept creeping into her mind, unheralded and unwelcome.

Gerald's fire truck was parked in the entrance to Killer's block and Angela could see what was left of Killer's house – nothing more than a pile of smoking burned timber and twisted rusty looking roofing iron amongst the stone and brick foundations with the chimney standing remarkably intact at the end that would have been Killer's kitchen. Gerald and his crew were standing around, their faces the same ashen grey as the landscape and one of the younger men was standing on the other side of the truck to his mates, dry retching on to the ground. Angela observed that you normally couldn't see Killer's house from the road but now that all the trees that surrounded his house and grew along the fenceline nearest the road had all been burned you had a clear view of the house, or at least the charred rubble, and she thought of how much Killer would have hated being able to be seen by anyone driving past, not that many people drove along the road that came to a dead end at the mountain top a couple of kilometres higher. There were a couple of shacks up there used as weekenders by people from the city and there were the occasional bushwalkers and twitchers who would drive up to the summit, but passing traffic was pretty much a rarity and, in many cases, when people did pass it was by accident because they had missed the turn off for the track to one of the holiday rentals that sat between Angela's place and Tony and Alyssa's.

Gerald was standing on the running board of the cab of his truck and he had the two-way radio in his hand and was speaking softly and the sound of the person he was speaking to came back crackly with lots of static. Gerald finished saying whatever it was that he had been saying and put the handset back in the cab and, seeing Angela, climbed down from the truck and walked up to her.

'I wouldn't go up there if I was you' he said.

'I wasn't planning to', Angela said, 'I just wanted to see for myself'.

'We think he's in there' Gerald said quietly and, as if he couldn't bring himself to look Angela in the eye, he gazed off to the middle distance.

'Killer?' she asked quietly, and Gerald just nodded.

'We're waiting on the police and ambulance to come.' Gerald said as if he needed to explain why he and his crew were standing around not doing anything.

'Ambulance will do him a lot of good and you know he hated doctors, always called them quacks. That's what he used to say, have to go down to Maitland to see the quack' Angela said and laughed nervously.

'Maybe not the ambulance, if they can declare him here at the scene it will be the government contractor that'll come to take him to the morgue.'

'Are you sure it's Killer? I mean, it could have been someone trying to shelter from the fire, could be anyone' Angela said and knew that she sounded desperate.

Gerald walked her to the front of the fire truck and pointed out a burned-out wreck of a motor vehicle parked close to where the house had stood.

'I reckon that's his old ute, the old Falcon. He must have gone down to your place, satisfied himself that he had done all he could and came back here to wait.'

'Where was he? His body I mean?' Angela asked.

'In the house. I don't know the layout, like where the rooms were or anything, but he's close to the fireplace so I'm thinking he was in the kitchen.'

'Not outside fighting the fire like Tony?'

'Look at the place, there's no way you could fight it. He knew how big the fire was and he knew what was coming.'

'Jesus', Angela said and leant against the front of the fire truck, closed her eyes and tried to imagine what it must have been like to see those flames come roaring down the mountain and she imagined Killer watching for a bit and then calmly walking into his kitchen and pouring some tea in his old battered and stained white enamel mug with the blue ring around the top and handle and she imagined that the old mug was probably there in the house and could picture it unscathed. She was tempted to ask Gerald if he saw the enamel mug and then thought better of it because it seemed such a strange thing to ask and it was something that nobody else would understand, the way she associated that mug with Killer when he was at home and relaxed and she hoped that when he stayed to face the flames, for whatever reasons he had, that he was calm and that he was not afraid.

'Do you want me to get one of the boys to run you back to your place in the truck?' Gerald asked. 'The police asked me to stay here until they arrived but I'm sure Barry will be happy to drive you.'

Angela wondered if Barry was the young bloke who was dry retching when she arrived. She had a curious morbid desire to actually go up to the remains of the house and to see what it was that Gerald and the others had seen. Obviously it was enough for them to recognise that it was a body but Angela wondered at the state it was in, how badly it had burned and thought that it must have been pretty bad if Gerald couldn't say for sure that it was Killer unless the body was face down and they knew that they couldn't move it until the police arrived so they never had a chance to see the face.

'I'm okay to walk,' Angela said, 'I just needed a moment to get over the shock. I expected it, I suppose, but it still doesn't feel real.' She smiled at Gerald and he tried to smile back but his eyes were still grim.

Angela walked back down the hill to her own house and tried to think of what she needed to do immediately and what could wait. She cleaned out the refrigerator and when she was done, she felt overwhelmed and helpless. Her first thought was to throw the rubbish in the garbage but the plastic wheelie bin that sat next to the garden shed was partially melted and then she thought that she could just dig a hole and bury the rubbish but she then realised that the shovel had been in the garden shed and when she went and looked through the wreckage of her shed, she found the shovel but the wooden handle was badly charred and when she picked it up, the handle just broke down at the bottom near the blade of the shovel. In the end, she took the bags of rubbish and dumped them some distance from the house where she hoped that the smell wouldn't be too bad. When she went back inside, she stripped the bed and put the linen in a bag to take back to Ingrid's to be washed and hopefully get the fire smell out of her sheets.

As Angela was loading the car, she saw two police cars go past her gate, there was a marked car with the grumpy constable from the Scout Hall in the passenger seat and behind it an unmarked car with two older male officers in business shirts who Angela assumed must have been detectives. A few minutes later a van with a sign on it that said Forensics made its way up the road and finally a white unmarked panel van with two men in what looked like overalls that must have been, Angela thought, the people from the morgue in the city, coming to take Killer away.

Killer had told Angela that he hated the police for a very long time, and she thought that having so many police and other officials poking and prodding him and fussing over his remains really would have gotten on his goat.

'Mongrel coppers' Killer had said to her, 'are the lowest of the low. There used to be this big fat sergeant down at Wallisville, back when it had its own cop shop, and the bastard took a dislike to me when I was just a little tacker. I used to wag school a bit because I couldn't read so good and didn't like doing me sums and stuff, but I liked learning about animals and minding the chooks and the sheep that the school had. Bastard of a headmaster used to like to give me the cane nearly every week for turning up to school in a torn shirt or without shoes and stuff like that. I got punished for being poor, got the cane because my old man was an alchy and we never had money and he'd bash mum senseless sometimes so she couldn't mend my clothes or stuff and for that I used to get the cane. So, I'd wag school and just hang around down the creek and somebody must have dobbed me in to old Parsons, the headmaster, so he called his mate, fuckin' Sergeant Whiteman and he'd come and find me and throw me in the back of the paddy wagon and take me back to Wallisville, but he wouldn't go straight there, no he'd take the long way, up the dirt road that loops around Austin's Drop and he'd get his sidekick, Constable Handsman to swerve the paddy wagon on the dirt and slam on the brakes and then take off so that I was thrown around in the back like a piece of meat. When they got me back to the station, Whiteman would tell me that I was filthy and stank so he'd put the fire hose on me and that hurt like buggery, and you gotta remember that I was only ten years old and if I gave him any cheek, he'd lay into me with a phone book and call me a 'white abo' and shit like that and then when he was done, when his arms were getting a bit heavy from all the bashing, he'd tell me to piss off home and not to hitchhike because he'd send Handsman to check, so I had to walk the fifteen miles home and then, because I'd missed dinner, I'd get another hiding from my old man unless he was too pissed to be bothered'.

'How did you survive?' Angela had asked Killer when he told her his story.

'I became a tough little mongrel. Whiteman stopped picking on me when I got older. I was never big, but I was a strong little mongrel and fat Whiteman knew that if he pushed me, I'd take his head off with one punch. I grew up pretty cranky at the world and coppers and especially with Whiteman and I kept telling myself that I was gunna get a gun and one day I'd put a bullet in the bastard, but it wasn't gunna be a sneak go like an ambush or anything. I wanted Whiteman to look me in the eye before I pulled the trigger. I wanted him to know that he was about to die and reason why and I wanted him to piss and shit his pants the way I used to when the bastard threw me in the paddy wagon.'

'So, what stopped you?' Angela asked, 'You know, getting a gun and shooting him.'

'Well, I probably didn't have the guts at first and then one day I was up at Karuah doing a bit of fishing and I bumped into this bloke who was quite a bit older than me. He was a blackfella and I think we were distantly related on my Mum's side. Anyway, we had a couple of beers and I told him about Whiteman and he said he had a similar experience and he hated the copper for years and years and then one day he said it dawned on him that by keeping all that hate, the copper won and so, one day he saw the copper who had since retired and he went up to him and shook his hand and he said that the copper shat himself at first and was then confused and my mate thought he'd grown ten foot tall with all the weight and hatred off his shoulders'.

'So, did you take his advice, did you shake Whiteman's hand.'

'No, the bastard only went and got himself killed in a car crash one night, pissed he was, they reckon, but I did go to the funeral and I did shake Handsman's hand and told him that I had no hard feelings and he looked like he just wanted to crawl under a rock. The old bloke from Karuah was right, I felt all the hatred just run out of me and it wasn't just the hatred for that fat copper but for the headmaster and my old man and just about everyone'

'Just about everyone?' Angela asked. 'Tell me more'

Killer chuckled and winked and told Angela that a bloke has to have some secrets.

'I guess you're taking them with you' Angela said to herself as the dust from the passing cars settled amidst all the other ash and dust around her.

Angela potted around for another hour or so, checking on what was damaged outside the house, which was just about everything and what was damaged inside, which was next to nothing other than things that needed a good clean to get rid of the ash and soot and when she was satisfied that she could do more, she loaded a few more things in the car and then set off for the drive back to Ingrid's for the third time in as many days.

As she closed the gate behind her and got back in the car, ready to turn on to the road, she had to give way to the procession of official vehicles that had gone up to Killer's place a little earlier, and the procession was led by the morgue van and then came the two police cars and then it was safe for Angela to pull out and join the tail. The uniformed driver of the marked police car gave

Angela a little wave and half smile as he drove past while next to him, in the passenger seat, Senior Constable Brenda Ramzan glared at her and Angela tried to think what she might have done to get on the wrong side of the police officer.

It felt to her like a rather bizarre funeral procession that should have been travelling much more slowly out of respect for Killer's last journey down from his mountain home and in her mind, Angela pictured the procession at a walking pace with a man out front in an old fashioned black suit with tails and a shiny black top hat that had, on the back, a long piece of black silk that was streaming behind him as he walked and, ideally, Killer should have been in an oak coffin that was inside a horse drawn hearse pulled by two black stallions with black leather blinkers and little black hats on their heads made out of the same sort of silk as the man at the front had on his top hat. Instead, it was all brisk and business like, an unremarkable panel van with two men in grey overalls heading back with their delivery, another day in the office and the police heading back to their station to do whatever it is that police do in times like these and Angela imagined that probably required a lot of paperwork, that she supposed the police hated, like reports to be made to the coroner and the next of kin sort out and notified.

If Angela had been asked about Killer's next of kin, she wouldn't have been able to offer much in the way of information. She knew that he was born in the district and had virtually spent his entire life within a couple of kilometres of home and she never saw him get any visitors apart from locals with animals to be butchered and he didn't seem to do much visiting himself. He never went to the pub at all and Angela suspected that Killer might have been a bit of big drinker in his wild younger days, but she had never seen him drunk. He did take the occasional drink, Angela remembered and laughed again at her turn of phrase, 'take a drink' she thought, how quaintly English as if he might enjoy a sherry on his veranda each evening after dressing for dinner when, in fact, the only drink she had seen him take was a couple of times when she offered him a beer on a hot day in return for helping her with some task or another around the yard and he would join her for a whisky on Hogmanay, but just have the one and he would be back home before it got dark. She wondered whether the drink was one of the demons he had managed to conquer.

Angela knew that Mick liked a drink and she had been told stories by one of her old tutors who supervised her thesis that Mick sometimes hit the bottle a bit hard, but Angela couldn't say for sure whether it was one of his demons or if, as the Irish like to say, he was just a man with a powerful thirst. Angela had found some solace in the bottle herself during the lost days after the 'mega crack-up' and she had preferred to have a few whisky's in the evening rather than the anti-depressants that left her feeling fuzzy headed all day and unable to think clearly which was worse than a quick short hangover that was usually cured by coffee and breakfast.

It took Angela years to get over the 'mega crack-up' but she thought that she was very good at hiding it from her friends and colleagues and she managed to get through the sort of heavy teaching load expected of junior academic staff that involved taking a number of tutorial groups each week consisting of bored first year students who, when she started teaching, she hoped she could inspire and within a few years had given up trying to be inspiring and had moved to drip feeding enough information so that her students might be able to submit essays worthy of at least a pass because if too many failed, the head of department might question her ability to teach.

Angela had actually been surprised when she was offered the full-time position albeit on a contract. She had never particularly liked her head of department. Professor David Parkinson was a graduate of Balliol where he had earned a blue and had rowed at Henley and he always lectured in an academic gown wearing the red and blue striped tie of the Balliol Boat Club and in winter, he sported his college scarf like some knight's flag proclaiming himself someone better than his colonial underlings, or the unfortunates amongst staff who might not be as low as the colonials but, by virtue of having studied at red brick universities in Great Britain, weren't up there with the men and women of Oxbridge of whom there were four or five in the English Department and another couple in Classics.

Professor Parkinson was in his early forties when Angela commenced work as a part-time tutor and had been at the university for fifteen years. She thought that he had a very large chip on his shoulder but couldn't work out what it was all about. It was only some years later when she started to have an affair with The Professor, Sophie's father Arthur, not Parkinson, that she learned that David Parkinson had been born into a family that was relatively well to do and were Yorkshire merchants who had built up a small chain of stores across the north. David's father, however, was a gambler and a philanderer who had managed to father a number of illegitimate children across Yorkshire in most of the towns where the family had stores. The elder Parkinson met an untimely end when he was killed by a jealous husband around the time that David was completing his doctorate on Chaucer at Balliol. The trial of his father's killer was covered in lurid detail in the News of the World and the family were further disgraced when it was discovered that in order to pay off David's father's gambling debts, many of which were to loan sharks and London thugs, that the business would have to be sold and the family were left close to penniless. David Parkinson came to Australia in 1980 and immediately cultivated the air of an Oxford don who looked down his nose at those he did not consider were his equals.

Parkinson had a strained relationship with Arthur, or the

Professor as all of his students called him. In fact, one of the things that galled Parkinson was the way the students always addressed Arthur as Professor but, in their disrespectful colonial ways would address him by his first name. Parkinson probably only tolerated the Professor because he was a Cambridge man, a product of Magdalene but he also cringed at the way the Professor had never lost his Geordie accent born amongst the shipyards on the banks of the Tyne.

Angela had started her affair with the Professor when he was sixty-five and she was thirty-eight and steadily working her way to completing her own doctoral thesis. She had known the Professor since she started at the university twenty years earlier and at no time imagined that she would have an affair with him. He had been her tutor when she was an undergraduate and she still has fond memories of sitting in his office with Louis, Andy and the others, drinking wine from paper cups and listening to the Professor declaim poetry in his deep bass voice. He had a passion for Blake but also a strong identification with D.H. Lawrence and his lectures on Sons and Lovers were passionate and insightful. It was his love for Lawrence that led Angela to make a diversion to Taos in New Mexico when she when in search of the footprints of Mick in Aztec. She sent the Professor a postcard from Taos on which she wrote 'the ghost of David Herbert is here, and I wish you were too.'

The Professor had a bit of a reputation for having an eye for pretty young undergraduates, particularly ones who had brains as well as looks and, for a long time in her early twenties, Angela would have said that she had neither in abundance and thought that she was fairly plain looking and even though she got consistent Distinctions, didn't think she was the smartest woman in the English Department. Angela didn't expect that the Professor would show any interest in her and never showed any signs that he desired her, even when they became colleagues following her graduation with honours.

She often thinks that her affair with the Professor was some delayed response to what she saw as being rejected by Andy. The fact that it was thirteen years earlier when Andy had taken up with the Professor's daughter, Sophie, didn't strike Angela as being a bit too much in the past to get some sort of revenge, nor did she think that with Andy somewhere on the other side of the world and out of touch with all the people they used to hang out with that it was really a pretty empty gesture but, then again, when Angela thought back to those days she remembered that they were filled with empty gestures. She was the one who made the first move on the Professor and in the tradition of all good clichés, it happened at the staff Christmas party that was held in David Parkinson's rambling old Victorian house perched high on the hill with ocean views over King Edward Park. Angela had not been drinking all that much and had seemed to have gotten over the post 'mega crack-up' boozing and was now completely focussed on her doctorate but had decided that the only way she could get through an evening of Parkinson's snobbiness was to give the expensive French champagne he supplied a bit of a nudge.

Later on, she couldn't quite remember the circumstances that led her to wake up in her own bed, the morning after Parkinson's party, with a headache made more painful by the sun streaming through her window and the loud and deep snoring from the large white haired and bearded head of the Professor as it lay on the pillow beside her. She looked around the room and saw that their clothes were scattered all over the floor in disarray as if they had been hurriedly removed and she had vague memories of being able to taste red wine in the Professor's whiskers and his hot breath.

For years the Professor had been skating on thin ice when it came to affairs with students and in more recent years, the university had been taking a much stricter view of any relationship between a lecturer and a student and any relationship had to be declared if they were pre-existing so arrangements could be made for independent marking and assessment Staff were told that they were not to commence any relationship with a student and, if they did, they could face disciplinary action by the Academic Senate. The Professor never used his power to award good grades to seduce students and was appalled to hear that some other lecturers would give out higher marks to students who slept with them, and to suggest that he might do the same was an affront to his academic integrity.

'I just have a weakness' he told Angela on more than one occasion, 'and I am a lucky man that my dear wife understands that I am only human, and I have my needs.'

Angela quite liked the Professor's wife, Rachel, who was also an academic and a poet who Angela thought was actually more talented than the Professor but allowed him to have the public spotlight as academic, poet, raconteur and Rugby tragic which was at odds with his northern working-class roots, which would make one suspect that he would be a League man. Rachel had taught at the Teacher's College that had become a College of Advanced Education and then amalgamated with the university. When the amalgamation occurred and the two English departments combined, Parkinson announced that he would not have couples working together and so Rachel took a job as a part-time lecturer in Sydney and caught the train several times a week to work until she eventually rented a small unit in Ultimo where she would stay three of four nights per week in an arrangement that suited both of them. Angela suspected that Rachel might have had a man of her own in Sydney.

Angela's affair with the Professor was pretty casual and Angela didn't think that she had any emotional investment in it until it was all over and then she realised that the Professor was more to her than just a casual lover and it was the meeting of the minds that she enjoyed much more than the sex which, despite the Professor's reputation as a womaniser was, to Angela's mind, pretty boring and pedestrian.

The Professor retired a couple of years into the on again/off again affair with Angela which, by then, was more off, with them meeting up occasionally for dinner and wine and sometimes he would stay over but more likely than not he didn't until things just petered out and there wasn't a break up or anything dramatic and they remained friends. Upon retirement, the university granted the Professor the title Emeritus Professor and allowed him to keep an office in the English Department and to make use of the university resources and clerical staff and in return he gave a couple of guest lectures and presented the odd prize, involved himself with the committee for the University Literary Award and Book Festival and also mentored junior members of staff and post-graduate students and Angela asked him to cast an eye on some of her lecture notes from time to time and suggest improvements.

She hadn't seen much of the Professor since she had moved to the mountain and she thought that she should make a point of catching up with him if he was up to it. She did some mental calculations and was astonished to realise that the Professor would now be in his early 'eighties and she had heard from someone in recent times that he was in poor health and that the copious amounts of wine and the rich English food he so loved, and the fish and chips for lunch most days, and the stilton cheese most evenings, had started to take a toll at last. She couldn't imagine a world without the Professor in it, certainly not the world of the university because to Angela, he was the university, he was the English Department and the staff refectory and the poetry nights put on by the English Students' Society and the Literary Festival and everything that had made Angela fall in love with words and she was worried that, if she did see him, if he was old and frail, that her words would fail her but if she didn't make an effort to see him at least one last time, to joke with him about his roving eye, to join him in mocking the pomposity of Parkinson or the seriousness of Angela's colleague and former classmate Angus Stuart who had finally become a professor himself, that it would be a greater failure and worse than a failure, it would be a betrayal and Angela didn't think that she could stand any more betrayals in her life even if she, for once, was the one doing the betraying.

Not So Much Leaving Home, As Going Home

The members of Kevin Cutler's crew who had been standing outside his shop when Angela arrived in town that morning had moved across the road to the pub and were all standing around the pub veranda with schooners in one hand and cigarettes in the other and Kevin Cutler was standing there in the middle of them like some tribal chieftain as they all turned to watch the sad procession of the morgue van, police cars and Angela, who thought that they probably knew who the van had been sent to collect, and she thought that if she was one of them that she would have felt guilty that it was another crew from another town that had gone up the hill to look for Killer's body. Angela made up her mind there and then that she would talk to Gerald and that perhaps between them they could organise a small memorial ceremony for Killer and for Tony. There would undoubtedly be a funeral for Tony, but it would most likely be in Sydney, where he came from and where he and Alyssa had their families, but something local, Angela believed, would also be appropriate.

The procession made a steady progress down the road along the dry creek beds and at a couple of spots along the route, there were large flocks of white cockatoos either in the paddocks close to the road or perched on the electricity and telephone wires to such a degree that the weight of the snow white bodies made the lines sag and Angela found herself singing *Wichita Lineman* to herself as she drove and was also amazed and found it a bit eerie that the cockatoos, that were normally so raucous when they were in a big mob, were all silent as if they were paying their respect to Killer as he left the district. Angela searched her brain to try and retrieve some information that she had heard once about the symbolic meaning of white cockatoos in indigenous culture and she thought there was something about the white cockatoo being the first creature to die or that it was the creature that welcomed the spirits of those who had died and maybe, all these cockatoos, Angela thought, were not so much farewelling Killer, but welcoming him and he wasn't so much leaving home as going home.

Home, Angela repeated the word in her mind like it was a mantra, hoping that in the repetition, she might have some sort of awakening, some sort of realisation of what home was, what it meant and then, perhaps, she might come to some understanding of what her home was, not just as a space, not just as something physical, a structure of brick and mortar, or weatherboard and iron, or even of mudbrick, but somewhere that was inside her, and she started to think that home might be somewhere she has not been yet, or even somewhere that she had been but just failed to recognise it at the time. She loved her little mudbrick cottage and was devastated when she thought she had lost it to the fire and then astonished and relieved to see that it was still sitting there, waiting for her but, at the same time, she started to realise, that when she saw her house still standing, and when the relief had passed, that she had felt not much of anything.

Angela considered that she knew what home was when she was a child and it was more than the house that she grew up and lived in. Home was also her grandparents' houses because in those places she always felt loved, even when her grandfather was being his curmudgeonly self, railing at the iniquities of the world and her grandma was all dour and gloomy in the way that only a Scottish grandmother can get away with, and then there was her Nan and Pa's house that perpetually smelled of cakes fresh out of the oven and mothballs on her Pa's cardigan. As a little girl, her world was the couple of blocks in Everton and it was her home and she had a name, and Mrs Shorten, who owned the corner shop called her by that name when she bought her little white bag of mixed lollies with the ten cents that her Nana would give her on a regular basis, and all the neighbours would call her by her name when she skipped past their houses on the way to play with one of her little friends further down the street or around the corner in the next block. Her home ran through her like a river of love, sometimes burbling along, sometimes deep and still and it had many tributaries the curled and weaved their way towards the one big river of love as it flowed to the sea.

Then Angela grew up and the world kept getting bigger like the lines in that Tom Waits song that was one of Andy's favourites, and he would play it until Angela was sick of it, and she wished that she could remember the name of the song because she would like to listen to it again and she remembered that it was on an album that had a yellow cover and the words of the songs were made to look like newspaper articles with the titles as the headlines and the text as the text and the albums name was, she thought, like the masthead of an old style newspaper. There was some television documentary she remembered watching once about science and the cosmos and it might have been presented by that boyish looking physicist who'd once been in a rock band that wasn't Queen, but another physicist, or at least she thought that he was a physicist and she remembered someone on the program who may or may not have been the physicist who wasn't Brian May, saying that the universe was expanding, but that it wouldn't expand infinitely and, eventually it would start contracting and, in fact, it may have started to contract already and when Angela remembered this as she was singing the Tom Waits song to herself, she thought that was an apt description of this thing, this feeling called home and how, from when you were a child, your home, your world just kept expanding, getting bigger and wider and further from end to end and then, at some stage, and for Angela it was five years ago, when she came to the mountain, the world started to contract until it was just her cottage with some occasional outposts and she would have once called Ingrid's place home when it was the old brick semi-detached owned by their Italian next door neighbour, but the new stark, light and clean apartment with its stainless steel benches and picture windows was too cold and clinical for Angela to call home.

It was to Ingrid's place that she was heading, last car in the line of the sad little procession, and she thought that even if she couldn't warm entirely to Ingrid's flash new apartment, it was Ingrid herself that was part of this feeling that Angela called home.

After the 'mega crack-up', Angela's mother thought that Angela should move back home for a little while to recuperate, but Angela was having none of it and just wanted to return to her own bedroom in the house that she shared with Ingrid over the road from the racetrack. It was a three-bedroom house that they had shared since they were students together and once they were earning some decent money, they decided not to look for another flatmate after Sally moved out to set up house with her boyfriend. Angela and Ingrid found some furniture from a discount store and set up the smallest of the three bedrooms as a guest room and thought that they were very grown-up at last.

'I'd feel more comfortable if you were at home with your father and I' Angela's mother said to her the day that the private hospital said that Angela was ready to be discharged.

'Ingrid will look after me' Angela said, and her mother looked concerned.

'She can't be with you all the time, she has to work, and it was a close thing last time, what if she hadn't been there?'

'For God's sake, I didn't take the bloody pills, I just said that I felt like taking the whole bloody bottle' Angela said to her mother, her voice just under control.

That's how Angela had ended up in the hospital in the first place. She had voluntarily admitted herself after Ingrid convinced her that she needed to be admitted. Angela had been feeling very stressed for some time trying to finish her MA and feeling that she was being haunted by the spirit of Siobhan and she felt that she had the weight of all of Siobhan's pain and suffering on her own shoulders. Angela was not sleeping and when she did, the dreams would come and they would always, at some point, feature Siobhan standing on the edge of the Gap. Angela's doctor had prescribed her some tablets to help her sleep and warned her about taking too many and also about the risk of mixing the pills with alcohol and how it could have a fatal result. The doctor asked Angela if she had ever considered harming herself and she said that she hadn't, and as she was saying this, she hoped that the doctor couldn't tell that she was lying.

When Angela was a teenager there came a day when she just couldn't stand the bullying of Louise Milligan any longer and she thought that the only way to avoid the constant torment, the unrelenting nastiness and bitchiness was to die, and she hoped that by dying, Louise Milligan would lose her mind to grief and guilt. The problem for Angela was that she couldn't make her mind up on the best way to end it all and she didn't want to do anything too gruesome because that wouldn't be nice for the person who found her and it would be extra hard on her parents so she discounted throwing herself under the express train to Sydney as it thundered through the level crossing that was just down the road from her Nana's place and where, maybe once every couple of years, people would take that option and Angela's dad would get cranky because the level crossing would be closed for hours and he had to drive the long way to work and back. She contemplated taking an overdose of pills but didn't have access to anything that she thought would do the trick other than headache tablets and she had heard a story about a girl who took a couple of boxes of headache tablets and then spent several days in hospital with her kidneys shutting down before she died a painful death. Angela didn't want to do anything as silly as one of the girls in her class who took a whole box of laxatives and then had to spend days in hospital with horrible stomach cramps and really bad gastric that required her to be on a drip to keep the fluids up, but wasn't life threatening and who she heard Lisa Mulligan describe as someone 'who really must have had the shits with life' and then laugh like she had made some great joke, when the poor girl was just someone who was very sad and it wasn't, Angela thought, something to joke about.

The boys seemed to have it easier in some ways, the teenaged Angela thought, with their access to ropes and knowledge of knots from boy scouts, they could usually do a thorough job of hanging themselves and quite a few of the boys in her class had access to their father's hunting rifles, or even had their own, but, as far as she knew, none of the boys at her school had shot themselves and the only boy in her glass to have died was Nathan Oldberry who had been killed in a car crash at the end of Year 10 when one of his older mates had let Nathan have a go at driving his Torana over on the island the other side of the steelworks and he had slammed the car at speed into a telegraph pole.

Angela did think of filling her pockets with stones and then jumping into the harbour because she remembered that was how Virginia Woolf had committed suicide. Angela had just started to read Woolf at the suggestion of her English Teacher, Mrs Wells and thought that Virginia was someone she might like to emulate and wished she was part of a group like the Bloomsbury set. She would have to find the right place and the right time to drown herself because, being a busy working harbour, there were always a lot of people around and if someone saw her go into the water, particularly fully clothed, they would probably come to her aid.

In the end, Angela had decided that this killing yourself business was really just too hard to organise, and she couldn't think of a method that was foolproof and could be achieved painlessly or without troubling anybody else. She also decided that Louise Milligan just wasn't worth it and that in future, whenever Louise was nasty to her, Angela would just laugh at her and tell her that she was just a moron like all the other girls she hung out with and that none of them would ever amount to anything but, of course, she never did say anything to Louise, but she did learn just to switch off and act as if she never heard Louise and without giving Louise the benefit of a reaction, the bullying seemed to come to an end by the end of Year 11. Louise Milligan was struggling in class and she might have been becoming a little self-conscious of her own serious shortcomings and that's why the bullying stopped.

The time she ended up in hospital was the culmination of a couple of days where Angela had just been overwhelmed with everything and, for so long, her thesis had been the focus of her every waking moment, occupying all of her time and her thinking and her emotions were all tied up in the Caldwell Street Push as if some unseen hands and unheard voices from beyond the grave were pushing her and driving her until she had completed and submitted her work, and then there was silence, and then there was emptiness.

Ingrid had been on afternoon shift at the hospital and had come home late at night to find Angela sitting in the loungeroom with a half full bottle of whisky and it was obvious that she has been drinking fairly heavily, and in her hands was the bottle of sedatives that her doctor had prescribed her when she said that she had been having trouble sleeping.

'What are you doing?' Ingrid asked.

'Nothing' Angela said and tried to push the tablet bottle down the side of the cushion on the lounge chair.

'Give them to me' Ingrid said in her best stern nurse voice that she used with the most recalcitrant patients and it had the effect of making Angela look to Ingrid to be like a small naughty child caught with something she shouldn't have. Angela reached down and dug out the bottle and handed it to Ingrid. 'How many have you had?' Ingrid asked.

'None'

'Are you sure. You mix these with booze and your respiration slows down and you go into a coma and then within minutes you die, or you vomit in your sleep and breathe in the vomit and you die' Ingrid lectured.

'Like Jimi Hendrix?' Angela tried to joke.

'I'm serious' Ingrid said.

'You don't have to worry about me. I'm a coward' Angela said. 'There was a moment or two when I thought about opening the bottle and swallowing the lot, but I couldn't do it'

Ingrid unscrewed the lid of the bottle and took one tablet out and broke it in half and put in on the table in front of Angela and put the bottle in the pocket of her scrubs. 'You probably shouldn't even have half a tablet but it's a quarter of your normal dose. I'm worried about you having these when you've been drinking but I don't want you withdrawing either.'

Angela just nodded and Ingrid noticed the tears welling up in her eyes and that her hands looked like they were shaking.

'You've got a choice' Ingrid said, and Angela looked up at her with questioning and worried eyes. 'We go to the hospital in Merewether tomorrow and you admit yourself as a private patient. I'll ring your GP first thing and get a referral. OK?'

'You said I had a choice?' Angela asked.

'You agree to do this, or I call an ambulance now and have you taken to Psychiatric Emergency Care.'

'The nuthouse?'

'PEC we call it, but yes, it's where the involuntary patients and the psychos go and it's not a nice place' Ingrid said thinking that some tough love might be what Angela needed.

The next morning, Ingrid drove Angela to the GP and picked up the letter and then drove to the small private hospital that specialised in psychiatric illnesses for the city's better off folk suffering from a range of illnesses including depression, anxiety and various neuroses, but who weren't dangerous or posed a risk to anyone other than themselves.

'Can you let Mum and Dad know?' Angela asked Ingrid while they were sitting waiting for the admission paper work to be completed.

'I'll drop in when you're settled in your room.'

'I wonder if there'll be a Native American chief who'll be willing to help bust me out' Angela said and smiled to Ingrid and then patted her arm. 'Thanks for caring.'

Ingrid said nothing and just patted Angela back on the arm and then put her arm around her shoulder.

The next morning Angela woke up and Ingrid was standing at the foot of her bed with the worried look she sometimes had and asked Angela if she had a good night and Angela said that she couldn't remember anything from the previous day other than being in the car with Ingrid and that something had happened the previous night but she couldn't remember that either and Ingrid told her that it might have something to do with the medication they put her on when she was admitted to force her to sleep and to stop her brain from working itself into a frenzy.

Angela liked the psychiatrist who was looking after her. Doctor Flores was only a couple of years older than Angela and seemed genuinely interested in Angela as a person and not just as a patient. While Angela was in the hospital, she had a session with Doctor Flores every day for the first few days and then every second or third day for the next three weeks until she was discharged. They had lively and interesting exchanges where they talked about Jung and Freud and they shared some favourite writers like Joyce and Beckett and Eliot, but Doctor Flores had never read any of Mick's works. Doctor Flores told Angela about some of her favourite Argentinian writers like Cortazar and when Angela had said that she had liked the short stories of Borges and thought that one day she would like to visit the pampas and see the gauchos in their villages, Doctor Flores scolded her gently and said that while Borges was an important writer, he also supported the junta during the dirty war in the seventies and how Doctor Flores's family had fled Buenos Aries when her oldest brother and his wife were disappeared because they were leftists, and how Doctor Flores later found out, they had probably been drugged and thrown out of a helicopter over the River Plate.

After that conversation, Angela felt very guilty for quite a while. She was guilty that she was lying in a hospital bed with such black thoughts when, for the most part, her life had been happy, and she had certainly not lived through times of fear in the same way that it must have been for Doctor Flores and her family and thousands of others in Argentina, and also in Chile, and in dozens of other places throughout the world, and how it must still be for people in some places in the world where fear is real and where stepping outside of your own front door could mean a nasty death. Angela felt guilty because she had never known poverty and had grown up with a hot meal on the table every day and money for clothes and books and records and family holidays. She felt guilty because she had never been physically, sexually or mentally abused as a child but knew that there must have been children that she knew at school who carried with them terrible secrets of what went on in what was supposed to be the safety of their homes and yet, these children, scarred and battered inside, went on with their lives and although many probably had breakdowns, at least they had a reason to break down and Angela felt guilty because she didn't think she had a reason.

Her parents visited her regularly and Angela would get annoyed and frustrated at the way her mother would sit and want to hold her hand and look at her in a pitying way and tell her how worried everyone was and how they just wanted her to get better and how perhaps she should get a less stressful job when she got out of hospital and how Angela's father had put in a good word for her with one of his mates down at the club who owned a business that sold bathroom supplies like taps and sinks and toilet pans and how he was willing to take Angela on for a couple of days per week helping out in the office with the ordering and invoicing and that it was good steady work with an opportunity for promotion to managing one of his stores because he had plans to expand.

'Mum, academia must be the most stress-free job in the world. It wasn't the job that put me here.' Angela said one day when her mother had been prattling on again about the bathroom supply business.

'I just don't think it's the sort of place for the likes of us' her mother said. 'I know they probably look down on you and that must hurt and no wonder you ended up, you know, wanting to end it all.'

'Professor Parkinson said that I was likely to be offered a full-time position in the new year. Not a tenure but a year by year contract. I will be paid full time which will give me time to study and publish articles as well as teach.' Angela said and smiled at her mother who gave Angela her pained and concerned look.

'Don't you think you should be thinking of settling down. Your father and I had been hoping for grandchildren you know.'

'And I'm only twenty-eight so there's plenty of time, but be warned, I don't know if I want to have children, maybe I never will.'

One day Angela bought a t-shirt she had seen in the markets in Paddington and it featured a picture of a woman's head and shoulders holding her hand to her mouth and with a look of surprise and it was like an illustration from a magazine from the forties or fifties with the woman sporting a hairdo from that period and, under the picture of the woman there was a caption: 'Oops, I forgot to have children'. Angela wore it to her parent's for lunch one Christmas and her mother told her that it was a shameful and disrespectful thing to wear on a day that celebrated the most important birth of all and where would we all be if the Blessed Virgin Mary simply forgot to have a child and Angela responded that she didn't get the connection because she, Angela, was certainly not a virgin and she also suspected that Mary had no choice in bearing a child no matter what the circumstances of that child's conception had been. The rest of the lunch was eaten in silence by Angela's mother who was putting on a sulk and a non-stop commentary from her father about how the first day of the Melbourne test match was likely to pan out and who might win the Sydney to Hobart yacht race that year. It was the last time Angela went home for Christmas.

When the little procession crossed the bridge into Maitland, the two police cars turned off and headed towards the police station in the side street and it was just Angela following the van containing the body of Killer. She had wondered if the van might have gone to the Maitland Hospital, but it continued on towards the New England Highway and Angela thought to herself that, of course, Killer would be going to a stainless-steel slab in the pathology lab at the hospital where Ingrid worked. The traffic out of Maitland was getting heavier and Angela got stuck behind a truck on the highway and soon lost sight of the morgue van. She turned up the radio when the news came on and the announcer said that there might be a chance of rain overnight and this might put out the fires that were still burning in the mountains to the north of the valley.

She was back in the flat before Ingrid got home from work and she decided that she would take her out for dinner to one of the restaurants along the harbour front, across the road from the units and hoped that they would be open on a Monday night because that was the night that a lot of restaurants closed. It would be a dinner to celebrate the fact that her house had been saved and to thank Ingrid for putting her up and to ask if she could stay for a bit longer until she could get power connected to her cottage and move back in and she tried to put out of her mind the thought that Killer wouldn't be there next door any more apart from in the form of some restless spirit that she hoped would be more like a guardian angel.

'So how do you really feel?' Ingrid asked when Angela gave her the news. 'Because last night you almost had the insurance money spent on a world trip?'

'I think you almost had it spent for me' Angela laughed and then looked a bit serious. 'I'm not sure how I feel. It'll never be the same again, not up there and it's not just because Killer is dead or Tony is dead and their houses gone, and I don't expect that Alyssa will return. It's something deeper, something more profound. I don't think I'll ever feel safe up there again, not in the same way, not knowing that this could happen again and I might not be so lucky next time, it could be my house that goes up or I could be the one lying on a slab and I don't think I want that just yet, I've got too much life left in me.'

'Well I'm glad you think so' Ingrid said.

'Anyway, I'm not going to make any big decisions just yet. Intellectually I know that I'm probably safe from fire for a couple of years until the undergrowth builds up again and there's also no point in selling now when the fires are fresh in everybody's mind, so I've probably got a year or two to decide about the next steps for Angela McGregor.'

They managed to find a restaurant that was open on a Monday

night and digging through the bundle of clothes that she had brought with her, Angela had managed to find a richly coloured and patterned skirt that looked like it might have been from Morocco or somewhere equally exotic and she matched it with a white cotton blouse and a big broad black leather belt and sandals and even borrowed some make up from Ingrid to complete the picture.

'You expecting to meet someone?' Ingrid had asked when Angela came out of the spare bedroom in all of her finery.

'I just felt like a change from spending most of my days in old jeans and t-shirts or flannelette shirts when the weather gets a bit chilly of an evening. My hillbilly rig I call that, and this is my hippy, arty, intellectual rig.'

Later in the restaurant, Angela thanked Ingrid once again for letting her stay in the apartment until she managed to get everything sorted out back on the mountain and Angela had said that she hoped that it wouldn't take all that long now that the worst of the fire had passed and that things would be getting back to normal in Allynsdale over the next few weeks.

'Is anything ever normal in Allynsdale?' Ingrid asked.

'Well, when I say normal, I mean normal for Allynsdale' Angela said laughing and using her chopsticks, spearing another piece of tempura prawn from the shared black lacquered plate that sat between them.

Grief, The Phoenix
and the Other Thing

The rains came just before Christmas and there were green shoots peeking through the blackened grass and early one morning, Angela saw a kangaroo with a joey's head sticking out the top of the pouch eating some grass that had newly sprouted near her back door, and she imagined that it might have even been the same kangaroo that gave her strength all those weeks ago when she had a panic attack while she was driving back to see if she still had a house or not.

The river was starting to run again after the rain and even if it was just a weak trickle, to Angela it was a sign that it was being reborn. Gerald disagreed and he said that the little rain that had fallen had not broken the back of the drought and it was only a matter of time, perhaps days, before the river dried up again and Angela told him to have faith because anything's possible and she should know as the owner of the house that the fire forgot to burn and then Gerald started to bore Angela with all the technical and scientific reasons why her house was spared when others burned and how it all had to do with wind vectors and temperature and hot spots and the speed of the fire front and the direction it was moving and the availability of more flammable fuel close by.

'Fires are lazy bastards' Gerald said, 'you'd think that they just power through because that's what it looks like when you're confronting it, but the truth is a fire will always seek out the path of least resistance, the path with the most fuel and oxygen and where it's hottest'.

Angela started to think that this might have been a good metaphor for her own life. To her friends it seemed that she had spent a good part of her life, particular in her twenties and thirties when it seemed to the world that she was so focussed on her career, on her studies, on her teaching and so passionate about her books that she burned with it all and that she was unstoppable when, for Angela, she had no idea what to do with her life and so just did the things that came easiest to her and this wasn't to say that she wasn't passionate and didn't enjoy being a scholar but to do anything else, another career or become a wife and mother was just so inconceivably hard.

In the three weeks that Angela had been back, she hadn't gone further up the road than her own driveway because she didn't think that she could bare to see the remains of Killer's house and it was hard enough to go past Tony and Alyssa's every time she left her own house. About a week after the fires there was a small notice in the Herald advising that there had been a private cremation at his own request for one Bernard Bernard formerly of Allynsdale. Angela didn't see the funeral notice herself, but Gerald pointed it out one day when she stopped for petrol, in a copy of the paper, he had kept for her.

'Bernard Bernard eh' Angela said, 'Who gives a child a name like that?'

Gerald shrugged and said that he didn't really know Killer all that well. 'We'd sometimes have a chat when he came to get petrol or tobacco, but he never gave away much about himself.'

'Privately cremated at his own request?', Angela looked at Gerald and raised her eyebrows, 'Well he was half cremated and that certainly wasn't at his own request and the crematorium just finished the job but I wonder who would have organised it and who would have known his wishes, I would have thought that he might have liked to have been buried on his own land and I wonder what they did with the ashes?'

'Gees you can have a black sense of humour sometimes' Gerald said, shaking his head.

Angela was still determined that she wanted to organise something as a way of saying goodbye to Killer and to Tony and she hoped that the people of the town would support her and she needed a bit of help in the organisation as she had never taken on a task like this before and she was unsure how to go about it or how even to get the ball rolling. Most of the events in the town were organised by Kevin Cutler and his family but, given the antagonism that seemed to exist between Kevin and Killer, Angela was not one hundred per cent convinced that any suggestion she made for a wake for Killer would be well received. The notice in the newspaper about Killer's cremation made no reference to any other family member and it looked like it had been privately placed because there was no logo or details of a funeral company like there normally would be on a notice like this. Angela had looked up the telephone book online and couldn't find any other Bernard's in the valley. There were a couple of Bernard's in Newcastle who may or may not have been family.

Angela had sent an E Mail to Alyssa and received a response within a couple of hours. Alyssa said that she was slowly recovering from the burns to her hands and that the doctors were very happy with the progress and expected there to be some scarring but not a lot and the worst part was that it seemed to hurt more as it healed than it had when the burns first occurred. Alyssa said that there had been a funeral for Tony and that he had been buried in the family plot in the Rookwood Cemetery. Angela imagined that there might not have been a lot left to bury, just charred bones. Angela told Alyssa about her plans to hold some form of simple acknowledgement of the loss of Tony and Killer at some stage in the near future and that she hoped that Alyssa would be able to attend but also understood that she might not be able to bear coming back to Allynsdale. Alyssa had said that her brother had gone up to the property with his big truck and trailer and had removed anything that was salvageable and that she was probably going to put the block on the market and wasn't sure if she had the strength emotionally to return to the property. Alyssa told Angela that she was staying in a granny flat at the back of her brother's place and that she was still going to the clinic at the hospital every second day but that Angela was welcome to visit her if she was in Sydney and Alyssa closed off her reply telling Angela that she would like to stay in touch and would write again and for Angela to send her the details of anything she organised for Tony and Killer.

There were a couple of buildings in Allynsdale that might be large enough for a modest gathering, not counting the Anglican church at the main intersection and the Catholic church that was on the road that went over the mountain to Cheltenham. Angela assumed, but couldn't be sure, that Tony, with his Italian heritage was a Catholic and when she asked Killer once about religion, he told her that he was a pagan and didn't believe in any of this god business, but he did believe in nature. So, ruling out the two churches, there was the Scout Hall where the evacuation centre had been established and there was the old CWA hall just near Kevin Cutler's shop and Angela thought that Kevin Cutler's wife, who she only knew as Mrs Cutler, was the boss of the Allynsdale CWA. There were no longer any Scouts or Cubs or Brownies or Guides in Allynsdale and the Scout Hall was owned by the council and you could book it by filling out a form on the council website, but you had to pay a hiring and cleaning fee to the Secretary of the hall committee who Angela discovered by looking on the website was Kevin Cutler.

Angela wasn't sure of the reasons why Gerald wasn't in the Allynsdale Bush Fire Brigade and had joined the brigade in the next village over the ridge but she was sure it was because he'd had a falling out with Kevin Cutler some time ago, but whether or not it had something to do with bush fire business or whether it was just because of the racist remarks Kevin would make about

Anila, Gerald's wife, she couldn't be sure, but what she did know was that there was no way that she could ask Gerald to approach Kevin on her behalf to rent the Scout Hall and she didn't really know anybody else well enough and the reason she was reluctant to ask Kevin herself was that he would just treat her the way that he always did, as a blow-in who had no business in Allynsdale.

There was always the pub and even if Singo, the publican, was one of Kevin's cronies, he wouldn't knock back the chance to make a few dollars from drinks and maybe a light supper of sausage rolls and party pies and some little triangle sandwiches and Angela was happy to fund all of it herself and the more she thought about, the more it made sense because she would have had to organise catering anyway and the only options were the pub or Mrs Cutler's café.

Angela decided that on the off chance that there might be a surviving relative amongst the Bernard's in the phone listing for Newcastle, she started to telephone them one by one and on the third attempt she struck gold. The telephone was answered by a woman whose age Angela could not determine and her thoughts were that the woman was probably younger than she was, but not by a huge amount and could have been somewhere in her late forties. The woman said that her name was Sarah Bernard and that she was Bernard's daughter and this totally surprised Angela because she had no idea that Killer had children and he never mentioned children in any of the conversations that they had over the years.

When Angela explained that she wanted to organise a small gathering so that Bernard's neighbours could show their respect and remember him with stories and anecdotes the way people did at wakes, Sarah laughed and said to Angela 'Do you actually expect that anyone from that place will bother to turn up?'

'I know he didn't have many friends', Angela said, 'but everyone around here seemed to know your father and I thought it might be nice. He was a good neighbour to me and helped me out quite a bit and there was another man who was also killed, Tony Conti, and I thought that it would be a joint memorial. Nothing too fancy, just whoever wanted to come along and maybe say a few things.'

'Well, there might be a few who might want to come and speak but they might not have things to say that you want to hear. He must have mellowed a bit in his later years if he was such a good neighbour' Sarah said without making any commitment whether she would come along herself.

'I have to come down to Newcastle a bit later in the week and I'd be happy to catch up for a coffee if you had time?' Angela suggested and Sarah took Angela's number and promised that she would get back to her in a day or two.

Angela had decided to bite the bullet and go and see Singo herself to ask about using the large back room for a function to celebrate the lives of Tony and Killer. Like a lot of country towns, the pub was often the focal point for any gathering and the back room had, over the years become almost like a de-facto town hall. The council used it when they wanted to brief locals on things like roadworks and repairs to the dozens of old rattly wooden bridges in the district, at election time the candidates would often hold meetings in the pub to outline their policies to the constituents and Singo had said that all the parties were welcome to hold their meetings in his pub except the Greens and they had to hire the scout hall. Allynsdale and the district was divided politically with most of the residents voting for the conservative parties because they thought the Nationals best represented the rural areas but there was also a growing contingent of mainly younger people and tree changers who were voting Green and the vote was consistently getting Greener at each passing election. Angela was a rusted-on Labor supporter and would happily tell anyone who'd listen that she wouldn't have been able to go to university if it hadn't been for the reforms under Whitlam. A lot of the people in the town thought that Angela was a Green because she lived in a mud brick house and was educated and was sometimes a bit aloof.

When she went to see Singo, it was one of the few times that Angela had set foot in the pub since the incident ages before with Kevin Cutler's nephew. Singo wasn't behind the bar and so she asked Chloe, the young barmaid, for a glass of iced water and then changed her mind and asked for a can of Coopers. Angela had seen Chloe around town and she also looked like a fish out of water. Her parents had arrived in the district around the same time that Angela had bought her place, but they lived a couple of miles the other side of town on the road to Cheltenham. Chloe's mother was an artist and had a studio at the back of their house and her father was an accountant who had his own business in Cheltenham looking after the local farmers and small businesses by helping them to pay as little tax as they could legally get away with.

'You're a teacher at the university, aren't you?' Chloe asked Angela as she put the can of beer down on the bar and reached in the fridge for a cold glass.

'Was', Angela said, 'I was an English lecturer'.

'What do you do now?' was the next question.

'Research work mainly, and I publish the occasional article and I review books for a couple of papers here and overseas. I don't earn a lot, but I don't need a lot. I also tutor kids for the HSC and when things get a bit tight, I even do a bit of cleaning.'

'What did you specialise in when you were teaching?' Chloe asked.

'Mainly Australian literature and I was considered one of the three or four top people on Randolph Stow in my day. I also loved some of the Irish writers from the twentieth century, Joyce and Beckett although Beckett was technically a French writer because he wrote in French.'

'I didn't know that. I read Waiting for Godot for school this year. I loved it. I tried to read Finnegan's Wake but couldn't get past the first couple of pages before my head was in a spin.' Chloe said and shook her head.

'Try Ulysses instead. It's still not an easy read but it's not impossible like Finnegan's Wake and if you really wanted to read Joyce, you should ease yourself in with Dubliners and the Portrait of an Artist, they're both pretty straight forward reads and they're good to set the scene of Dublin at the time and of what the main themes are in the later works. Once you've had a go at them, go back and read Finnegan, but read it aloud and phonetically and it will start to make sense, particularly if you can do a reasonable Irish accent.'

It was the first time that Angela had talked about literature to anyone for a long time and she couldn't remember ever talking about it with anyone in Allynsdale apart from Alyssa who liked to keep up with the latest novels and she would go to her favourite bookstore in Sydney every couple of months and come back with bags of book that she would devour and then lend to Angela if she thought they were any good, and so Angela's main reading was books that had been sent to her for review or anything that Alyssa had seen get a positive review in the Herald or Australian. Angela couldn't believe that of all the people she would be talking about books, it would be the young barmaid in Singo's pub, and she realised that she had probably unfairly thought of Chloe as being the sort of girl who'd work in the pub and marry a local farm labourer and be pushing out her first kid before she was twenty.

'So, you like reading?' Angela asked.

'Yes, and writing. I write poetry but please don't tell anyone around here, they already think I'm strange enough.' Chloe looked around the empty bar to make sure that there was nobody to hear her confession.

'Do you show people your poetry or go to any readings?'

Angela asked.

'They have a reading in the art gallery in Maitland once a month and I've been going to that regularly since I got my licence. Some of the poets are really good and a few said that my poems have a lot of promise which I suppose means that they're not that good yet. I'm going to uni next year and I'm going to do creative writing.'

'That's terrific, you'll love it.' Angela said and suddenly wished that she was eighteen again and about to start all over at uni and at life and she thought that she might have done it differently if she had a second chance but how differently she wasn't sure. Perhaps she wouldn't have given up Andy to Sophie without a fight. She had been enjoying the talk so much that she almost forgot why she had come to the pub in the first place. 'Is Singo around?' she asked Chloe.

'He's had to go to Maitland to see a man about a dog, as he put it. Should be back by lunchtime so I can help out in the kitchen.'

'I wanted to see him about booking the back room for an evening next week.'

'That shouldn't be a problem' Chloe said and reached into the shelf under the cash register and pulled out a blue covered desk diary and opened it up and asked, 'any particular night?'

'Maybe Wednesday, less people here than Thursday or Friday.' Angela said. Most of the people who drank at the pub were paid on a Thursday, so it got busy and, of course, Friday was always busy, being the end of the week.

'Done,' Chloe said, writing in the diary.

'I'll want a bit of catering as well, just some sandwiches, pies and sausage rolls.'

'You'll have to chat to Mrs Singleton about that. She should be downstairs in a tick to get ready for lunchtime. What's the occasion?' Chloe asked.

'Just a little get together to remember Tony Conti, my

neighbour' Angela said and thought that she'd not mention Killer.

'That was terrible', Chloe said, 'and Mr Bernard as well. He lived near you, didn't he?'

'He was my neighbour on the other side' Angela said and left it at that.

'Well he deserves to be remembered too' Chloe said, and Angela's heart melted at her kindness and she couldn't help a tear escaping from her eye and running down her chest.

Angela finished her beer and said to Chloe that she would talk to Mrs Singleton before the end of the week when she had some idea of the numbers to expect.

There was an Allynsdale Facebook page where the local community members posted all sorts of information about the events that were occurring in the town and Angela put up a post advising of the get together to remember Tony and Killer and she E Mailed Alyssa with the details and asked people to respond within the next couple of days for catering purposes. She was a bit surprised when Kevin Cutler and his wife were two of the first people to say that they were coming and Angela suspected that as much as Kevin and Killer didn't get on, Kevin would be worried about a gathering of the community occurring where he didn't play a leading role and he even messaged Angela saying that he would be happy to say a few words if she liked. Angela also received a message from Rodney Cripplegate that appeared to be taking her to task for organising something off her own back and he suggested that this was his job as the ward councillor and that she had to understand that the event didn't have the endorsement of the council but he would probably attend in the capacity of a private person and Angela replied, sarcastically apologising and saying that she was sorry but she didn't know that Council had to give permission for groups of people to meet at the pub and that, in future, she would ask permission from the mayor and tell the mayor and general manager that this was at the instigation of

Councillor Cripplegate. Angela didn't get a response.

As promised, Angela drove to Newcastle and arranged to meet with Sarah at one of Sarah's favourite cafés that sat over the road from the main beach and had terrific ocean views. Angela was ten minutes early and Sarah arrived precisely on time and she looked younger than what she had sounded on the telephone and was immaculately dressed in a grey two-piece business jacket and skirt with a white cotton shirt, and her hair and make-up were perfect but also understated. Angela felt a little shabby in her old jeans and t-shirt and no make-up but was pleased that at the last minute she decided that it might be a better look if she put on a bra under the t-shirt. Sarah walked straight up to Angela in a business-like manner and held out her hand for Angela to shake as she introduced herself.

'So, you knew my father?' Sarah asked.

'Bernard Bernard?' Angela asked, 'Yes we were neighbours for the last five years, but I only learned his name recently, everyone called him Killer.' Sarah flinched a little at that name.

'Why did they call him that?' she asked with a tone of suspicion.

'He was sort of the unofficial butcher for a lot of his neighbours. Most of them were city people like me who wanted to live in the bush and quite a few were into self-sufficiency and raised animals to eat, chickens mainly but also the occasional steer or lamb or goat. When they wanted the animal killed and butchered, they would bring the animal to your father and he did a good job too.'

'If they can't bear to kill and butcher the animals they raise, they've got no business eating meat' Sarah said quite emphatically.

Angela let that one pass without comment. 'I didn't know that he had children, I suppose I didn't know all that much about his past although it sounded like he had a rough childhood?' Angela asked.

'And I hear that in court every single day, it's all because of my bad childhood, Mum and Dad didn't love me, I didn't get

Christmas presents, I wasn't allowed to have a dog, and nothing to do with the choices I make as an adult.'

'You're a lawyer?'

'Crown Prosecutor. Worked my way up from Police Prosecutor studying law by distance education.'

'Your father would have been proud.' Angela said, smiling.

'I doubt it. I sometimes think I took on my career just to spite him, but it was all my choice, my decision.' Sarah said and while she spoke, she was gazing out to the ocean.

'And your mother?' Angela asked, hoping that she wasn't crossing over some unspoken line.

'I'll have to start calling you counsel for the defence', Sarah said and turned back to look at Angela and she was smiling but it was a sad smile Angela thought. 'She died when I was little. For a long time, I blamed his nibs, still do to some extent, but they were as bad as each other and big drinkers with it, from what I can remember. I was only seven when Mum died. They had a big row and Mum took off in the car and she had been drinking like she always did. You know that bridge just past Wallisville, where you do a sharp right, cross the river and then do a sharp left? Well she didn't turn fast enough, went through the timber bridge railing and car landed upside down in the water and there was six or seven feet of water in the river. She drowned. The coroner reckoned she had broken her neck in the crash but there was water in her lungs. He couldn't say if she was conscious or not when she went in.' Sarah sipped her latte from the glass that had been put in front of her by the waitress while she was talking.

'You were lucky she didn't take you when she left.' Angela commented.

'Yep, pure luck. I don't think it was intentional. In the heat of the argument and because of the grog, I think Mum might even have forgotten that I existed. Well, I was shunted off to an Aunty on Mum's side down here and for a couple of years bounced around between family members until DOCS got involved and the caseworker found some family from Dad's side who lived down the lake in a nice house and were prepared to take me and I stayed with them for the next ten years until I went to the Police Academy.'

'Did you see your father much?' Angela asked.

'Around Christmas he would visit. The people I was staying with were like his second cousins and I think there was some bad blood.'

'We're having a small get together at the pub in Allynsdale next Wednesday, nothing formal but just a chance to acknowledge your father's passing and that of another local man, Tony Conti. I understand why you might not want to come but you'd be more than welcome and there might even be some people there that you know.' Angela said.

'Thank you', Sarah said shaking her head, 'but what's in the past should stay in the past. There's probably not that many of the old people left living up there and, to be honest, I don't want to hear the old stories, all the suspicions and accusations and, well, there's no way now to know what was true and what wasn't.'

'I'm not sure I follow?' Angela looked puzzled.

'Dad had his demons, that's for sure, and yes, his childhood was rough, and his old man used to beat Dad and Dad's Mum pretty brutally from what I can gather, and this went on until Dad was fourteen or fifteen and then his father died and so it stopped. The story is that Dad helped his father on his way.'

'How so?'

'My grandfather was a violent drunk who'd drink anything he could get his hands on, and when he was broke, he'd drink metho if that's all he could get. One night in the middle of winter he disappeared and wasn't found for a couple of days and when he was, he was stone dead, just under the bridge near old Molly Thompson's place, although back then she would have been a young woman living with her parents. The local doctor signed the death certificate and said that he died from exposure having passed out when he was paralytic. The bloke who found him, Charlie Cutler, you probably know his son Kevin, reckoned that the old bloke had a big wound to the back of his head like he had been hit with an iron bar or something and that the doctor and the undertaker hushed it up because nobody liked the old bloke and they all assumed it was either Dad or his Mum or both and nobody wanted to see them get in trouble with the law.' Sarah stared hard at Angela while her words sunk in.

'Did your Dad ever admit it?' Angela asked.

'Not to me and not to anybody else as far as I know. What I do know is that Charlie Cutler made Dad work for him, chopping wood and stuff and never paid him and told Dad that he was free to complain to the cops because Charlie might have a story or two to tell himself and Dad was already being picked on by the Sergeant in Wallisville so he buggered off out west for a few years. After his own mother died, Dad came back and lived in the house and took up with Mum. Old Charlie Cutler was dead by then, but there had been whispers that Dad was a murderer and for a while, Kevin would tell anybody who moved into the town to keep away from Dad, but I think, in the end, it suited Dad to be a bit of a hermit.'

'He had friends. He was a bit of an eccentric old coot but there were people who liked him and there are people who'll miss him.' Angela said and gazed down the beach to the crumbling art deco façade of the municipal ocean baths and thought about the way we all have facades and how, over time, with wind and rain and the salt of many tears, those facades also crumble until they expose the raw building materials underneath the cheap plaster of our existence.

'You sound like you were quite fond of my father and I suppose you must think that I'm a bit cold and heartless, but he was never really my father in the sense that he was someone I could go to for guidance or advice, or who was there to praise my achievements or to correct my faults.'

Angela shook her head and told Sarah that she wasn't there to judge her and that she understood, or at least thought she understood the way that Sarah felt and that she also appreciated why Sarah wouldn't want to come to the memorial gathering and Sarah told Angela that she appreciated meeting her and they said goodbye with neither of them making any agreement that they would stay in touch. Sarah shook Angela's hand and left the café. Angela wondered who would inherit Killer's block and assumed that it would be Sarah as his closest relative and thought that Sarah would probably put it on the market.

Ash Wednesday

Ingrid drove up to Allynsdale after work on the Tuesday before the memorial gathering and told Angela that she had taken a couple of days leave so she could help with the preparations and be there the next night for Angela. Angela thanked her for doing this given the fact that Ingrid had never met Killer or Tony. It had been ages since Ingrid had been to stay and over the years that had only been a couple of times and, even then, she had been the only house guest that Angela had and so she had taken to calling her spare room, Ingrid's room.

As they sat on the flagstones outside the kitchen, drinking white wine, Ingrid commented on how strong the smell of bushfire was, and Angela told her that there were still fires burning in some of the more inaccessible areas of the Tops and they might smoulder away for weeks or even months.

They sat quietly the way old friends do, sharing the silence with nothing needing to be said and if they spoke, it would have just been useless words used to fill in the gaps between the animal and bird sounds and Angela was tiring of the uselessness of words. Angela thought about smouldering fires that seemed benign but could flare up anytime. She remembered visiting some friends of her father who lived very close to some old coal mines in the Valley and not far from the house where the friend lived there were these huge mounds of what looked like coal but was greyer and some of the mounds appeared to have whisps of smoke coming from them and her father's friend's wife said that they were called chitter dumps and the children were not to go near them because they might look like they'd be fun to climb, but they were burning on the inside and if you climbed on one, you could fall through the loose chitter and be burned to ash and nobody would know where you were or would be able to find you.

Maybe I'm a chitter dump, Angela thought when she remembered the story, because I look cool and solid on the outside but on the inside, I am just burning waste, rubbish, a by-product of coal and coal is carbon and so are diamonds and that's who I've become, she thought, the unseen burning ash of diamond waiting for some redemption. Angela believed strongly that she somehow needed to be redeemed but her biggest problem was that she could not put her finger on what it was that she needed to be redeemed of.

'What was she like?' Ingrid asked, interrupting Angela's wandering thought of coal and diamonds and chitter and redemption.

'Who?'

'Killer's daughter, you said that you had coffee with her the other day' Ingrid said with the chastising tone she sometimes used when she didn't think that Angela had been listening to her.

'Hard to say', Angela said, thinking aloud. 'She was pleasant enough I suppose and very professional. She's a lawyer, a prosecutor and used to be a policewoman...'

'Police Officer', Ingrid interrupted, 'we don't use gender specific terms for occupations or professions anymore'. Angela shot Ingrid a look that seemed to ask if Ingrid was serious or taking the piss.

'Officer then. Anyway, she was happy to talk about her father, not that she knew that much about him. She said that a lot of the people around here thought that he had killed his own father back years ago when Killer could hardly have been more than a kid himself.'

'That explain why he didn't have many friends in the town, at least amongst the old families' Ingrid suggested.

'I think it was more than that. Sarah said that it was Kevin

Cutler who made sure everyone was told that Killer was a murderer, but Killer reckoned Cutler hated him because he was part Aboriginal and that Kevin was just a racist prick.'

'We don't say "part aboriginal", a person either identifies as being indigenous or not and some people find it offensive as if you're talking about racial purity and saying that some people are more indigenous than others.' Ingrid said hoitily.

'I can't take a trick, can I? Anyway, that was how Killer described himself and I'm just repeating what he said.' Angela sniffily replied and then topped up her wine glass. 'I'm glad you came up' she said to Ingrid, smiling and raising her glass.

They talked late into the night with just the moonlight to illuminate them and like they often did, there was a lot of nostalgic 'do you remember when' or 'what happened to so and so' and Angela was always amazed at how much Ingrid knew about all of their old friends and where they were.

'I didn't know if I should tell you', Ingrid said when they were well into their second bottle of wine, 'but I saw Andy the other day.'

'Andy Mac?' Angela asked quickly and looked closely at Ingrid in the darkness. 'Whereabouts?'

'Stockton of all places. I was having a late lunch with some friends at the café, you know the one right on the beach that they're scared will get swallowed up by the ocean.'

'Yair, go on.'

'He came walking down the road near the Surf Club and stood looking at the ocean for a while and then went walking up along the beach.'

'Did you speak to him?' Angela asked and tried to hide the excitement in her voice that Andy might be back in town.

'No, but it was him though'

'What did he look like?' Angela asked quickly.

'Old, well older. His hair is completely white and cut very

short, almost a crew cut, and he's put on a bit of weight and he was dressed in khaki chinos and polo shirt with blue boat shoes, you know, the ones with the rope soles and the white piping.'

'So, he's lost the combat boots?' Angela laughed.

'He looked like a really prosperous middle-aged man, but you know there was something that looked like sadness in his eyes, and the way he gazed out to sea for several minutes was as if he was hoping something that he had lost would materialise.'

Angela felt a sinking in her stomach like she felt when she was a teenager or a young uni student and someone she was keen on proved to be more interested in someone else. When Ingrid talked about Andy's sadness and the way he looked like he was looking for something he had lost, she had a fleeting hope that the something might have been her but then, of course, she realised that what he would be looking for in Stockton would be the memory of Sophie, because that's where she lived and he once told Angela that he loved walking along the beach with Sophie and never realised that every time he mentioned her to Angela, it was like another little nail being driven into Angela's heart until there came the time that so many nails had been driven there, she didn't think she felt a thing, but knew, then and there, as Ingrid spoke, that this is what the chitter dump had been holding the whole time, the memory of Andy and the hope that she had more than thirty years ago that it might bloom into love and how it was all her fault because she never said anything because she was scared and she was not sure what she had scared about – certainly there was the fear of rejection but also the fear of feeling stupid as if she had misread Andy's friendship for something else and as she got older she knew that she always had trouble with signs and signals from other people and that's why she preferred her own company to save the embarrassment of a misread cue, a misinterpreted word or gesture.

'Why didn't you speak to him, find out what he was up to these days?' Angela asked and Ingrid thought that there was a sound of desperation in her voice.

'What would I say? I doubt if he would remember me anyway' Ingrid said slowly and quietly.

After Andy had broken up with Sophie, Angela tried to reach out to him a couple of times, but he just seemed cold and distant. He had moved out of the house he shared with Patrick and Georgia and moved into a shared house with a couple of would be musicians Angela was acquainted with who were friends with Lucy and had gone to school in the same country town as Brendan and, like Brendan and Lucy, were serious potheads. Angela called in a couple of times to visit Andy, but he would just sit and pull cones and stare at her until she felt uncomfortable. Andy did get his act together in the end, after he had moved away to Sydney and Angela heard that he had finished his M.A. but had put his aspirations to be a poet on hold when he got some good job as a researcher or something in the United Kingdom and might have even been studying again but none of the people she knew had any contact details for him.

'He really was the one that got away, wasn't he?' Ingrid asked.

'It was never meant to be' Angela said, not quite believing her own words.

Ingrid announced that the wine had made her sleepy and that she was turning in for the night. Angela sat up for an hour or two listening to the music on her media player that reminded her so much of her student days. She listened to Joy Division and was almost hypnotised by the bass and drums on songs like *Heart and Soul* and thought about the way that Ian Curtis was forever young in the minds of her generation, while they were the ones slipping through middle age into their dotage and she smiled when she remembered the way that she would rip off her parents for playing the old records of their favourite musicians from the fifties because some of the records were more than twenty years old, and now, she spends a lot of time listening to records recorded more than thirty years earlier. She wondered what Andy might have been listening to and thought that his tastes would be the eclectic mix they always were and that he would listen to the old bands but would probably be into new young bands, particularly indie bands and singers.

Angela had a dream that night that she was living with Andy in a big house on the ridge to the west of the city in a house that, in her dream, was remarkably like the house the Professor and his family and lived in and she and Andy were married and were both lecturers at the university and that Andy was a respected poet. They had a daughter, in her dream, a precocious blonde girl in her late teens or early twenties who Andy indulged, and who Angela fought with, and when she woke from her dream, Angela was confused and disturbed because, in the dream, the daughter had the same face as Sophie.

She didn't tell Ingrid about the dream because Ingrid could get all funny and want to interpret them for Angela. One Ingrid's contradictions, that Angela found endearing, was the way, at one level, she was all hard and practical and called a spade a spade which came from years of nursing in the emergency room while, on the other hand, she got into heaps of new age thinking that Angela liked to call hocus pocus. 'Symbolic wisdom is the prisoner of the madness of dreams' Angela once said to Ingrid, quoting Foucault, but, when asked, couldn't explain to Ingrid what she meant by it and Ingrid said that she was surprised because, being an English Literature academic, Angela spent most of her time looking for the wisdom in the symbols contained within words.

The gathering at the pub was scheduled to start at 6 pm and people would be invited to say a few words about Tony and Killer but Angela had nothing formal planned and she convinced Singo to support the gathering by suggesting that if it started at six then some of the people who came would probably stay on drinking and some of them might even order a counter meal for their tea. Singo was up for anything that might mean a few extra dollars and he used to tell people that he only kept the pub running as a favour to the town, as a place for them to meet, but Angela suspected that the four poker machines that Singo had in the small room out the back on the way to the dunnies probably turned over a bit of cash given there was always at least two locals sitting there feeding dollar coins into the slots and she had heard that most evenings Kevin Cutler's wife could be found in front of one of the machines with a can of Diet Coke in her hand that would last most of the night while she disposed of the profits from the café.

Ingrid and Angela were at the pub by five and set up a table with a vase of lilies and framed photographs of Tony and Killer. The photo of Tony had been E Mailed by Alyssa along with her apologies and the photo of Killer was one that Angela had. Tony's photograph was taken on his wedding day and he looked smart in a dinner jacket, wing collared shirt and black tie while Killer, on the other hand, was in his singlet and shorts and leather hat and he is half turning towards the camera wagging his finger at Angela who had taken him by surprise when she took the snap. Angela had asked around the town and nobody appeared to have any photographs of Killer. Angela checked with Mrs Singleton who said that the sandwiches had been made and that there were mini sausage rolls and party pies in the oven warming up. Satisfied with the food, Angela went into the main bar and gave Chloe one hundred dollars and told her that she wanted to open up a bar tab and to let her know if it needed topping up and that the open bar would be from quarter to six to six thirty to allow everyone to get a drink and toast the memory of Tony and Bernard.

Angela spent the next forty-five minutes worrying whether anybody would show up and how embarrassing it would be for her if there were no takers to her invitation. She was also expecting someone from the local newspaper to come and take some photographs and write an article about the gathering. The journalist Angela had spoken to seemed very keen to do the story and said that it was good human-interest material but was disappointed when Angela couldn't give her a lot of details about Tony or Killer, who Angela referred to as Mr Bernard. The journalist said not to worry too much about it as she was sure that there would be a lot of people at the gathering who could fill in the gaps.

Kevin Cutler and his wife were the first people to arrive at the gathering and Kevin was wearing a cleaned and ironed firefighting uniform shirt that had a name badge proclaiming him as Brigade Captain.

'Can't say I always saw eye to eye with Bernard', Kevin said to Angela, 'but he was a member of our community, the same as Mr Conti even though he hadn't lived here with us very long.'

'Guess that makes me a blow-in as well?' Angela asked.

'Doing little things like this are important for the district' Kevin said, and his wife nodded agreement, 'and it is welcomed by the community in a way to bring us together after such a tragic event.'

Gerald and Anila walked in while Angela was talking to the Cutlers and not wanting to join in on the conversation, Gerald gave a nod and a little wave to Angela and then went to the bar to get himself and Anila a drink. Over the next fifteen or so minutes, more and more people arrived and most of them went to the bar and got drinks and when they were told that there was a bar tab, they came and thanked Angela personally. Chloe, behind the bar, made sure that everybody knew that it was Angela who was paying because she didn't want the people to think that this was a result of Kevin Cutler's largesse. After he had spoken to Angela, Kevin had made his way to the back corner of the room and sat at a table with his wife and waited for other people to join him.

The first person to join the Cutlers was Rodney Cripplegate and Angela noted, with some amusement, that Rodney also wore a name badge proclaiming that he was Councillor Cripplegate. It was always the men, she thought, who needed to wear their name badges that proclaimed some title or organisation as if there identity was tied up in their job, even if it was a voluntary job like fire captain or councillor and how the badges were unnecessary in such a small community because everyone knew who everyone else was anyway and how people like Cutler and Cripplegate thought that their roles gave them some broader, general authority outside of the specific thing they represented. Angela had never worn a name badge except those ones that are printed on cardboard and put inside a clear plastic holder with a clip that you wear at conferences so that the other conference goers know who you are. Not that Angela went to a lot of conferences in her lecturing days. She had been asked to give a number of papers and she enjoyed listening to papers on topics that interested her, but she hated all the mingling about and small talk that came with the territory and her lack of networking probably didn't help her career.

'You're doing remarkably well' Ingrid said, as if she had been reading Angela's mind. 'All this mingling and small talk with strangers.'

Angela had been a little tetchy with Ingrid all day and Ingrid thought that this was probably because Angela was nervous about the gathering. The truth was that Angela was all emotional about Andy being back in town and angry with Ingrid for not speaking to him when she saw him at the beach. She didn't think that Ingrid had liked Andy all that much back in their younger days and it wasn't as if Ingrid had said anything, but it was the looks she would give him and the way that she didn't hang around with Angela at the uni bar when Andy was with them, and when he started seeing Sophie, Ingrid was outraged at the way they both carried on together, quite shamelessly, when everyone knew that

Sophie lived with her boyfriend and Ingrid wondered how the boyfriend felt about all of that carry on and was disappointed that Angela seemed to be hurt and jealous when, in Ingrid's eyes, and using a word she thought she might have learned from a Jane Austin novel, Andy was nothing more than a cad.

Angela was annoyed when she heard some loud laughter from up the back of the room and realised that it was Kevin Cutler and his young firefighting charges and she noted that a couple of them had more than one schooner in front of them and she thought, of course, they're not here to show respect to Killer but to drink as much as they can while the tab was open at the bar.

'They're not bad kids really', a voice said to Angela's side and she turned to see Gerald next to her and beside him was Anila. 'Most of them are pretty decent and come from good homes. It's just when they're with Cutler, they think they have to fit in, that they have to act like him and that's why they carry on like that but get them alone and they're all just polite young country boys.'

'Except for Cutler's nephew' Angela said remembering the night she copped his abuse in the pub.

'The apple that lies in proximity to the tree' Anila said and Gerald laughed a little.

'A fair enough translation' Gerald said to Anila who just smiled.

'Does he have kids of his own, Cutler?' Angela asked.

'No. Apparently they can't. Some medical reason' Gerald said.

'On his part' Anila added.

'Shoots blanks?' Angela said and Anila looked puzzledly at Gerald.

'It means he's infertile', Gerald said, 'something wrong with his spermatozoa.'

Anila nodded to show that she understood the analogy and then she also chuckled a little. 'Blanks, I like that, like blank bullets, harmless.'

'Probably explains a lot', Angela said to Gerald, 'the town's alpha male can't recreate himself, so he tries to build the young men in his fire crew in his own image. God help the town.'

Angela looked up at the clock that hung on the wall next to the portrait of the Queen and some unknown local in what looked to be an army uniform from around the time of the First World War and she recalled that the room also served as the gathering place for Anzac Day ceremonies where the day would start with Kevin Cutler leading a parade through the town dressed in his fireman's uniform on which he wore the service medals of some distant relative.

It was time to get the formalities under way and Angela banged a spoon against the side of a glass to get everyone's attention and when there was sufficient quiet, she began to speak, a little nervously at first.

'I want to thank everyone for coming along this evening to share their memories of Tony and Bernard, who most of you knew as Killer. We're not going to make this a formal occasion because neither Tony or Killer would have wanted that. I would like to acknowledge the traditional owners of the land we're gathered on and pay my respects to elders past and present and to also acknowledge that Bernard, Killer, identified as a first nations person and this, I believe, was where his mob came from.' Angela got a dirty look from Kevin Cutler who whispered something to Rodney Cripplegate who also curled his lip.

'I guess I'm a blow in like Tony but for the last five years both Tony and Killer were my neighbours and it's as if we had our own little community, up on the hill, that was part of Allynsdale and sometimes a bit separate. As neighbours we relied on each other and I am going to miss my neighbours. Alyssa, Tony's wife, couldn't be here with us today but she sends her warm regards and thanks. I understand that some of the people here sent her cards and flowers to wish her a speedy recovery and also for Tony's funeral that was held recently. Alyssa's burns, she says, are starting to recover slowly and she plans to come back and visit when she can, but she also told me that she will probably stay in Sydney now where she can be close to her family. What I'd like to do is to ask anyone who'd like to speak to come up and say a few words.'

Nobody made a move, and everyone stood looking at Angela until eventually Kevin Cutler stood up and made his way to the front of the room to the sound of a few of the young blokes saying things like 'good on you Kev' and 'that's the way Captain.'

'I just wanted to say a few words on behalf of the town' Kevin started, and Gerald leant close to Angela and whispered, 'the unelected lord mayor, does this at every function'.

'I want to thank Angela on behalf of Allynsdale for organising this afternoon and taking it on herself. We would have gotten around to organising something ourselves, I'm sure, but we're still recovering from the fires and that recovery will probably take a long time. Unfortunately, we couldn't save Mr Bernard's home or Mr Conti's but, by some miracle, Angela's house was pretty well untouched which I suppose means she was meant to stay here with us and become part of our community.'

'I think she already was, Kevin' Gerald said, and one or two people clapped and said 'yes', and Kevin gave Gerald a dirty look.

'Being part of this community means being part of its institutions, part of its fabric, not just having your house here' Kevin said pointedly back at Gerald. 'It's about being one of us, being like us, sharing with us, and that takes time. I didn't know Mr and Mrs Conti all that well, but I am sure that they were very nice people and they had made a commitment to living here, with us all, and I'm sure they would have tried to become part of the community in time. It was a tragedy what happened to Mr Conti and it's a tragedy that was unnecessary and will happen time and time again unless people listen to advice. I told Mr and Mrs Conti that they should evacuate, and they didn't listen, well, at least Mrs Conti listened and that's a small consolation. We have order in our town for a reason, we do things a certain way for a reason and knowing that order, is what I mean by becoming part of this community.' From up the back of the room, there was some clapping and Cripplegate said 'Hear, hear!'

'And my father?' said a voice from the doorway. Angela looked across thinking that she recognised the voice and there was Sarah standing in the hallway, looking imposing in her smart business suit and Angela realised for the first time how tall Sarah was and she also seemed to have inherited Killer's muscular wiry frame. Kevin Cutler didn't know where to look or who to look at.

'I'm Sarah Bernard, a few of you might remember me from when I was a little girl although it's been more than thirty years since I lived in the district, actually it is coming up to forty years since I left, just after my mother died and I'm sure many of you remember that event.'

'Please come in Sarah, you're very welcome' Angela said, and Kevin gave Angela a nasty look as if she had somehow, by inviting Sarah in, usurped his authority.

'My father always considered this to be his home and it's where he wanted to die, so I suppose he got that wish at least.' Sarah continued with the confidence of years at the bar. 'My father kept pretty much to himself and he had his reasons, but I have heard from Angela that he was on friendly terms with a lot of the newer people in the district and was respected for his helpfulness and his knowledge'. A few people sitting near the front nodded and Angela recognised them as some of the tree changers who were scattered around the district and she also knew that some of these tree changers who had made the effort to come to the gathering had lost their own homes in the fire.

'I wish I had known my father better, particularly these last few years. He had his demons, and I don't doubt that for a second, and he may not have conquered them, but from what I hear, he did a good job keeping them at bay, despite the efforts of some of the people who are here in this room this afternoon' and with that, she looked pointedly at Kevin Cutler who was turning red and looked like he might have liked to have hit Sarah, and Angela noticed and remembered hearing rumours that Cutler was known to give his wife the occasional backhander.

'The man that was recently described to me', Sarah smiled at Angela and continued, 'was a man that I believe had mellowed over time and through his connection to his home, to this place and to nature. He was a man who had become thoughtful of others and I understand that after Angela had taken the good and proper advice of Mr Cutler to leave as the fire was approaching, my father went back to Angela's place and did some things to make it safer and helped it survive the fire. He then went back to his own place where he perished, and I don't doubt for a minute that he had no intention to leave because, as much as he had mellowed, I am sure that Dad still had his stubborn streak.' Angela noticed that where tears starting to well in Sarah's eyes and she knew that if Sarah started, she would soon follow.

'I'm not going to make excuses for my father. In his young days I believe that he had an untamed wild streak to him and I know that he used to try and use alcohol to keep his demons in check, and when he drank, they grew larger and larger and I knew that he could be aggressive and I know that he and Mum would drink together and she would goad him until he snapped and then he would be full of remorse because he should have known, better than anyone, the scourge of a drunken bully on a family, because that was how his own father was. My grandfather was a nasty vicious man by all accounts. Nobody knows for sure how my grandfather died, and I know that you all have your theories, you've all heard the various stories because one of the institutions that Mr Cutler here is so proud of is the institution of gossip. Maybe my father was involved somehow in his own father's death and maybe he wasn't, and the thing is that none of us here know the truth and now we'll never know.'

'I know what my own father told me, and he wasn't a liar' Kevin Cutler said angrily, and Angela was worried that there was a growing air of hostility in the air the longer that Sarah spoke, and she also thought that she would wear the blame for Sarah being there.

'I'm a Crown Prosecutor', Sarah went on, 'and before that I was a police officer for a number of years. If I learned anything, it was that the truth isn't always simple and there are many ways to tell a story and all the stories can be true and, at the same time, they can all be lies. I said that my grandfather was a violent bully and you know, in my life I've seen a lot of bullies who were the victims of bullying themselves. Men who witnessed their fathers beat their mothers end up becoming wife beaters themselves. Tell me Mr Cutler, did you father beat your mother?'

'That's enough!' Rodney Cripplegate said, jumping to his feet. In front of Sarah, Kevin was breathing heavily, his hands balled into fists. Angela looked at Sarah and saw that she was standing lightly on the balls of her feet and moving her head gently but the muscled in her arms were taught and ready to spring if Kevin Cutler tried anything.

'Councillor Cripplegate, as I live and breathe. I haven't seen you for years. How long has it been? That little girl, she would be in her late teens, early twenties now.' Sarah said and smiled, and the rest of the room looked puzzled.

'I was acquitted, you know that, there was no evidence just politically motivated slander.' Cripplegate said.

'A politically motivated eight-year-old girl?'

Cripplegate turned to face the room and raised his hands. 'Right, you all have to leave, this function is over by orders of the Council.' Sarah laughed.

'You preposterous jumped up little redneck shit. The publican

can kick us out if he wants, or someone can call the police, but you have no authority. My aunty told me about you. You were the one who used to chase my mother around the playground shouting at her, calling her names. What were they? Do you remember? Wasn't it coon or bong or darkie or abo? Something like that. Calling her names until she cried and wouldn't go back to school anymore.'

A couple of the young tree changers had stood up and had moved to a position where they could defend Sarah if they needed to and Cripplegate was also red in the face and there were flecks of spit on his lips. The young blokes from the fire brigade, sitting up the back, didn't know where to look. One of them, a young fellow that Angela only knew as Danny suddenly stood up and stormed out and as he got to the door, he turned around and pointed to Cripplegate and said 'I always knew, always knew that you were a fucking rock spider. You're fucking finished mate, fucking finished in this district.'

Another of the young firefighters, Danny's mate, Sooty, stood up and there were tears in his eyes and he walked up close to Kevin Cutler and pointing to him said to the room 'He's no better. What about the initiation into the brigade? We all had to go through it. Captain Cutler's welcome he called it, getting your balls and knob smeared with boot polish that Cutler would rub on and then getting one of the others to do stuff to you while they all watched, you know, sticking things up your backside.' Sooty fell back in his chair sobbing great convulsive sobs.

Angela was standing next to Gerald and asked quietly 'is it true, does this happen in fire crews?'

'Only in Cutler's crew', Gerald said, 'Only here in this forsaken hole. The other units are professionals who look after their crews and do a fantastic job. This lot are a rabble, show ponies, and it's not the fault of the young blokes like Sooty and Danny. It's all they've known since they were kids.'

'I'm not staying here listening to this shit' Cutler said and walked over to his wife and grabbed her by the upper arm and she yelped a little and told him to take his hands off her and Cutler said 'You're my fucking wife, do as you're told' and then one of the tree changers who Angela always thought was a bit of a hippy jumped behind Cutler and thrust his other arm up behind his back forcing Cutler to let go of his wife. 'You're all pieces of shit, the fucking lot of you' Cutler said and left the hotel and his wife was left rubbing her bruised arm not knowing what to say or who to turn to.

'Secrets, secrets and lies, I remember my father saying that when I was a little girl.' Sarah said calmly. 'Cutler talked about the fabric of the community as if he was the stitching that held it together. Him and Councillor Cripplegate here. Secrets and lies. The happy little community pretending that everyone got on so well. I think my father knew your secrets and that's why he stayed living here. He wasn't going to be pushed out by the likes of Kevin Cutler or this piece of shit' she said pointing to Cripplegate. 'Dad wanted to stay here and shine a mirror at all of you. I think he probably thought that the fire would sweep all of you away, well, all the hypocrites anyway and I know that he wished no harm to those who had shown him kindness and he would have been devastated that Molly Thompson lost her house. There are good people here too, and it was people like Gerald over there who saved the town'.

'He wouldn't let us' Sooty sobbed and one of the other young fellows shook his head to tell him to be quiet. 'No,' Sooty said, 'they deserve to know the truth. We got up the road towards the fire and then Captain Cutler went down a couple of fire trails away from the fire front and then back around the next gulley and up the ridge where the fire had already passed, and he stopped the truck and said that we should just sit and monitor the radio for a while. We could hear Gerald on the radio calling for other units to come and defend Allynsdale, defend our own town and Cutler told us to stay put and wait and he said that Gerald's such a big man, thinks he's so good, let him save the town. We waited for a couple of hours and then went back the way we came but the wind had changed direction and we were caught in a flash over and I thought I was going to die, and Mr Cutler was just shitting himself and not saying anything. Danny was driving and he got us through unhurt and when we got close to town, Mr Cutler made Danny swap seats so that Mr Cutler could drive into town as the hero.'

There was dead silence in the room, and it seemed that nobody knew what to say. Angela turned and looked at the picture of Killer wagging his finger at her as if he was admonishing her for being the cause of all of this, but she thought that there was a sparkle in his eyes as well and she felt that he was out there, somewhere looking down on everything, pleased with the way the truth came out in the end.

A few of the people were filing out and Rodney Cripplegate stood staring at Sarah like some standoff in an old school western. Sooty and his mate walked past and as they got close to Cripplegate, the mate spat on him and then kept walking

'You haven't heard the last of this' Cripplegate said and left.

In the end there was just Angela, Ingrid, Sarah, Gerald and Anila in the back room and off to one side, not sure what to do with herself, was Mrs Cutler.

'I think I need a drink after that', Sarah said, 'do you think they'll serve me?'

'Chloe, the kid behind the bar's lovely. Not sure about Singo though' Angela said.

'He's sweet', Gerald said, 'he can't stand Kevin or Rodney, just doesn't say anything because he likes to keep the peace.'

'That's the problem sometimes' Sarah said and led them all into the front bar where Chloe told Angela that there was still some credit on her account. Sarah looked over and saw that Mrs Cutler was still in the back room like she was unsure of what to do. Sarah went over and spoke to her quietly for a few minutes and then came back to the group.

'I'll have to pass on that drink. I'm going to take Mrs Cutler somewhere safe, in the city. I'm on the board of one of the refuges and they should be able to take her, otherwise it will be a hotel for the night.'

'I'll follow you, at least to Wallisville, just to be on the safe side.' Gerald and Alyssa wished Angela and Ingrid goodnight. They both had a drink of white wine and Ingrid asked Angela if she wanted to go back home or head to Ingrid's until it all blew over.

'I'm staying here, it's home and besides, I've got Killer looking out for me.'

A Long the River Run Was Love

And Angela thought this, and these words were true – that the water would run through the valley again and that the valley would turn green again and the people would smile again and maybe Andy would come back to the beach again and maybe someone else will be there who will recognise him and tell him that Angela is safe in her little mud brick house in the mountains and that she survived the fires that killed her neighbours and that perhaps he should go and find her and then maybe she might laugh again, might smile again like she laughed and smiled all of those years ago, late at night in Harry's Bar where she drank black beer because it seemed a radical thing for a woman to do as it had been the beer of the miners and wharfies and sailors of her town when she was a girl, and how she smoked cigarettes that she rolled herself because it was cheaper and also because it seemed to be a bit radical and different to the girls she went to school with who all ended up engaged and with jobs in insurance offices before they were twenty and who all smoked tailor made mentholated cigarettes and drank West Coast Coolers and Midori and Lemonade and who'd never heard of Molly, either Molly, Molly Bloom or Molly that was Siobhan and who ended up leaping into the darkness that may have been a leap of faith or perhaps a leap of no faith off the cliff they call the Gap into the Tasman Sea that some people pretend is the Pacific Ocean but isn't really.

And Angela thought this, and these words were true - how Mick could have told Killer's story in such a way that it was holy and had some meaning and that it was prophetic and that the fire symbolised something and that perhaps the whole town had to be cleansed by the fire, disinfected by the heat of the flames and the smoke, but it was true that the flames didn't reach the town, apart from old Molly Thompson's and she had never hurt anyone and she didn't need to be burned clean and had nothing for which she needed to be redeemed and neither did Tony Conti who was incinerated along with his house while Angela's was spared, and she was even more consumed with guilt than she had been before the fire and her counsellor told her that she had nothing to feel guilty about and Angela told her that she didn't know half of it and she was feeling guilty for things that she couldn't even remember doing or saying but must have done or said, how else would she have developed the guilty feelings that she had carried all of her adult life.

And Angela thought this, and these words were true – that the river would run again from the mountains to the sea and wash the valley clean and carry all of the secrets of the town to the harbour and deposit the secrets far from the city, far from the land, deep in the ocean underneath the storms and tides and waves, settling into the sand or gravel or whatever it was on the sea floor, never to be seen again, gone and finished forever, lost to time and even to the meaning of time.

Somewhere, a long time ago, Angela remembers catching two buses to the university. The first, blue and crowded, eight thirty in the morning and the shop girls are full of gossip, and the office men, hot in their collared shirts and ties, are reading the newspaper and giving angry little frustrated looks when someone carrying a big bag of books sits on the narrow bench seat next to them and makes their newspapers rustle, and they sigh and when they do a sour tobacco smell comes from between their mean thin lips and it is late February and it is still hot and there were fires earlier in the summer, but not too bad, and it is still warm, unseasonably so, and the office men are beginning to perspire, dark spots emerging in the armpits of their polyester shirts and the office men don't wear deodorant so, in Angela's nose there is the musty smell of their sweat mingling with the overpowering perfume of their cheap aftershave, their Old Spice or their Brut33 that they would have received eight weeks earlier as a Christmas gift from their mothers, or grandmothers or wives or girlfriends or children and they hope that the bottle will last until Autumn when they will not perspire or smell so much and Angela smells her own smell, the Femfresh her mother insisted that she uses and has used for almost all of her high school years and which she will soon dispose of on the advice of the Women's Collective which is one of the first groups she joins during O Week, along with the Drama Society and the Film Society and the Wilderness Society and the Amnesty Club and the Poetry Society and the Fencing Club even though she has never picked up a sword in her life but thought that it looked romantic and elegant and she might meet some nice people and maybe even find a lover who is athletic and intelligent and perhaps a little arrogant who might drive a little sports car, like the MG that one of her teachers used to drive and who all the girls thought might have been a poofter because he was well spoken and well dressed and never sleazed on to any of the Year 12 girls the way some of the other younger, and not so younger male teachers would. The first bus went all the way from Everton and Angela knew that when she got to town that she had to get off at Walton's and cross the road and get the 100 bus to the university although one of her friends had suggested that she could have gotten off at Tudor Street and cross the road to the pizza shop, where she was later to go with Andy, and get the 225 but Angela didn't know about the pizza shop that morning and she knew even less of Andy and his place in her dreams for the next thirty years.

The people outside of Walton's waiting for the buses were mainly students like Angela who had come into town from the various suburbs to the south and were changing buses and there were a lot of them because it was the first day of the first term and Angela tried to look cool and was hoping people weren't guessing that she was a first year and she thought she could tell the first years because some of them seemed to be still children in her eyes, particularly the gawky and gangly group of boys who were chasing each other and throwing balls and were carrying their books and pens in school ports and were only distinguished from the real school children who were also waiting for a bus because they weren't wearing school uniforms. In the window of Walton's there were displays of furniture that were ignored by the students, but later in the day the window shoppers would come to look and browse and go inside and prod and poke and scratch their chins and walk around a lounge suite or bedroom suite or entertainment unit from every angle and when they made up their mind would talk to the shop assistant and fill out some papers the way, for years, Angela's Mum and Dad had whenever they replaced some second hand furniture with a new piece that would be paid for every fortnight to a man who came to the house on a motorbike with a big leather satchel and leather bound receipt book and Angela's mother told her that she should buy something on hire purchase as soon as she could afford the repayments so she built up a good credit reputation with Walton's and so, when she married, she could buy nice things for house from her husband's wages. Keeping house, her mother called it, this thing that women did, that Angela would do one day and the only consolation her mother had about Angela going to university was that she might meet a better class of boy to marry, one with prospects, one with an emerging career, perhaps in accounting, who could get a steady job that had progression over time and promotions and pay rises that could coincide with the birth of children who would grow up in a nice house in the suburbs, maybe even down the lake but close enough to home for regular visits to their grandparents.

The steelworks were making clouds again as Angela waited for the 100 bus and they rose, big fluffy puffs like cotton wool against the clear blue summer sky. Later on Andy would tell her that it was steam caused by the water cooling the coal being baked into coke in the coke ovens and how nobody much liked to work in the coke ovens because it was always hot and steamy and the gas given off could make you sick or kill you and how the worst place to be was up on the lids and men died there from the fire and the gas and the falls and how it was all the wogs who liked to work there on a seven day roster with plenty of doublers and Andy knew these things because when he was a boy, before the university, he worked at the steelworks in one of the rolling mills where he dreamed of being a poet like the Professor and his circle of friends who had put out a book that Andy had read at night in the mill, and where he tried to find poetry in the steel but the steel was already in his heart, but Angela didn't know Andy then and when she did know him, later on in second year at the university, she showed him off to her mother even though he wasn't her boyfriend then and never really ever was and her mother was not impressed and thought that he was dirty but it was just that he was scruffy with his big bush of uncombed curly hair and his curly black beard that nestled on his chin and his jeans with the holes patched with red paisley fabric and combat boots from the disposal store because he couldn't afford Doc Martens and his lack of manners when it came to food, and Angela's mother said there must be nice boys at the university like Mrs Farrell's son, Wayne, with his nicely pressed and spotless polyester shirt with short sleeves and his brown slacks and briefcase and neatly parted hair and his car that he washed and polished on the front nature strip every Saturday morning and how Wayne Farrell had no time for wasteful things like poetry and that poetry was alright for girls to enjoy but not for husbands and fathers who needed to know how to change the washer on a tap and adjust the spark plug on the Victa lawnmower and how, according to Angela's mother, Andy probably knew none of these things, him with his head in his books and his fancy words and strange clothes and Angela did not know if Andy knew these things because she never talked about them but suspected that he might know some things from working in the steel mills that Wayne would never know like fear and danger and noise and smoke and light and fire and the rough words and rough hands and gentle hearts of men who work in places such as these.

The bus came that first morning and Angela counted out the thirty cents for the fare and handed it to the driver in his blue peaked cap and blue shirt with epaulets and pressed blue shorts who handed her the ticket and she made her way down the aisle to find a seat and smiled to the other university students because she was now one of them and had a library card with her name and number and a bus pass that said she was a student and a knapsack with prescribed texts for Drama and English that were to be taught that day with Classical Civilisations the next and Philosophy the day after that and so she didn't have to carry all of her books, just the ones for the day so she had *Hedda Gabler and Other Plays* in the Methuen edition that she had read the weekend before and *Beowulf* in the Penguins Classics edition translated by Michael Alexander that she was half way through. Later on she would love *Tristram Shandy* and *Tom Jones* and then *Ulysses* and *The Four Quartets* until she fell back in love with Mick, who had never really left the pile of books beside her bed that she packed up in the first term of uni to take to her first student digs in a house with an unmown yard and cracked and faded weatherboards and a rusty tin roof that was prone to leaking, and ash and soot and coal dust everywhere and where, at night, she and her flatmates talked all night and drank flagon claret by candlelight and listened to scratchy lp's by Joni Mitchell and Laura Nyro and Nico and how she became surprised that Andy liked these women singers too, when all the boys at Everton High only ever seemed to like songs by men like Ted Nugent or Cold Chisel and never heard the voices of women let alone listened, yet Andy seemed to listen, and this she liked.

She saw him that first day, in the Student Union, walking through the crowd, at ease with himself and his place in the world and seeming to say hello to every second person he passed in the crowded corridor that ran the length of the refectory to the coffee bar that overlooked the bushland with its little creek. It was her second year before they spoke, when Angela and Andy were in the same class being taught by the Professor and there was Lucretia there as well and Louis and Brendan who Angela dated once before he had dated Lucy, but it was all so long ago and there was the girl from the Trotskyite party who'd argue about class with the Professor and Andy would sit back in his chair and gaze out the window looking bored at all the politics because he was a poet, he said once, and the only people who bang on about the working class are the ones who've never lived that life and didn't know that it was real and how he hated that the life he had tried so hard to escape could be reduced by earnest students to an abstraction and Angela thought that she might be falling in love with him a little bit but was never going to say that because he might think that love was an illusion an abstraction, or at least the way it is talked about and Angela had nothing to compare with how she felt except her books and knew that it wasn't something mad, that she was no Cathy and he no Heathcliff and there was nothing in Mick to help her, or Eliot, or the classics, or the plays she studied in Drama, or in Shakespeare, and the films she watched were either silly and corny designed to entertain silly girls or were heavy and dark and brooding European films without happy endings and laden with sorrow, and that's not how she felt when she sat with

Andy in class or the bar or sharing the bus home or sharing a meal in the refectory or pizza at the little Italian place near the bus-stop in Tudor Street.

Angela remembered parties as if it was just one big huge party that seemed to go on every weekend for her first three years at uni and it was at these parties that couples would pair off and some of them even stayed together and some of them were even together thirty years later with their smart children and nice houses in the better suburbs of the capital cities and very few of them stayed in their home city and those that did never mingled very much with their old uni friends unless they had gone into similar professions and the mingling was mainly with other parents of similarly aged children and Angela had never found a partner at these parties, not one for life or even a part of life and had soon grown tired of the one night stands that never promised love or anything that even approached what she thought that love might have been, and she had been mindful to ask Andy what he thought love might have been, given he thought of himself as a poet and sometimes poets think that they're experts on love, even if Angela could never find answers in any of the poetry that she had read.

And then Andy had met Sophie, one night in Harry's Bar, after an English class on D.H. Lawrence, and mother love, and Oedipal subtext, and suffocation, and the brutality of coarse men. and Andy had said that he hated the way that Lawrence had portrayed the miners as brutal and coarse without making any suggestion as to the cause of their brutishness and coarseness and how it was their work that made them that way and that the father in the book had been dashing and handsome in his youth and there were signs that he had loved his wife when they were first married and the Trotskyite girl carried on with her rubbish about the Professor being a class traitor and Andy had told her that she was full of shit because she thought that working class people had to stay working in the pits and the steelworks and dying in these jobs because they were working class and yet it was alright for the Trotskyite girl to go to university and perhaps enter a profession because she was already middle class and would probably always be middle class and Angela wanted to tell him how inspiring he had been and how much she had agreed with him and she was going to tell him in the bar that night and maybe even invite him home for a drink when the bar closed and she had used the last of her savings to buy a bottle of whisky because she knew that he liked to drink good whisky but could rarely afford it and she hoped that it might serve to ease her planned seduction and then Sophie walked into the bar and flashed her whiter than white teeth smile and flashed her firm and toned whiter than white skinned thighs and laughed at his jokes and stroked his hand and cruelly dismissed the boy that she accompanied to the bar in the first place and then Andy was lost to Angela for good.

Something went wrong with Sophie, and Andy wouldn't talk about it, but he disappeared inside himself for a very long time, lost with his words in his little notebook where he was always jotting down ideas for poems, or so he told Angela, and he stopped washing for a while so he always had that stale smell of urine and bong water and Angela later thoughted that the urine smell was not like the tang of Mr Blooms kidney breakfast but something earthier but also unpleasant and then Andy disappeared for good and Angela pretended that she didn't care and didn't notice and besides, by then she was totally engrossed in her thesis and exploring the world of the Caldwell Street Push but not knowing that the Gap was waiting over the horizon and Siobhan and her madness and obsessions that became Angela's madness and obsessions and the voices in her head screamed at night and she didn't sleep and the doctors gave Angela drugs to help but the voices compounded even with the help of the drugs, the laughing and taunts of Seamus Plunket and his acolyte and the despair of Siobhan who was not Molly because approached the world with passion and joy and lust and all the thing that Angela wished she had, whereas Siobhan approached the world with fear and apprehension and doubt and all of these were the things that Angela owned and carried with her until the mega crack up and silence and eventually calm.

Andy was out there all the time and Angela pretended not to notice his absence and pretended that she didn't care and even once when someone at the university mentioned Andy, wondering what had become of him, Angela pretended that she didn't know at first who this Andy was until the questioner reminded her that she had been in a couple of the Professor's classes with Andy and expressed surprise that Angela could forget him and Angela said that he hadn't made much of an impression and that night she went home and dug out an old photograph from the student newspaper of Andy reading some poetry one night in the bar and she cried and she remembered that the poetry wasn't all that good but people applauded because they were kind and Sophie was there, so it must have been in that year when Andy had met her, but early on because as the year progressed, Andy disappeared more and more into the world of Sophie and Angela sometimes suspected may have been even madder than her own world just before the mega crack-up, and that was saying something.

In London, Angela had daydreams of bumping into Andy somewhere old and he would be surprised that she had finally left Newcastle to see a bit of the world and he would offer to take her around and show her all the sites, both the popular tourist sites and the obscure ones as well and they would drink in the pubs that famous poets had drunk in and Andy would tell her that he was successful in some job to do with the arts and that he had missed her all this time and how Sophie had been such a big mistake and how he had paid a dear price and, in her daydream, Angela would take his arm as they walked along the Thames Embankment, and it would be Autumn, and the light would be soft and there would be leaves at their feet and Angela would say that she too had paid a big price but it was alright now because they had found each other again and Angela would tell Andy that she was going to New Mexico and Andy would say that he would come because he had never been there and one of his friends had told him of a wise man, a Native American spirit man, who lived in a pueblo outside of Taos who makes your dreams come true and that Angela and he should go an visit and put their trust in the winds of the New Mexican desert and that this would be their world making pilgrimages to place where all of Angela's favourite writers had lived and worked and she could immerse herself in more than just the words, but the smells and the tastes and the sounds and laughter of children and the crying of old people and sunrises and sunsets until there was no more need for words.

New Mexico, Angela dreams of New Mexico and Mick and David Herbert and Andy is unreachable as all of them. She thought that there was too much sky out there, blue, dazzling with barely a cloud, going on upwards forever and the earth, under her feet, the colour of straw also went on to far horizons where mesas shimmered in a heat haze and driving down from Denver, Cody Pommeray on her mind, the black top I25 disappeared in a shiny silver mirage drawing her deeper into the country, following dry rivers because the tears had all run out long ago, and later, back home, in the months and weeks before the fire, the river had also run dry and the world was turning brittle, just one spark, she thought, just one spark and thought she remembered a song from long ago that had that line, just one spark to light the fire and then she would know that it had all been an illusion, her shelter on the mountain because as Ingrid had said to her once 'you can run as much as you want but you can't run away from yourself' and it was Ingrid who had seen Andy at the beach where he might have been looking for Sophie and if it was Angela who had seen him, she would have said, she imagined, she dreamed, that he had no need of Sophie because, in the end, Sophie only ever brought him sorrow and Sophie only ever bought Angela sorrow and Angela hoped that Sophie never knew the sorrow that she brought to others, that Sophie would never know that sorrow.

And Angela thought this, and the words were true – that the hospital staff seemed kinder somehow and the nurses smiled at her as they did their rounds but sometimes spoke to her as if she was a child and little did they know that there were days when she wanted to be a child again, a second, second new start, another new beginning, a reset to back when she had choices to make and how those choices might have been different and she wondered if the kind nurses had heard of Nietzsche or Kundera and if they knew about the eternal return and how it leads back to the same places and the same choices so that Angela thought that even if she could become a child again that there would be nothing different, and she would still be here in this bed, in this ward and Andy would still be out there, somewhere in a world that she could no longer face and that Killer would still be dead in the forest.

'It's raining', one of the kind nurses said to Angela as she held out the little plastic cup with the tablets that were prescribed so that Angela would no longer feel or dream, and the larger cup with water and Angela looked at the water and thought of rivers, 'up in the mountains, they say there's good soaking rain' and Angela smiled and nodded her head and tried to imagine the rain that she had not heard or seen so long.

And now the rain will come again, and the river would run near her house, the river would have a soul and a spirit, and the rain would soak, at last into the blackened ground and the new shoots would emerge, trembling green fronds bursting out of the burnt ground. Vines would grow, clasping like tight hands around the charcoaled remains of Killer's house and he and his world would be reclaimed at last and Angela hoped that the rain would bring peace to Killer's soul because she had begun to believe again in the concept of the soul and knew what Mick had meant when he had the old man say that his was a strange country and she thought that her soul wasn't the desert lands of Mick's west, or his tropical island or the verdant rolling hills of Suffolk or even the hustle of London where Andy had not emerged the way she dreamed he would, or the crystal brittleness of New Mexico and the wisdom in an old man's eyes. She knew her soul was in a cottage near a river that was running again and that at the end of a winter's day she could return, at least into her dreams, to sit in front of a fire, patting Osana's old grey head as he purred in her lap and she knew that a long the river run was love.

The End